Praise for *New York Ti...*
Lindsay M...

"McKenna provides heartbr...
development that will move...
military background lends authenticity to this
outstanding tale, and readers will fall in love with the
upstanding hero and his fierce determination to save
the woman he loves."

—*Publishers Weekly* on *Never Surrender*

"Talented Lindsay McKenna delivers excitement and
romance in equal measure."

—*RT Book Reviews* on *Protecting His Own*

"Lindsay McKenna will have you flying with the daring
and deadly women pilots who risk their lives... Buckle
in for the ride of your life."

—*Writers Unlimited* on *Heart of Stone*

Praise for *USA TODAY* bestselling author
Merline Lovelace

"Merline Lovelace rocks! Like Nora Roberts, she
delivers top-rate suspense with great characters,
rich atmosphere and a crackling plot!"

—*New York Times* bestselling author Mary Jo Putney

"Lovelace's many fans have come to expect her
signature strong, brave, resourceful heroines and she
doesn't disappoint."

—*Booklist*

"Ms. Lovelace wins our hearts with a tender love story
featuring a fine hero who will make every woman's
heart beat faster."

—*RT Book Reviews* on *Wrong Bride, Right Groom*

Lindsay McKenna is proud to have served her country in the US Navy as an aerographer's mate third class—also known as a weather forecaster. She was a pioneer in the military romance subgenre and loves to combine heart-pounding action with soulful and poignant romance. True to her military roots, she is the originator of the long-running and reader-favorite Morgan's Mercenaries series. She does extensive hands-on research, including flying in aircraft such as a P3-B Orion sub-hunter and a B-52 bomber. She was the first romance writer to sign her books in the Pentagon bookstore. Today, she has created a new military romantic suspense series, Shadow Warriors, which features romantic and action-packed tales about US Navy SEALs. Visit her online:
lindsaymckenna.com
twitter.com/lindsaymckenna
facebook.com/eileen.nauman

A career Air Force officer, **Merline Lovelace** served at bases all over the world. When she hung up her uniform for the last time, she decided to combine her love of adventure with a flair for storytelling, basing many of her tales on her own experiences in the service. Since then she's produced more than ninety-five action-packed sizzlers, many of which have made the *USA TODAY* bestseller lists. Over twelve million copies of her works have been printed in more than thirty countries.

When she's not tied to her keyboard, Merline enjoys reading, hitting little white balls around the fairways of Oklahoma and traveling to new and exotic locales with her husband, Al. Check her website at merlinelovelace.com or become friends with Merline on Facebook for news and information about her latest releases.

COURSE OF ACTION: CROSSFIRE

Lindsay McKenna
and
Merline Lovelace

HHARLEQUIN® ROMANTIC SUSPENSE

ISBN-13: 978-0-373-27923-4

Course of Action: Crossfire

Copyright © 2015 by Harlequin Books S.A.

The publisher acknowledges the copyright holders of the individual works as follows:

Hidden Heart
Copyright 2015 © by Nauman Living Trust

Desert Heat
Copyright 2015 © by Merline Lovelace

Recycling programs for this product may not exist in your area.

Printed in U.S.A.

H HARLEQUIN®
™ www.Harlequin.com

CONTENTS

Dear Reader,

Welcome to the beginning of summer, with vacations, beachy weekends, great books to read and, in just a few short weeks, the Fourth of July. On this holiday, we pause from our normal schedules to give thanks to the ongoing sacrifices that people around the world make to bring freedom, honor and a joyful life to as many as possible.

It is a pleasure to share with you this action-packed and emotional military-themed 2-in-1 *Course of Action: Crossfire* (#1853), written by *New York Times* bestselling author Lindsay McKenna and *USA TODAY* bestselling author Merline Lovelace. In this latest duet, two men must face overwhelming obstacles if they are to find—and hold on to—true love.

Do look for our other adrenaline-pumping romances from Harlequin Romantic Suspense out this month! In *New York Times* bestselling author Carla Cassidy's *Cowboy of Interest* (#1852), a grieving sister realizes that the man accused of her sister's murder is innocent, and is the one person who can help her find justice. Beth Cornelison's *Colton Cowboy Protector* (#1851), the first book in The Coltons of Oklahoma, is a suspenseful tale of a woman fulfilling her deceased cousin's last wish regarding her young son and who then becomes the target of an assassin. Don't miss Amelia Autin's *King's Ransom* (#1854), a lush tale of a foreign king who must seduce—and protect— the One Who Got Away.

As always, we'll deliver on our promise of breathless romance. Have a wonderful June and happy reading!

Sincerely,

Patience Bloom

Senior Editor

HIDDEN HEART

Lindsay McKenna

Dedicated to just some of my wonderfully loyal
readers, whom I love sharing my books with.
Thank you for being who you are! These are readers
who all contribute to my Facebook Fan Page
or to my free quarterly newsletter, which you can
sign up for on my website, lindsaymckenna.com.

Elena Amell, Cynthia Reifel, Linda Little, Faye Farmer,
Joann Prater, Lori Weber, Shelley Jensen,
Emma Metz, Dianne M. Quattlebaum, Lisa Bickley,
Mary DeLeon, Jean Saucier, Betty Tanner, Pam Stack
of Authors on the Air, Lucie Fleury Dunn, Sina Buckner,
Shawn Leinhart, Kerrie Liddicoat (Australia),
Felicia M. Ciaudelli, Pegg S. Godsil-Coatney,
Constance Roehl, June Williams (UK), Abe Koniarsky,
Amarylious McAlpin, Therese Scacchi Lopez,
Robin Driscoll, Angela Rabin, Veda Funk,
Danielle Schenk-van Lujin (Netherlands),
Lisa Newman, Marcie Bryant, Julie DeLap,
Veronika Spagnolo, Debb Lavoie, Rebecca Jensen,
Regan Wiard Zick, Tammy O'Holloran,
Jeanne Morris, Yrrehs You C. Lapaz (Philippines),
Robin Dubach Mlckovsky, Debbie Shields,
Berkeley Metz, Cathy Casey, Maureen Wolverton,
Melanie Ley, Debbie Hankins, Stephanie Hyacinth,
Kay Courtney, Linda Dawson Uhrich, Starr Hill, Pamela
Plessinger, Sue Peace, Cheryl Bishop,
Patricia Wheeler, Patricia Slate, Kathryn Sheets,
Debbie Hankins, Ruth A. Chestnut,
Judy Meece Kendrick, Loretta Ferris-Uszacki,
Janice Caver Burton, Jeren Touch-Werner,
Daphne S. Sampson, Reno Sweeney.

Chapter 1

"I'm hit! I'm hit!"

Ben Moore's scream of surprise slammed into Sergeant Dan Taylor's earpiece.

It had been an ambush in an icy area where it had snowed.

The blackness of the early December Afghan night lit up as another Taliban RPG screamed into their previous ditch position against their enemy. His Special Forces A team, comprising twelve seasoned Army personnel, had fled to an empty Shinwari village, taking refuge in a few mud and stone huts. They were outnumbered and outgunned.

Dan cursed, digging the toes of his boots into the fine, silty dirt as he hurled himself around the corner of the mud house. Ben, who was like a brother to him, lay at the opposite corner, rolling on his back, his hands jerking around. He'd been struck down by a bullet!

No! God, no! Not Ben! God, please...

As Dan skidded onto his knees, the night lit up with
yellow and orange fire while another RPG landed in
the house in front of them. He winced. Rocks, dirt and
dust showered him, and he crawled rapidly on his hands
and knees toward Ben. His ears throbbed, lost sound
and then his hearing partially returned. In the light, he
saw a black, shining flow spurting outward from Ben's
neck. *Oh, Jesus!* He'd been hit by shrapnel or a bullet
in the neck. With his gloved hand, Dan lunged forward,
trying to cover the torn carotid artery that was spurting
blood several feet into the air. His heart was pounding,
sweat stinging his eyes, his breath coming in ragged,
tearing gulps.

"Lie still! Lie still, Ben!" he pleaded hoarsely, knees
near Ben's head and shoulder. Ben's eyes were wide
with confusion and shock, no doubt aware of what had
happened. Ben was one of their 18-Delta combat medics. Tears mingled with Dan's sweat, the tracks streak-
ing down through the dust on his bearded face. Pressing
his gloved hand against Ben's neck, his fingers continu-
ally slipped in the warm blood.

A bullet snapped past so near Taylor that he could
feel the heat of it against his own neck. Ben was moan-
ing.

"Ah, God," Ben rasped. "I'm hit...bad...Dan...bad..."

"Get your hands away from it!" Dan pleaded hoarsely,
leaning close, trying to stop the artery from bleeding
out. "Don't move! Dammit, don't move! Ben! Let me
try to stop it!"

The burping ring of AK-47s filled the night air around
them amid the deeper, more resonant sounds of the M-4

rifles used by the A team. Dan saw Ben beginning to lose energy, his eyes growing hooded, his hands dropping listlessly into the dirt. The human body contained approximately eight pints of blood. A wound like this could bleed a person out in two or three minutes if it couldn't be stopped.

"Hang on, hang on!" Dan cried hoarsely. He called Captain Jamie Curtis, but he didn't answer. Was he hit, too? Dan tried Warrant Officer Carter Jackson. *No answer.* Half their team was down and wounded. Help was on the way—two Apaches were thundering toward their compromised position. Would they get here in time?

Dan screamed to the comms sergeant, Franklin, to get two medevacs in here. Frantically, Dan tried to pull a battle dressing from his cargo pants pocket while holding his other hand tight against Ben's neck. *Son of a bitch!* He yanked it free. Terror worked through him. The flashes from other RPGs fired in their direction made Dan feel helpless. It wasn't something he felt often, and he hated the sensation. Ben's blue eyes, now cloudy and less focused, met his, almost imploring. "D-dan..."

"Shut up, Ben! Save your strength! *Fight! Stay with me!*" he rasped, quickly fitting the thick battle dressing against his neck. If Dan put too much pressure on the wound, he'd choke Ben to death. Pressure on a wound was always what stopped the bleeding, but the neck was the most vulnerable part of a human's body. There was no way Dan could put a tourniquet around Ben's thick neck—he'd asphyxiate him. Dammit! Tears blurred Dan's vision as he placed both hands around

Ben's neck, watching how quickly the white of the clean battle dressing darkened.

"D-dan…listen…" Ben whispered. He tried to raise his hand, but failed. "Listen…"

"No!" Dan snarled. "You're going to make it, Ben! Just let me keep the pressure on it! Don't talk!" His throat ached with pain, a lump so large, he thought he was going to choke on it. Dan saw Ben give him that look. He'd seen it hundreds of times since they'd joined the Army at age eighteen. It was that amused look, that patience he had by the truckload, as if he was a father putting up with a petulant child. In this case, him.

"Listen…" Ben whispered, forcing his fingers around Dan's wrist. "Cait…"

Dan squeezed his eyes shut, his head falling downward toward his chest. Ben's voice was thin…weak… God, Ben was bleeding out and he couldn't stop it from happening. Another sob of desperation tore out of Dan and he stared through his tears at his friend. He seemed at peace now. There was no more terror in his eyes, the fight bled out of him.

"W-what?" Dan rasped, watching the clean, white edges of the now-slippery battle dressing disappear as Ben's blood soaked through.

"T-take care of Cait for me? Don't let her marry a military guy. Protect her? She needs your help, Dan. Be there for her—" Ben's fingers weakened on Dan's wrist "—b-because…I won't be able to…"

Dan saw the life flicker out of Ben's staring eyes. He sobbed, throwing the battle dressing away, dragging Ben into his arms, holding him, cradling him in the middle of the firefight. Dan couldn't stop crying and calling out

his best friend's name. Ben was dead. Oh, God…Cait…
Ben's younger sister…they were so close…so close…
His heart felt as though it was being torn into bleeding
pieces within his chest.

He dragged Ben's lifeless body back against the wall
of the partially destroyed house. Somehow, and Dan
didn't know how, he managed to get Ben wedged in
between the two broken mud walls in order to protect
his body. A team left no man behind. Hearing shouts
in Urdu coming toward him, he turned, grabbing his
M-4 out of the fine grit and dirt, swinging it around.
Rage filled him.

He screamed into his mic to Franklin that Ben was
dead. Bled out. In two and half minutes a fine, damn
brave man—his best friend—was gone.

Shadowy figures moved around other destroyed mud
houses toward his position. All Taliban. Above him, he
heard the thick whumping sounds of two Apache combat helicopters swiftly racing toward them. They were
the team's only hope of getting out of this alive.

Dan wasn't going to leave Ben's side. He'd make
his stand here. He'd fight to keep his best friend from
being taken by the Taliban. They'd strip his body, hack
him up and then behead him. It wasn't going to happen.
Kneeling near where Ben lay, Dan raised his M-4 and
sighted. Sweat stung his eyes, his heart torn apart by
grief and adrenaline. They could all die here. The M-4
jerked heavily against his shoulder. The acrid, burning
smell filled his flared nostrils.

He saw a shadow fall to the ground, screaming, his
AK-47 flying out of his hands. Teeth clenched, snarling
a curse, Dan partially hid between the thick mud walls,

holding his M-4 steady, taking out one, two, three more Taliban troops out of the firefight.

His team was getting overwhelmed. Dan had no idea the size of the force they were facing, but it wasn't small. His earpiece was exploding with screams, orders and calls from his brother operators. They had been ambushed! This was supposed to be a quiet night, moving along in their two Humvees and a supply truck. But it had turned into a nightmare and they were now fighting for their lives.

Dan had no idea how many others were dead or wounded. He could pick out other M-4 rifles being fired at different points around the small village. They had spread out into a diamond formation, protecting their flanks, not able to move from their positions without opening up a flank the Taliban could pour into and kill all of them.

The sawlike growl of the Gatling gun being fired from beneath the Apaches began. The rounds were dangerously close! Dan ducked, watching the .50-caliber rounds chunking through the empty mud homes, dirt and rocks flying into the air in all directions, now shrapnel. He heard the screams of the Taliban troops struck by them. Satisfaction soared through him.

And then Dan caught movement near the house where he knelt. The next thing he knew his right leg was collapsing beneath him. Shocked, he twisted around, lifting his weapon, firing at the enemy soldier who had fired at him. *Son of a bitch!* The soldier was slammed backward by the bullet from Dan's M-4.

Dan watched the man fall like a puppet into a heap. The vibration of the Apaches told him they were immediately above him. His whole body vibrated with the sound of the combat helicopter drifting overhead, hunting the enemy. The Gatling guns on the two stalker helos were pointed away from them. The pilots had the Special Forces team identified on their TV monitor, and they now had a bead on the enemy, cutting them down like a scythe slicing through a field of ripe wheat. Dan now noticed that his leg was numb. Lowering his M-4, he slid his left hand across to his right thigh. Blood met his exposed fingers. He'd been hit!

The vibrations of the Apache's blades pummeled his entire body like invisible fists. Dan leaned back into the wall. *How bad was it?* His mind swung between shock and watching for enemy. The combat helicopters were rapacious predators, hunting down the enemy with on-board infrared, sighting and killing them.

I'm bleeding out.

Dan almost laughed. Hysteria jammed into his throat. He grabbed for the tourniquet on the left epaulet of his cammies, jerking it free. He had to get it around his right thigh, above the bleed. It was an inky-black night except for flashes of light from above like bolts of lightning spewed from beneath the bellies of the hunting Apaches. Dan saw the bleed. It, like Ben's, was spurting out like a geyser. There was no pain. Cursing, he dropped his M-4 beside him and yanked the tourniquet around his leg. They'd all been taught how to apply a tourniquet to a bleeding limb, tightening the strap enough to stop the flow.

Dan called Morales, the other combat medic, letting him know he was hit and had a tourniquet in place. He didn't know if Morales was alive or not. Every Special

Forces A team had two 18-Delta combat medics. Ben was dead. He called hoarsely for Franklin, giving him his location, the type of wound he had and his present condition.

Dan jerked the tourniquet tight. His teeth clenched as the pain ripped up into his thigh and raced raggedly into his torso. The bleed was lessening. He tightened the tourniquet more, the strap in his dirty, grimy gloved fists, slick with Ben's blood and his own. *Tighter! Tighter!* Or he'd bleed out just like Ben.

And then who would take care of Cait? For a moment dizziness assailed Dan. He blinked through the sweat that leaked into his eyes, his breath raspy, black dots dancing before his eyes. No! He couldn't faint! Not now!

The spurting had stopped.

Dan felt momentary relief. He slumped against the mud wall with Ben nearby. Keeping his gaze roving around him, he saw no more enemy in the area. The Apaches were hovering above their diamond pattern, invisible watchdogs in the black sky above them, loud, the thumping vibration continued to rhythmically beat against his body. They'd stopped firing. The powerful vibration jammed like fists through him, and was all Dan could hear and feel.

He called hoarsely for Morales once again.

No answer.

How many of his team were left alive? Were they all wounded? How many had died?

The pain drifting up his leg became nearly overwhelming. Dan closed his eyes for a second. He saw Cait's face, her shoulder-length red hair, that riot of freckles across her nose and cheeks.

He had met her when he was eighteen years old—
he'd come to Hawaii for training. She and her brother,
Ben, had seen him on the beach where he was learning
to surf. They'd struck up a conversation and, for Dan,
it was like meeting old friends once more. He couldn't
admit it to Ben, who was six feet tall like himself, but
he was drawn to Cait's clean, natural beauty, her wide
green eyes, the color of the Pacific off the coast of Oahu.
She was so full of life.

He cursed softly as his gloved hand slipped on the
tourniquet. Opening his eyes, he could tell there was
no more bleed. It slowly dawned on him that something
white was sticking up and out of the torn cammie fabric across his thigh. What the hell was that? And then,
in the next minute, Dan's slowing mind recognized it
as his thigh bone, the femur. It was broken and jagged-
looking, sticking up out of his flesh.

The shock settled in. He was in serious condition.
He called for Morales, giving him more info about his
condition.

No answer.

Finally, Franklin came back.

"Dan, only five of us ambulatory. We'll get to you
in a second. Two medevacs just landed. We're coming
for you and Ben…hang on…"

Dan tipped back his head, feeling tiredness seeping through him like a slow, black, moving river. He
closed his eyes and acknowledged Franklin's transmission, telling him that he'd lost a lot of blood. And that
Ben was dead.

"Not sure I'll be conscious…" he muttered, his last
transmission. The rhythmic whumping of the Apache's

blades comforted him as he closed his eyes. They were on guard above them. They'd protect them, and the medevac Black Hawks were now on the ground and would save the wounded.

As he thought of Ben, he felt as if his heart had been torn out of his chest. They were both twenty-nine years old. They'd been together for five years on this Special Forces team. They were tighter than fleas on a dog. They were supposed to rotate home in another week. Back to Honolulu, Hawaii, for a well-deserved thirty-day leave. They'd see Cait, go surfing together and have beach picnics, laughter, good times and fun.

Tears leaked out of his tightly shut eyes. He felt weaker, knowing that the bleed was staunched but not stopped. He could still slowly bleed to death. Where was Morales? He needed a medic. Dan had to stay alive to tell Cait and her family what happened to Ben.

Ben's family was so tight. A good family, unlike his own. Ben's mother was an ER doctor at a civilian hospital in Honolulu. His father was a retired Marine Force Recon colonel. Cait was a physical therapist working over at US Army Tripler Medical Center, helping soldiers who had been wounded get their limbs working again.

All of those memories flowed through Dan's short-circuiting mind. He wasn't worried about his mother, Joyce, who lived in Honolulu. She was an embittered woman, angry at the world. His father, an alcoholic, was dead. Tears leaked down his bearded cheeks. Dan felt suddenly cold, felt the iciness moving up from his feet and into his lower legs. Was this how Ben had felt as he was bleeding out? It must have been. Oh, God, was he dying?

Cait! Behind his eyelids, Dan saw her oval face, that stubborn chin of hers and that wide, smiling mouth. How many times had he entertained kissing that lush mouth of hers? How many times had he ached to make love to her? But he never had. He never would. She was Ben's little sister and Ben had asked Dan to guard her, make sure she stayed away from military guys who wanted her for only one thing.

Dan never told Ben that he coveted Cait for himself. She was so fresh, innocent and happy. He always felt better around her. Whether she knew it or not, she lifted Dan, made him feel good about himself. She was the optimist. He was the brutal realist. He'd harbored dreams of telling her he loved her. But Ben would have lost it and their friendship would have been destroyed. So Dan said nothing. And now, as he lay slowly bleeding out, Dan felt grief because he would never be able to tell Cait that he'd fallen in love with her at eighteen and held a torch for her in his heart until his dying day.

That was the last thing Dan remembered thinking before he lost consciousness.

Everything was hazy. Pain drifted up Dan's leg and into his lower body, making him groan. Weak, he struggled to open his eyes. His nostrils flared, catching hospital smells like anesthetic and bleach. Why couldn't he open his eyes?

"Dan? It's Cait. Don't fight so hard. You're coming out of surgery. It's all right. You're alive. You're safe…"

Cait's voice was low and soft, so close to his ear. The

sensory experience, combined with her warm hand touching his cheek, oriented Dan. His heart pulsed strongly when he heard her smoky tone. He swore he could even smell her scent, so sweet, reminding him of spicy cinnamon. Her voice was barely above a whisper. So close to his ear. He hungrily absorbed the warmth of her long fingers gently stroking his cheek, as if to soothe the tension he held within him.

He was *alive*? Was he? His mind was in pieces and Dan couldn't put anything together. The pain was like a deep, agonizing toothache drifting up his leg. He felt heavy and he was thirsty. Moving his lips, he became aware his throat smarted with pain and it was dry. God, he was so thirsty! Compressing his lips, he tried to speak, but nothing but a croak came out.

"Dan? You're in recovery. Stop fighting, okay? You're safe. You're home here with me. It's Cait."

The moment she cupped his cheek with her palm, he stopped struggling. And as she lifted her hand away, moving her fingers gently through his long, clean hair, his scalp prickled with pleasure. His entire body went limp and he groaned, unable to open his eyes.

Cait!

Maybe he wasn't dead after all. Her touch felt so damned good. Steadying. Stabilizing. She felt so very close to him. And like a starving animal, Dan eagerly inhaled her scent deep into his body, and it fed him, helped him focus.

Minute by minute, Dan's mind started to hinge back together. The more Cait stroked his head, rearranging his hair here and there because it nearly touched his shoulders, Dan acquiesced to her light ministrations.

Some of her words ran together. He didn't care what she said—it was Cait. He loved her so damn much and he'd never told her. Never. It would have hurt Ben to know that he ached for Cait.

Ben...

Blips and flashes exploded behind his shut eyes. He saw Ben, heard himself screaming at him, running to his side. The whole scene downloaded from his spinning brain and suddenly, Dan was there, not in recovery. Cait was with him. He could hear her soothing voice speaking to him, but he was back in the village, trying to stop Ben's bleed. There was such anguish that roared through him—his body jerked and then tensed. Cait's hand gripped his shoulder firmly, her voice low, fraught with anxiety, near his ear.

Dan couldn't hear anything except the explosions, the M-4's throaty roar, the popping of AK-47s and the thumping of Apache helicopters racing toward their compromised position. *No! No! Ben couldn't die! He just couldn't!*

A low animal cry tore between his thin, contorted lips. His entire body jerked in response. Pain exploded in his leg and it raced up into his torso, sucking the breath out of him. Cait's husky, urgent voice broke through his barrier of agony. Dan tried to hold on to it, fought to follow it even though he couldn't hear what she was saying. He tried to concentrate on her fingers moving soothingly across his tense shoulder, trying to calm him down.

Ben died! He died! He'd bled out! A moan, like that of an animal being tortured ripped out of Dan. He was too weak to move. Too weak to open his eyes. And how he wanted to see Cait, but he couldn't. The last thing he remembered feeling was Cait's lips pressed against his sweaty brow, her voice trembling with emotion, her hands cupping his sweaty face. Anguish, grief and loss plunged Dan into a spinning, darkening hell and he knew nothing more.

Chapter 2

Cait Moore tried to fight back her tears as she watched Dan Taylor slowly become conscious. Her brother, Ben, was dead. Word had reached them a week ago. No one had told her and her family how he'd died. Looking at Dan's face, the deep tan, the slashes on either side of his thinned mouth, she knew he would know. Maybe it would give her and her family some desperately needed closure. They'd buried Ben three days ago at the National Memorial Cemetery of the Pacific at Punchbowl Crater on the island of Oahu. Her heart ached with loss for her big brother.

She stood watching Dan, who was in a slightly elevated position on the bed. He'd come out of seven hours of surgery at Tripler Medical Center, his second surgery in seven days. Cait had found out that they'd planned to amputate his leg during his first surgery

at Landstuhl Medical Center in Germany. Dr. Allison
Barker, who was an exceptionally talented ortho surgeon, had stopped the amputation. When Dan had arrived at Tripler, Allison had put screws into Dan's leg
instead, saving it from amputation.

Her heart swelled with feelings for Dan. Beneath
his tan, he had an unhealthy pallor. Her gaze drifted to
the two IVs, one in each of his arms. One was a con-
tinuous morphine drip because bone pain could only
be addressed with this opiate. The other was feeding
him the necessary fluids and nutrients he needed to
stay alive and recover. He wore a blue hospital gown
that emphasized the breadth of his shoulders and his
powerful chest.

Memories assailed her as she stood, her hand lingering on his arm, feeling the sprinkled dark brown
hair beneath her fingertips. Would Dan ever be able to
surf again? Allison and her surgical team worked on
soldiers and Marines whose limbs had been destroyed.
Dan would become Cait's patient at some point because
she'd pleaded with her boss, Dr. Jackson Berringer, to
allow her to work with him. Cait was grateful Jackson
had granted her request. She was a damn good physical therapist, and she wanted no one else but her to help
Dan to recover his ability to walk and do the things he
had done before being wounded.

Absently she moved her fingers slowly up and down
Dan's ropy forearm, watching his lids quiver. He was
finally coming out of the worst of the anesthesia. She
couldn't settle her roiling feelings, which swung between her grief at Ben being dead and her relief that
Dan had gotten out of that firefight alive. Tears stung

her eyes at the thought that Dan could have been killed, too. She wiped her tears away and sniffed. He couldn't see her crying. He'd ask why, and she couldn't tell him. How long had she loved this brave soldier? Ever since she'd met him.

Cait made a frustrated, muffled sound, forcing her tears away. Dan's eyes would open at any moment now. How she loved him. And he didn't know. She'd never spoken of it to him. Ben had wanted her to consider Dan a brother, but she never had. Her big, overprotective brother would have been crushed if she'd ever admitted that she had, over time, fallen hopelessly in love with Dan.

Everything had changed now. Cait knew Ben had always worried about her falling in love with a military man. He'd warned her they were out for sex and sex only, that she needed to marry a medical doctor because they were more stable and reliable. They would respect her for her keen intelligence and she wouldn't have to worry about her husband being killed in combat, making her a young widow.

Ben had wanted her to be happy. And to have a good, stable marriage. But it had become so tough on Cait, every time they came home on leave, to pretend and hide her feelings from Dan. And keep the secret from her brother.

Her hand stilled on Dan's forearm. How many times had she dreamed of Dan loving her? Kissing her? Cait's gaze drifted to his strong, chiseled mouth that only now was beginning to relax. The morphine drip was giving him some badly needed relief from the nerve pain.

Suddenly, he opened his eyes.

Cait moved closer, fingers wrapping around his wrist, watching his gray, cloudy gaze. He was drifting in a morphine cloud.

"Dan? It's Cait." She smiled down at him, reaching out, grazing his cheek and pushing his long, nearly shoulder-length hair behind his ear. His gray eyes suddenly became raptor-like and fastened on her. Her smile grew. "You see me?"

"Y-yeah…Cait…"

His voice was hoarse and rough. "It's okay, Dan. You're coming out from anesthesia." His dark brown brows dipped. "Am I speaking too fast for you?" Cait knew words ran together when anesthesia still lingered in a person's body. Her heart mushroomed with powerful emotions, wanting to kiss him, but he was conscious now and he'd remember if she did. And how could she explain her actions to him then?

"N-no…fine…where?"

"Tripler Medical Center. Honolulu." She didn't want to stop touching Dan. At the very least, there was the healing value of touch with physical therapy, but her need to touch him ran much deeper.

His large, black pupils widened as she ran her fingers through his mussed but clean long hair. The nurses had washed it, but it needed to be combed. Cait knew Special Forces A teams grew long hair and wore beards so as not to stand out in the Middle East.

She watched his eyes grow dazed and then slowly wander back to her and actually look at her. Cait couldn't stop smiling. How badly she wanted to kiss Dan, welcome him home, celebrate that he'd survived.

"H-how long since…since I got wounded?"

"Seven days. They kept you in a drug-induced coma after taking you out of the field, Dan." She saw his eyes grow to slits, felt the shift of energy around him. He remembered the firefight. She could sense it and see it in his wrinkled brow, the hardness coming back to his gray, murky eyes. "I'm sorry," she whispered. "Ben didn't make it...but you did." Cait swallowed and fought the tears flooding her eyes. "You're alive, Dan. And you're going to live..."

At that moment he jerkily lifted his hand, his roughened fingers weak but still able to lift and capture her hand.

"I tried to save him, Cait...God...I tried..."

"It's all right." She wobbled, heard the grief and guilt in his gruff voice. "No one's told us what happened... only that he died in a firefight."

Dan closed his eyes, fingers tightening around Cait's slender hand. She wore a hospital uniform of blue scrub pants and top. Her beautiful red hair was up on her head in a loose, askew topknot. She wore pink lipstick, but the flush across her cheeks was natural. Her scent, the cinnamon shampoo she used, the steadying firmness of her warm skin beneath his cold fingers, helped him focus. Hearing the stress, the grief in her low, tortured voice, brought up his own anguish over Ben's death.

Dan stared up into her green eyes glistening with unshed tears. She was fighting back those tears, and it ripped into him. He'd never had any defense against Cait. He was vulnerable to her at all times. His fingers tightened around hers.

"He didn't feel any pain, Cait. He got hit in the neck." He stopped. His voice had become harsh with agony.

"I—I tried to save him... I'm sorry... I wanted to so damned bad but..." Dan choked, tears burning in his eyes. He turned away, embarrassed that tears ran down his face. He released her hand but Cait caught it, wrapping her fingers tightly around his.

"It's all right, Dan. I know you did everything you could. God...I'm so grateful you're alive..." She choked back a sob.

Just having Cait's strong hand around his helped. Dan couldn't stop the tears and finally pressed his face into the pillow. He couldn't bear to look at her since he knew grief was written in her features.

Finally, as he got a hold of his floating, amorphous emotions, Dan forced himself to turn and look into her shadowed green eyes. "I—I'm so damned sorry, Cait..."

"Hush," she whispered, lifting her hand, gently smoothing out the wrinkles on his tanned brow. "It's all right. Ben died doing something he loved, Dan. And you were with him." Her eyes grew misty. "At least he died with you there. That had to be a comfort for him."

Dan shoved the grief down deep inside himself. "Yeah...I was there. I tried." Her fingers trembled slightly as she continued to graze his brow, his cheek, her touch so featherlight. Dan felt like a dying man who was being given absolution by a saint. He lifted his lashes, staring into her warm, anguished gaze— Cait had never looked so beautiful, so fresh and alive, as right now.

"Are you in pain?"

Yeah, his heart felt like hell, writhing with anguish. "A little," he mumbled. "I'm on morphine. I can feel it dialing back the pain."

She smiled a little. "Yes, you are."

When she continued to hold his hand, Dan felt a gratefulness he couldn't give words to. How like Cait to intuitively know he needed her right now. She wasn't a physical therapist for nothing. At Tripler she was considered the best of the best. And she'd been helping soldiers recover from lost and wounded limbs since she was twenty-two and now she was twenty-eight.

"You're an angel," he rasped, holding her eyes, watching her pupils enlarge. "You've always been my angel." Dan forced himself to stop. He was blithering because the morphine had loosened his closely held emotions for her. He saw surprise on Cait's expression and then the joy that suddenly shone in her pale green eyes.

"I like being your angel," she managed shyly, her voice strained. "In fact—" she squeezed his large, rough hand "—I've been assigned by your ortho surgeon to help you through recovery, Dan. I'll be with you all the way…"

Oh, yeah, his leg. He'd forgotten about it until just now. His emotions, his mind and heart had been on Ben dying and how it was affecting Cait. She took his hand and laid it against his belly and he squeezed her fingers in return, a little of his strength returning. This was the first time there had been any real intimacy between them, man to woman. Dan tried to ferret out the unexpected joy he saw banked in her eyes. Did Cait *want* his touch?

Maybe it was his opiate-drenched mind, Dan told himself. Cait had had other relationships over the years, all with civilian men, who'd come and gone. What on earth had he just seen in her eyes? She kept grazing the flesh of his hand and lower arm, as if wanting to touch him. It felt like more than a medical touch. But was it just her normal bedside manner? Dan didn't know, and he was too drugged right now to think two coherent thoughts in a row.

"Are you thirsty?"

He nodded. "Thirstier than a camel." When Cait released his hand, he wanted to reach out and capture it once again. But he didn't. Dan ached for continued contact. Wanted so much more of it—and her. Even now, he could feel himself stirring beneath the blue blankets across his lower body. Even on morphine. He had it bad for Cait. Dan savagely suppressed his sexual desire.

Cait rolled the tray over to his bedside, filled a glass of water and placed a straw in it for him. She lifted the straw, placing it between his lips. The gesture was so damned sensual Dan felt his body respond again. He drank the entire contents of the glass. He ended up drinking one more glass before he was sated.

After pushing the tray aside, Cait sat on the side of his bed, her hip inches from his. Dan could see a tent of covers over his lower legs from his knees to his feet. "How are your parents doing, Cait?" His voice was stronger now. His brain was actually functioning up to a point.

Cait's expression saddened. "They're suffering, Dan. If you'll allow me, I'll tell them what you just told me. That you were there with Ben when he died." She reached out, fingers skimming the hand resting on his belly. "It would help them so much."

"Yeah, go ahead." Dan saw moisture in her eyes again,

her grief on the surface. "His last words," he rasped, "were about you. Ben asked me to take care of you."

Her fingers closed around his, and he saw how badly Cait needed to be held and comforted. She would have to be the strong one for her devastated parents. Who was there to comfort her? He wanted to be the person to do that. But Dan could barely do anything right now. He was so damned helpless trussed up in the bed, not to mention physically weak. It took every bit of his strength to speak, to squeeze her fingers. Wanting to do more, unable to, he saw her strength, saw her swallow back the tears and give him a tremulous smile of gratefulness.

"Ben was always overprotective about me." She shook her head.

"Because he loved you."

"I know." Cait closed her eyes. "I miss him so much. I was so looking forward to you two coming home."

It felt as though a knife had sliced open his heart. All Dan could do was cling to her fingers, somehow convey his guilt. "I'm sorry, Cait. You can't know how much…"

She sniffed and sat up, pushing red tendrils behind her ear. "We need to concentrate on you now, Dan."

Dan watched her struggle with her emotions, place them gently aside for Ben, her whole attention now focused on him. It felt good. Fortifying. Necessary. "My mother? Joyce?"

"Oh, I talked to Joyce earlier. She couldn't get off work at the software company to come and wait for you to come out of surgery. I told her no worries, that I'd be here for you. She was relieved. She'll be here tonight after work to see you."

Dan grimaced. "Just as well." Worried, he asked, "Did she yell at you?"

After years of abuse by her alcoholic husband, Joyce had become a testy and defensive woman. Soon after they'd moved from Rush City, Texas, to Honolulu, his father had died. It had been his dream to move. His father had sold their small cattle ranch and dragged them to Hawaii in order to fulfill his wish. His mother hadn't wanted to leave her extensive family in Texas. And Dan had been in the Army six months later when his father died of a massive heart attack here in Honolulu while out on a golf course. Dan had come home on emergency medical leave to bury his father and listen to his angry, bitter mother curse her husband at his graveside.

Now, Dan worried that Joyce had taken out her bile on Cait.

"She was upset, which is understandable, Dan. She wanted to be here." Patting his hand gently, Cait said, "Joyce is worried about you."

Biting back a curse, he growled, "Just as well she's not here, Cait. I'm not up to dealing with her. All she can do is say the sky is falling, that life sucks. She's like a toxic black cloud that overshadows everyone within five minutes."

Dan knew Cait was more than aware of Joyce's depression and mood swings. She had tried to get her some help, but his mother was stubborn and angry. She was in control of her life, finally, and that was that.

Cait give him a doleful look and a tremulous half smile.

"She's been abused, Dan. But let's not talk about that right now. I know Dr. Allison Barker, your ortho surgeon, is going on rounds right now." She looked at her watch. "It's 0800. She should be here any moment now. She'll tell you about the state of your leg."

Dan had lost track of time and days. His whole world centered on Cait. She wore an ID badge clipped to her left pocket, indicating she was hospital staff. "Okay," he said. "Are you on duty?"

"Yes, beginning at 0900. I asked Dr. Barker if I could come and stay with you until you became conscious. She said yes."

"Nice waking up to an angel," he said thickly. Her eyes sparkled.

"I'm glad you think of me as your angel," Cait teased, smiling.

Her smile went straight to his grieving heart, lifting him, making him feel hope. The love he held for Cait wanted to be known. Dan quickly squelched the urge to tell her how he felt. "Yeah, I've always thought of you that way, Cait. I know some of the soldiers you've helped, talked with them, and they say the same thing about you—that you're an angel. You've helped so many people."

"And now, I get to help you." Cait caressed his shaven cheek, holding his cloudy gray gaze.

A doctor in her early forties quietly entered the ward. She was a brunette with blue eyes and she wore a white lab coat. The talk among some of the other men in other beds farther down the line stopped.

"Oh, here's Dr. Barker," Cait said, standing. She smiled down at Dan. "She's the best."

The tall, spare woman approached his bed. She offered her lean hand and Dan weakly raised his.

"You're looking awfully good, Sergeant Taylor. I'm Dr. Barker. I was your ortho surgeon for your injured leg. Are you up to a little talk about the surgery I performed?"

"Yes, ma'am," he said. Dan liked her warmth. She wasn't like so many doctors—cold and robotic. Her alto voice conveyed her concern for him.

Opening his chart, Barker said, "You were hit with a bullet in the right femur, Sergeant. You'd lost nearly four pints of blood. They took you to the hospital in Bagram, where they stabilized you. The next day, you were taken on a C-5 flight to Landstuhl Medical Center in Germany. I have a good friend there—Dr. Travis. He's an ortho surgeon like myself. He called me because he said your broken femur was so bad that he thought he needed to amputate it."

Dan scowled, sudden shock hitting him. He couldn't lift the tent to see if his leg was still attached or not.

"Oh," Barker said, following his gaze, "your leg is still there. I told the ortho to stabilize you, do what he could, and bring you here where I'd do the final operation on you and determine whether or not we could save your leg." She smiled a little. "And we did save it. Me and my team. But Dr. Travis is a brilliant ortho surgeon and he helped make my job possible."

"I still have my leg?"

"Sure do, Sergeant. And you're going to keep it." Her brows went down. "But because you've got a lot of screws in the bones, holding the femur together so it can knit and grow strong once more, you're in for a lot of bed time."

"How long?" Dan tried to steel himself, watching Cait who had stood back, her hands at her sides, her expression open and vulnerable.

"Two months minimum, Sergeant. It's a very difficult recovery and that's why so many surgeons amputate. Your recovery time is going to be a lot longer, a lot more painful, but I have a great PT here." She motioned toward Cait. "And she felt saving your leg was a viable option. So did I. Cait will be your PT specialist, Sergeant. I know you know one another, so that's a plus. Cait said you are fast friends."

"Yes, ma'am," Dan said. "We've known each other for eleven years." *And I've loved her all that time.* He glanced over at Cait, whose eyes glimmered with unspoken joy, and he managed to lift one corner of his mouth to show he was glad, too.

"These first two months are going to be a special hell, Sergeant," Barker warned him. "You're lucky—I understand Cait plays a mean game of Monopoly. You play Monopoly, Sergeant?"

Dan grinned a little, trading a glance with Cait. Her cheeks were flushed now. "Yes, ma'am. She usually beats the pants off me."

"Well," Barker said, smiling a little, "be prepared to play a lot of Monopoly these next two months. You're bed bound for the first six weeks, and you're going to be bored out of your skull. Miss Moore can't begin PT until we can get you ambulatory, and that won't happen until the six-week mark. So get your mind wrapped around that, Sergeant Taylor, for the long haul. Okay?"

"Anything to keep my leg, ma'am." Dan held the surgeon's gaze. "Thank you for saving it…"

Giving a curt nod, Barker said, "It was my pleasure. I'll see you tomorrow morning." She moved on to the soldier in the next bed.

* * *

Cait tried to get a hold of her emotions. She walked from the swimming pool area at five o'clock, finished with her last soldier of the day. Wanting to see how Dan was, she'd promised to have dinner with him tonight. How she looked forward to seeing him! She hurried through the massive medical center and made it up to the third-floor Ortho. When she entered the ward, she saw Dan had been placed in Fowler's position, and he looked sad but alert.

"Hey," she called softly, "how are you doing?"

Dan lifted his head. Instantly, his heart took off with joy. "Better now that you're here."

Grinning, Cait came over and looked him over. "How's your pain level? Holding?"

"Yeah. Nurse was just in and adjusted the drip." Cait's red hair was now tamed into a ponytail, the tendrils lovingly caressing her high cheekbones. "I'd give anything to get a shower, though."

Cait sat down on the edge of the bed gently, not wanting to cause his leg any discomfort. "Hasn't the nurse given you a bath yet?"

"No." Dan grimaced and rubbed the seven-day growth of beard on his face. "I'd like to get cleaned up. Is that possible?"

"Do you mind if I give you a bath and a shave?" She held up her hands and she smiled. "I'm well trained."

The idea of Cait doing that for him damn near sent Dan into a boiling cauldron of heat and need for her. "Sure…"

Cait stood. "Be back in a minute. I know there's a nurse who's out sick today on the Ortho ward, and that's probably why you didn't get your bath. I'll ask the head nurse if she minds if I take care of you instead. Be right back."

Within ten minutes, Cait was back with everything she'd need. Using the rolling tray, she set up what she'd need to shave his face.

"I didn't know you did this kind of thing," Dan muttered, apologetic, his throat tightening with sudden emotions. Cait had brought over a small washbowl of warm water and applied the shaving foam to his face, which felt like sensual foreplay to him.

"Well, you've never asked what I do here," she teased lightly, her palm light against the side of his face while bringing the razor downward from his temple to his jaw. "Now," she said, smiling into his eyes, "don't talk while I'm shaving you, okay? Just sit back, relax and enjoy it…"

Dan closed his eyes, head against his pillow, drawing comfort from her quick, light touches. Cait was so close, her hands delicate and yet firm against his flesh. Sparks of heat zigzagged down through him. This was intimate. This is what he'd always wanted to share with Cait. In no time, she'd scraped the beard free from his face. Dan was sorry it was over as she gently patted his face clean with a warm, damp towel.

"Are you always going to shave me?"

She laughed and took a warm cloth, gently finishing cleaning up his face. "Only until you feel stronger. Maybe a day or two more. Why? Was I that bad?" She tilted her head, studying him. "No cuts."

Dan managed a sour smile of sorts. "No…it was good. Thank you…"

Cait gave him a serious look. "Have you ever been bathed before, Dan?"

He stared at her. "As in a hospital bath?"

"Yes."

"No...never. Why?"

"Because—" she cleared her throat "—it's kinda intimate." She gestured down toward his lower body. "Everything gets washed." She gave him a worried look. "I don't know if you want me to do this. Would it be embarrassing for you? Uncomfortable? Maybe you'd rather wait and let a nurse you don't know do it for you?"

Dan noticed how Cait's face turned red with embarrassment. "Oh" was all he managed to choke out. And then he searched her eyes. "You don't have to do this, Cait. It's all right. I understand." Because she'd never seen him naked. Never seen his whole body. The thought filled him with a sudden shaft of boiling desire. His dreams were coming true in real life. Only, as he saw Cait's face and expression, he said, "I'm okay with it. But are you?"

She shrugged. "Listen, I bathe guys in the ortho ward. Sometimes, when they're short a nurse and I don't have a PT patient, I'll come up here and lend a hand. I'm game if you are."

He was more than game, but he tried to look serious about the issue. What was he going to do if he became erect? Still, Cait wasn't totally innocent...and she was a professional. "Okay," he said gruffly. "Let's do it."

Cait nodded and leaned over him, pulling him slowly into a more upright sitting position in order to start the process. "I'll untie your gown and then I'll pull the curtains around your bed so you have privacy."

Dan nodded, his skin tightening as her fingers flew over the three ties against his back, releasing them. Suddenly all his torrid thoughts, all the hot dreams of loving Cait he'd had through the years, rose unbidden. Dan watched as she pulled the long, light green curtains around his bed. When she turned, he saw how serious she'd become.

"Are you sure about this?" he demanded. Because he loved her, cared for her and never wanted to hurt her or make her feel embarrassed. He was the antithesis of his alcoholic father, would never want to harm someone he loved.

"Well," Cait said wryly, pulling the gown off him and keeping the covers in place around his waist, "this is a bit uncomfortable for me, but don't worry. I'll deal with it."

"You've almost seen me naked, Cait," he teased, leaning back, closing his eyes.

"That's true. And I know what a man looks like. So, you just lie back and let me get you cleaned up. You'll feel so much better afterward."

Dan nodded. "Well, if it gets to be too much—" he pried his eyes open, seeing how flighty Cait had become as she retrieved the towel, wash cloth and soap on the tray "—you can stop at any point. I'll be okay with that, Cait."

She gave him an amused look. "Maybe if I was a greenhorn eighteen-year-old I'd have issues, but I'm not eighteen anymore, Dan. We're adults. We'll handle this. Now, close your eyes and just enjoy this warm wash cloth and the wonderful scent of Ivory soap. Okay?"

And enjoy her hands on him… Already he could feel

himself hardening. He swallowed. "Yeah...okay...but I'm not made of stone..."

He lay back and tried to relax as she soaped down his neck and shoulders, that cloth so soft and warm feeling. He couldn't help but think this was beyond any fantasy he'd ever had about Cait. And as much as Dan tried, he couldn't stop his body and mind from thinking of Cait as his lover as her hands skimmed across his powerful chest and torso. It felt as if she was loving him, exploring him, not just washing away the stink. His morphine-laden mind dreamed whether he wanted it to or not.

"Just relax," Cait said as she moved quickly, washing Dan's upper body. His eyes were closed, but she could tell that he was affected by her touch. His skin kept tightening where she washed his body. It was pure, unadulterated pleasure to see this man's body. She hurt inwardly to see the scars, the cuts and old bruises discolored with age. His body was a story of combat. Cait had secretly wanted to touch Dan in this way, a loving way, caressing him. Her throat felt parched as she patted his upper body dry with a soft, white towel. Afterward, she placed another dry towel across him to keep him warm.

As she pulled down the sheet and blankets, positioning them up and over the tent, her heart started hammering. He was erect. This wasn't anything new to Cait. It happened. But this was Dan, the man she'd secretly loved for so many years. And he wasn't the average man at all. It sent unexpected heat pooling into her lower body. Cait was well aware that Dan was powerfully masculine, but his arousal made him even more potent.

Feeling shaky inside, her breathing shallow, she quickly began to wash him from the waist down. As her fingers slipped around his erection, she felt him tense and then try to relax. Her heart leaped, and she imagined him inside her. Something told Cait that Dan would be a gentle lover, a man who knew how to please a woman, giving her pleasure, as well, and not just satisfying himself.

Finally she was done washing him. She quickly placed a small towel across his body. She noticed the ugly red welt of the surgery scar and the pins over half his thick, treelike thigh. Cait's mouth was dry and her heart was hammering with need. Now she ached for him. She'd gone two years without sex. *Two years.* But this man required more than just physical attention. He was wounded, and she had to control her desire. Easier said than done as her body longed for him to touch her, fill her with himself.

Chapter 3

Where was Cait? Dan lay sweating in a pool of pain in his bed, his leg hitched up, and he was unable to move. He hated the catheter and hated being confined to bed. He didn't sleep at night because of the nightmares about Ben's death. If he so much as twitched the wrong way, those damn screws would feel as if someone had poured scalding water around each of them, the agony nearly unbearable. He could always opt for more morphine and knock himself out for hours at a time, waking up feeling half-alive. Or half-dead.

He was desperate to see Cait. It had been two days since she'd washed him, blushing the entire time. He didn't dare tell her how good her hands had felt on him, sick son of a bitch that he was. Even now, he was thinking about sex. With her. But he'd been thinking of that with Cait forever.

It was after dinner and the ward was quieting down. Most of the men were lucky. They were not prisoners to their beds because they'd had their injured legs amputated. They were mobile in their wheelchairs, going for physical therapy daily while he was left alone in an empty ward. He envied them in one way but was glad he still had his leg, so he suffered in silence. Never would he ever take walking for granted again. Or being able to move around. Or getting up and out of bed when he wanted to.

"Hey," Cait called from the door, walking to his bedside, "how are you doing, Dan?" She automatically slid her hand over his shoulder.

"Cait...you aren't a dream, are you?" he croaked.

She grinned. "No. Some guys, when they know they're coming to work with me in PT, have nightmares, though."

He grunted and turned his head toward her, drinking in her fresh, clean look. Her red hair was gathered into a loose topknot, slightly askew, giving her a girlish look. She was wearing the unflattering light blue scrubs, but they couldn't hide her willowy body from him. "You're never a nightmare in my dreams." Damn, but he was loose lipped. Seeing the surprise flare in her eyes, Dan muttered, "It's the morphine. Never mind me..." Well, it was a lie, but he didn't want Cait to realize how much she meant to him. Had always meant to him. His flesh radiated heat where her small, slender hand rested. She was gently grazing her fingertips up and down his forearm, as if to soothe him.

"Really? Dreams about me? Tell me about them?"
Not a chance. They're X-rated...

He needed to distract her so she forgot what he'd said. He licked his dry lips and gestured weakly toward the nearby table. "I'm thirsty as a horse. Could you?"

"Sure."

Her hand left his arm and Dan groaned inwardly. He wanted Cait to keep her connection with him. The deep, aching pain in his leg went away when she made contact with him.

Coming back with a glass and straw, she placed it between his lips. "So, you have dreams about me, huh?" She gave him a wicked look, watching his Adam's apple bob up and down as he chugged eight ounces of water in no time. Pulling the straw from his lips, she felt her breasts tighten. Dan had such a male mouth, chiseled and strong. Cait lost count of how many times she'd dreamed of him kissing her.

"Well," he muttered, wiping his mouth, "a few. Can I have another glass of water, please?"

Cait returned, sliding the straw between his lips once more. Heat flared in her lower body as her fingertips brushed the corner of his mouth by accident. Instantly, she saw his eyes narrow, the burning look in them startling her. Cait knew the look of a man who wanted his woman. Dan wanted her? Shaken, she held the glass steady as he drank the entire contents.

"You were really thirsty. Why weren't you drinking through the day?" she asked, pulling the tray over and setting the emptied glass on it.

"I don't know," Dan grumbled irritably. He gripped the covers and released them. "I hate being trussed up like a pig going to slaughter."

Cait smiled softly, coming closer, one hand on his

lower arm and the other resting on his shoulder. "It's very hard, Dan. I wish…I wish I could do something more to help you, but you're on my appointment list in a little over five weeks from now."

"You could sleep with me." He raised his brows, eyeing her hopefully. At first she blinked. And then she flashed that wide smile of hers, eyes dancing with mischief. Dan had joked around with her a lot throughout the years. She thought he was teasing her, but he wasn't. Still, it was nice to see her reaction. To see the interest in her eyes. There was no other way to interpret what he saw, and it filled him with a rush of hope he didn't dare think about. "Not every night, of course. But it would sure be nice to have you in my arms, beside me. That way I could forget about my constant pain."

Cait gave him a rueful look and shook her head, touching his jaw, which needed a shave once again. "You haven't changed at all, have you, Dan?"

He swallowed a smile. "I'll never change, Cait. What you see is what you get." Dan patted the mattress. "Come sit by me, right here." Damned if he didn't see momentary hesitation laced with outright yearning for him! *What the hell?* Was he so drunk on morphine that he was imagining her reaction? He had to be. Cait had never given him any outward sign that she was the least interested in him as a man. *Until now.* Dan swallowed hard, falling into her shimmering green eyes.

"Well…" Cait hesitated, looking toward the rest of the ward, "it wouldn't be right…against regs and all."

"Is that all that's stopping you?" He said it half in jest, half seriously. And he wasn't smiling. Her smile slipped, worry coming to her eyes.

"I'm a by-the-rules girl, Dan. You know that. And I know you guys in Special Forces don't do rules, and like to break however many of them you can get your hands on." She forced a smile, looking at her watch. "I've got to run…"

"What? A new boyfriend?" He kept his teasing light, just as he always did.

"Boyfriend?" Cait wrinkled her nose. "Not a chance, Dan. I'm done with men."

"Uh-oh," he murmured, giving her a wicked look. "Then that means I'm out of the running, too? No longer a contender for your hand, Cait?"

Her smile instantly softened. She reached out, touching a strand of brown hair near his ear, tugging on it. "When haven't you been the one?" she demanded, her voice oddly husky, her smile slipping. "I need to run, Dan. I'll try to drop by tomorrow sometime. Get some sleep. I worry about you." She leaned over, giving him a chaste kiss on his cheek.

Dan felt shock ripple through him as her warm lips grazed his flesh. He could smell her scent, smell her spicy cinnamon shampoo. His lower body roared to life. At least this time he was covered from his waist down. As she eased away, Dan caught her hand. "Hey," he growled, "I need at least one kiss a night to help me sleep. You'd do that for me, wouldn't you, Cait?" He looked solemnly into her widening eyes. "Just one kiss. Anywhere you want to plant it on me. It's a natural sleeping pill, didn't you know?"

She grinned and tugged his hair playfully. "Get out of here, Taylor! You're that same bad boy I've always known. With your usual bag of tricks."

Dan released her hand. "And you love me because of that. I know you do, Cait Moore."

Her smile slipped a lot, her eyes growing somber. She squeezed his hand. "Yes, you've always been the good bad boy in my life. You make me laugh when no one else can. And you make me smile."

"And I'll keep doing it," Dan promised, easing his hand from hers even though it was the last thing he wanted to do. "Give me a kiss once a day so I don't turn into a frog, and I'll keep you smiling and laughing."

"What a deal!" Cait chortled, stepping away. She lifted her hand. "Sleep tight, Dan. Dream sweet dreams, okay? I'll see you tomorrow evening."

"I don't want to turn into a frog, Cait," he called as she walked toward the door. As his voice carried down the row of other beds, he noticed how her cheeks reddened and she was suddenly shy. Cait shook her head, gave him one last warm look goodbye and left.

Dan's heart leaped when he saw Cait enter the ward at 1800 hours the next evening. He'd just eaten with the rest of the patients in his ward, and most of them were settling down to watch the TV at the other end of the long, rectangular room. Cait arrived wearing a dark green T-shirt with cap sleeves, loose white trousers and sandals. She carried a Monopoly board under her arm and a flowery decorated bag over her other shoulder. Her hair was caught up in a ponytail this time, long and swinging behind her. Dan's heart took off and so did his lower body.

"I swore I was going to get a Monopoly game in with you this week," she said, pulling the tray over and placing the board on it. She smiled and looked him over. "You got a haircut."

"Like it?" He'd badgered the nurse until they sent a woman up to cut his hair late this morning.

"Well, it sure is a change from the surfer-dude look."

"You don't like it?"

"It's just different. I'm so used to seeing you with your hair down to your shoulders, Dan. You know, fitting in over in Afghanistan or when you were surfing." She brought the tray over and positioned it so that as he sat up, it was close enough to reach but allowed her to sit on the edge of the mattress opposite him.

"You mean I've lost my drop-dead good looks?" Dan wriggled his eyebrows. "I no longer entice you?"

Cait laughed. "I can rely on you to lift my spirits." She placed the money along her side of the board, put the pieces on the board as well as the dice. "And you just look, well, more handsome."

Pleasantly surprised, he said, "You'll be proud of me. I shaved myself today. I survived my time with the electric razor."

"You look very much like a suntanned model who could pose for a men's health magazine."

"Even with my leg strung up?"

"Yes," she swore solemnly, trying not to smile. She gestured to the items on the board. "Choose your piece."

Dan looked at the shiny gold metal pieces. "I like cars—I'll take this one." Cait's cheerful mask slipped for a moment. Instantly, he knew she was grieving for Ben. His heart contracted with pain for her. "How about you," and he nudged her hand, "what's your choice?"

There was nothing he could do to assuage her grief.

Hell, he'd cried over losing Ben last night. She had to be in pain over the loss of her brother. Cait's eyes were suspiciously bright and he wondered if she'd cried recently. Dan wanted to do something…anything…to comfort her. But he couldn't do much in his present state.

"Ohhh," Cait murmured. "I think I'm gonna take the french fries. I intend to be the top mogul here by the time this game is over."

"Detroit will beat you out," he promised, waving the car in her direction. He grinned, his heart lifting. Every time Cait looked into his eyes, Dan swore he felt yearning coming from her. She was close enough that he could smell her and she smelled so good. She'd always worn a local perfume that sent him into a crazed mode of need. The scent was subtle and combined with her feminine fragrance.

She rallied. "Have the guys in here told you I'm a mogul who wins nearly every game I play with them?"

"Yeah, Bradford was telling me this morning when I got my hair cut that you were a ruthless Boardwalk titan."

She rubbed her slender hands together, grinned and said, "Oh, yes, I am."

"He said you're the Queen of Monopoly on this ward."

"That I am." Cait gave him a playful look. "And now, country boy from Texas, you're in my sights."

How he wanted to reach out, slide his hand around her slender neck, draw her forward a little, meet her halfway across that tray and kiss her senseless. Dan knew he could. He was a skilled lover with plenty of practice. "What's the perfume you're wearing, Cait?"

"What? Oh." She suddenly smiled and touched the nape of her neck. "Pikake. Why?"

"It smells really good on you," he said. A blush colored her cheeks.

"I've worn this same perfume forever. You know that."

He shrugged. "Well, maybe I'm older now and appreciate it in new and better ways."

This time, Dan didn't tease. He was dead serious and leveled a look at her that made it clear that he wanted her heart, body and soul. Her eyes widened and she blinked once, as if in shock for a moment over that very realization. And then she recovered, flushed redly and nervously touched her ponytail. "I—well, it's called Arabian jasmine. Remember? I told you a long time ago when you first smelled it and liked it? The story behind it?"

He nodded, moving the piece slowly around in his hand, fantasizing it was Cait's skin he was grazing. "Yes, in the nineteenth century, Princess Ka'iulana of Hawaii loved it." It had a spicy note to it and made Dan's body hum with need.

"I don't think you forget anything," she accused, nodding.

"Not when it comes to you, Cait. No, not a thing." Dan knew he was on dangerous ground because she seemed shaken by his sudden seriousness. He was rarely somber with Cait, always the jokester and prankster in her life instead. She suddenly lost her cheerfulness and sighed, the metal piece between her fingers.

"W-when the Army sent two officers to my parents' home…and then my mom called me later…" She blinked and touched her brow. "Dan, I was so afraid you'd died, too. I asked Mom about it, and she said she didn't know. Only Ben was dead from what the officers said. I was so panicked about it, I called Joyce to ask if she'd been notified of your death..."

Grimly, he reached out and captured her hand beneath the tray. "I'm too damned mean to die. I was born and raised in Texas, Cait. It takes a lot to kill someone like me."

He watched how she brightened, giving him a look of such longing it nearly broke him. It was then that Dan realized Cait needed to be held. Her mother had her father to console her. Cait had no one. But she had him, whether she realized it or not.

"Hey," he called gently, "do me a favor right now."

She frowned and fought tears that wanted to fall. "What?"

Dan released her hand and gestured toward the curtains. "Close them? I want some privacy with you, Cait." He knew he sounded in charge. Stern, almost, but Dan wasn't going to ignore Cait's needs any longer. He just couldn't. It was eating at his soul, squeezing his heart until the level of pain was far worse than the constant, gnawing ache in his leg. She hesitated and Dan pleaded with her. "Please? The guys aren't gonna say anything."

She slipped off the bed and pulled the long curtain around in a U-shape until they were completely enclosed. Cait wiped her eyes as she came over.

Dan pushed the tray aside and it rolled on its own toward the end of his bed. He captured her hand. "Come here," he ordered in a roughened tone, urging her to come and sit on the bed near his good hip. "Up on the bed here with me."

He wasn't about to give Cait a chance to say no and he used his strength to get her to lift her hip and settle it on the left side of the bed. He held her confused gaze and opened his arms.

"Remember when you were nineteen, and you'd been stood up by that boy? And I was home on leave? I found you out back on the beach crying your heart out. I sat down with you and pulled you into my arms." He searched her moist green eyes, noting the tremble in her lower lip as the grief overwhelmed her once more. She gave a jerky nod of her head. "Good," he soothed in a low tone. "Now come here. Let me hold you for a little while, Cait. I'll just hold you…"

She gave him a worried look, resisting. "Dan…your leg. If I move the wrong way it will cause you horrendous pain—"

"Ask me if I care," he said gruffly, gathering her slender form into his arms. Clenching his teeth, he felt pain shatter through his leg as she carefully eased forward, lying across him, her one hand against his upper chest, her head resting on his right shoulder. Nothing had ever felt so good to Dan. It was a dream come true even if he was going to pay for it with the agony the movement was costing him.

"Okay, I'll be careful." Cait relaxed against him, nuzzling his broad, powerful shoulder. The green cotton fabric of his gown was rough against her skin, but she didn't care. Nostrils flaring, she dragged in Dan's scent—the perspiration caused by his almost constant pain, a clean soap smell and his own, unique masculine fragrance that woke up her lower body.

"There," he said roughly, pressing his jaw against her hair, "now relax. No one has held you since Ben died. Let me at least do that for you, Cait..."

His growling words shattered her in an unexpected way, and she felt a sob jerk out of her as she pressed her face against the thick column of his neck, feeling his arms hold her more tightly, as if to somehow protect her from all the anguish that bubbled up at odd moments every day. Sometimes, she'd be helping a soldier with exercises when she'd suddenly burst into tears, embarrassed, having no explanation for them. With Dan, as the hot tears spilled down her cheeks, her fingers moving convulsively into the fabric across his chest, Cait felt no shame, no need to explain. Just...relief.

Dan closed his eyes, feeling the sweet curves and hollows of Cait fitting against his hard body. With every sob, his leg ached painfully, but oddly, just having her in his arms, able to comfort her, took so much of that burning nerve pain away.

Dan didn't know what was going on except that Cait was healing to him in every possible way. Sliding his hand across her back, following the curve of her graceful spine, nothing had ever felt this good. He could feel her skin tighten beneath his fingertips, even with the barrier of her shirt between his fingers and her velvet flesh. She started to cry harder now as he caressed and fussed over her. He knew now that since Ben's death, her parents hadn't been able to support her. They were too deeply mired in their own shock and anguish to reach out and help Cait, too. But he could.

Dan caressed her damp cheek, uttering soft, calming words to her, feeling the press of her small breasts against his chest. His erection stirred to life despite the nerve pain gnawing ferociously away in his thigh. Dan didn't care. He'd crawl over cut glass for this woman, who had always held his heart in her slender, beautiful hands. Cait had helped soldiers to heal over the years. He wasn't a healer, that was for sure, but Dan knew he could give Cait momentary shelter in his arms, a little TLC that she so desperately needed and deserved.

Turning his face toward hers, Dan inhaled deeply, as if dragging life into his body. His heart suffused with quiet joy. Her hand had inched upward, near his collar bone, opening and closing as she wept and released so much withheld grief. Her body shook and he continued to minister to her, his heart pounding with need for her. Dreams did come true, Dan realized, feeling that his lower body was fully awake now. He felt guilty even thinking about sex with Cait when what she needed was this: his touch, his quiet words of comfort. His whole world upended in these fifteen minutes. It was Cait who was always taking care of others. She probably hadn't ever thought of him holding her, silently loving her in his arms, and she surely didn't know how much he wanted her on every damn level he could name.

With trembling fingers, Cait tried to brush the tears off her cheek. Dan eased his hand downward and his large thumb dried the area with one stroke. Tiny sensations of fire radiated from where he'd caressed her. Cait wanted to stay in his arms, just to be held by him. She slowly extricated herself and sat up, giving him an apologetic look, trying to wipe her eyes dry.

"You needed a good cry," Dan said, his voice thick.

She licked her lower lip, tasting the salt of tears across it. "It's been a long time coming." Cait reached out, finding his hand and squeezing it. "Thanks...you always seem to be there for me, Dan. Every time I get in trouble, there you are to pick up the pieces of me." She tried to smile but failed and just gave him a tender look of gratefulness.

"I do have a habit of doing that for you," he agreed. Every time Cait broke up with her civilian boyfriends, he always seemed to be there, home on leave when it happened. Cait was right about picking up the pieces, but it was something Dan wanted to do for her. He always had ways of bringing a smile to her face, bringing laughter back into her life. During his thirty-day leaves, he, Ben and Cait would spend every day surfing on one of the many beaches on Oahu while she got over the worst of the breakup. Dan would leave, going back into deployment in Afghanistan, knowing that he would never have a chance for Cait's hand.

Until now. He felt terrible even thinking that way with Ben dead only one week. Dan told himself he should feel bad about thinking in those terms but, dammit, he yearned for Cait as if she were a lost piece of himself. He wondered just how much she was drawn to him. Was it just compassion for him or more than that?

He knew Cait was not a one-night-stand woman. She took a long time to get into a relationship and they tended to last for years. Ben's death and her grief meant Cait's interest in him, if any, couldn't be like the dreams and fantasies he had about her. About them as a couple. About a serious forever relationship with him.

Cait slowly moved off the bed, trying not to disturb his wounded leg beneath the tent. She released her ponytail, smoothing the strands and then pulled her shirt back into place over her hips. "You're in pain, aren't you?"

Dan grinned sourly. Hell, yeah, he was in pain. But Cait couldn't see where he really hurt. "A little," he lied.

"You're looking pale," she said worriedly.

"I'm damn well not using more of that morphine, Cait." He gestured to the Monopoly game. "Do you feel like playing? Or maybe you'd like to go home?"

She cleared her throat and whispered, "Can I take a rain check on the game, Dan? I feel so exhausted now."

Of course she did. He gazed tenderly at her. "Get out of here. I'll see you tomorrow sometime, okay? And, yes, we'll reschedule the game and I'll beat your pants off another time." He grinned wickedly, and Cait responded positively, a slight pinkness tingeing her previously wan cheeks. Her lips curved ruefully and she managed a slight smile in return.

"I owe you, Dan..."

And how he wanted to collect on that debt. What would Cait say if he told her the truth: that he wanted a chance to have a serious, ongoing relationship with her? That he'd always loved her? That he wanted a chance to explore what they had with one another?

Chapter 4

Dan was lying in a pool of sweat, the pain in his thigh nearing the threshold of having to punch that friggin' button to put more morphine into the IV drip to give himself some relief. It was barely 0700 and the other men in the ward had already gone for the day, leaving him alone. They were further along in the healing process. Five Army soldiers who had each lost a leg were in the ward. They didn't have to go through six weeks of hell lying in a bed, screwed together with nuts and bolts, but Dan was still grateful to have his leg.

By 0730, each of the five of them had left either in a wheelchair or on a set of crutches to go down the elevator to the chow hall. He was stuck waiting for his breakfast, which always tasted awful. The pain was coming in scalding waves, so damned excruciating that all he could do was breathe shallow and fast, teeth clenched, the sweat rolling down his face. His gown was soaked. He hated hitting the morphine button. The damned stuff took his head out of the game and he drifted in a white cloud of nothingness. He despised the opiate.

The door to the ward opened. Dan recognized Dr. Ann Moore, Ben and Cait's mother. She was dressed like a typical physician in a white lab coat over dark blue scrubs. Dan knew this had been coming ever since Ben had been killed. The serious look, the grief in Ann's face warned him things were going to get a lot worse.

"Dan? How are you doing?" Ann asked, giving him a weak smile of hello and coming to his bedside.

"Been better, Ann," he rasped. Oh hell, this was going to be a monumentally emotional encounter. Dan saw she'd been crying. Ann was an internist at a nearby civilian hospital.

She grimaced and looked over at the IV. "You're in a lot of pain. Have you given yourself some more morphine?"

He grunted. "No...not yet. Hate the stuff."

"It's not fun," she agreed somberly, reaching out and gently touching his shoulder briefly. "You should hit it. Pain actually stops the body from healing itself."

"Yeah," he muttered, "that's what Cait keeps telling me." Dan pressed the button. Not because he wanted to, but because he could see the emotional storm stirring in Ann's brown eyes. She had red hair like Cait, was tall and slender where her daughter was a head shorter than she was. Ann was in her midfifties and Dan could see Cait's face in hers. Only, there was a chasm of difference between the two, and Dan tried to shield himself from what he knew was coming.

"I didn't come to see you until now. I know Cait has been over here every day checking up on you. I was hoping you were sufficiently along in your healing to talk to me for a minute, Dan." She gave him a pleading look, her fingers tightening on his lower arm. "Please… can you tell me how Ben died? I've been going crazy imagining horrible things. Please tell me what really happened."

Dan felt the first hints of morphine easing his bone pain. His heart twisted in his chest. "I told Cait. Didn't she pass it on to you and your husband?" he grunted.

"She did tell us the basics. I need more information than she gave us. I just can't sleep at night, Dan. I lie there imagining things that are horrifying to me. If I just knew the truth…"

Because Cait was equally grief stricken, Dan thought, she might not have shared everything he'd told her with her parents. He owed the Moores this moment. The agony in Ann's eyes, the tightening of the muscles in her face as she tried to prepare herself for whatever he might say, it broke his heart.

"I'll tell you what I can," he rasped, "given that we're black ops. You know what that means, Ann."

She bit her lower lip. "Yes…yes I do…"

Dan closed his eyes, unable to stand the suffering in her face. In a low, tortured voice, Dan told her what he could, emphasizing that Ben had felt no pain and died with him at his side. It hurt like hell to even speak about it. Worse even, because of that damn bone pain gnawing constantly at him. Yesterday, Cait had come into his arms and cried her heart out, soaking the shoulder of his gown with her tears. Now, Ann was here, and tears dripped down her face as he finished a shortened version of the story. Her hand grip his arm firmly and then released him.

"T-thank you, Dan. I'm so sorry I had to ask you. I know how much you loved Ben. You two were like brothers."

Tears burned in his eyes and it took everything he had to hold himself together. The only good thing was that they were alone, the ward already emptied out for the day.

"Ben will always be a part of me, Ann," he managed, beginning to feel that vague, floating feeling, the pain in his leg becoming muted. He saw anguish in her eyes as well as anger and frustration. Dying on a battlefield wasn't pretty. She was a doctor and she now understood how Ben had died.

"Wasn't there anything else you could have done for him?" she asked in a wobbly voice.

Dan felt as if a bomb had gone off between them. He stared up at her, angry at the accusation that he hadn't done enough to save Ben. Instantly, he reminded himself that Ann had lost her only son. She would never see him married. Never see him with his children. He tried to wrestle his own shock over her question and put it into context.

Grief, Dan knew, did odd things to people. There was no such thing as normal behavior anymore. Ann was a solid, quiet, person, a good physician, a loving parent and a good one. He felt blindsided and gutted by her question.

"Ann, I did my best under the circumstances," he growled, his fists tightening in the bed covers at his sides.

"Y-yes, of course you did. It's just...God, I miss Ben so much."

"I do, too."

* * *

Cait dropped in midafternoon to check on Dan. He was staring darkly out the window next to his bed, the sun slats looking like prison bars sliding silently across his bed. Something was wrong. His brows were drawn together and there were beads of sweat across his wrinkled forehead. His large hands gripped the bed covers.

Her heart ached for him because she knew how much he disliked taking morphine. It knocked him out and Dan didn't like not being in control, awake and alert. He must have sensed her because he lifted his chin, staring in her direction. She managed a soft smile of welcome.

"Hey, I was just on the floor and thought I'd swing by for a moment." She reached out, running her fingers gently across his fist. "You're in pain?"

Dan felt so much of his anger, hurt and guilt dissolve beneath Cait's quiet, husky voice and her cooling touch. He wasn't about to tell her about her mother's visit to see him earlier this morning. Cait still looked exhausted from yesterday when she'd cried while he held her. She didn't need what Ann had said to him on top of everything else. Dan suspected Ann hadn't told her daughter about her visit.

"Yeah, bad morning" was all he said. "I'll be okay. Stop looking so worried. Okay?" He hungered for her presence because Cait always brought that calm ocean feeling with her. She was like a rock, so damned stable and reliable, which was what he needed right now, feeling out of sorts over Ann's veiled accusation. He opened his hand, turning it over and gripping her extended fingers. "Nice to see you. Did you get any sleep last night after you left?"

Cait managed a one cornered hitch of her mouth. "A little. I really needed that cry, Dan. Thanks for being there. I never expected you to offer to hold me, but it was so nice, exactly what I needed." Leaning over, Cait chastely kissed his cheek, looking deep into his dark, pain-filled eyes. "You are such a hero to me in so many ways, Dan." Her voice grew hoarse. "Thanks for holding me yesterday… Nothing has ever felt so good to me." She slid her hand over his rough jaw. "You've always been there for me. Always…"

"I wouldn't want it any other way, Cait." Closing his eyes, feeling like a needy beggar, Dan absorbed her tender touch and her healing words. Her mother, Ann, thought differently about him. He was no hero in her eyes, that was for damned sure. Asking him why he couldn't save her son's life. Accusing him in so many words of not having done enough. Damn, that hurt. It hurt more than he ever wanted to let on. He'd never expected that from Ann.

And Cait, whether she knew it or not, melted that hurt within him with just her quiet presence, her touch. Now it was Dan who wanted to turn toward her, throw himself into her arms and sob. Because he was close to doing just that, his throat tightened up, a lump forming.

"Do you need another hit of morphine? You're so pale and you're sweaty."

He saw concern for him in her tender green gaze, felt what he thought was love. It had to be the drug's influence, Dan sternly told himself. They'd never talked about loving one another. Dan ached, literally, from his heart down to his lower body, to kiss those full lips of hers, to feel her heat, share it and give it back to her, to love her until she screamed with pleasure.

Dan knew he could make her feel good. He knew he could love Cait enough to take away the sadness that was banked in her eyes, if only for a little while. Love was an antidote to pain. And Dan had never wanted to love a woman more than he did this one. He curved his fingers gently around hers.

"Yeah, I'll take a hit of the juice. I just don't like getting knocked out by it."

"I know," she soothed. "I've got a few minutes. Get the morphine into you and I'll give you a massage." She held up her hands. "I do it all the time for the guys who do PT with me. Knotted muscles, cramps, that kind of thing. Your shoulders feel so tight. Does your neck feel stiff?" She pulled a small bottle of lotion from her pocket, holding it up toward him. "I always carry this with me because as my patients start pushing unused muscles, they get horrible cramps. It's the fastest way I know to ease their suffering, soothe those overworked muscles and get them back to their exercises."

Her care, like a cooling balm, defused his anger and guilt over Ann's visit. "Hey, I could use a massage, thanks." God, he felt like a greedy fox in the hen house. To have her massage him? *Unbelievable.* Wonderful. He lay back and hit the button, searching her radiant eyes and finding an unnamed emotion in them. "Thanks, Cait. You don't have to do this."

"No worries, Dan. I've got twenty minutes before my next patient downstairs." She reached around his neck, loosening the tie, pulling the gown gently downward, exposing his upper chest. Patiently, she eased each of his arms out of the short sleeves and folded the material down around his waist. "There," she murmured, opening the lotion and spreading it on her hands. "Close your eyes. Just enjoy."

He was in heaven. Her hands were cool and gliding across his neck and shoulders. Cait was surprisingly strong, those slender fingers of hers pushing, manipulating and gentling his tight muscles. A groan rolled through him. Cait had magic hands and as he lay there, feeling the cloudiness of his fantasy-filled mind, he couldn't help a deep moan of pleasure rolling through his chest. His skin felt as if it were on fire, felt like a sponge pulling energy from her, absorbing it as if he were dying.

Never had he relaxed more than he did when her hands glided across his neck and shoulders. As Cait began to knead, pull and coax the muscles in each of his arms, Dan had no idea how tense he still was from the firefight. He had still been carrying it with him until she melted it away beneath her knowing, healing hands.

He was glad they were alone. The guys in the ward were down for lunch in the cafeteria at the medical center. He appreciated the intimacy that swirled and deepened around them with each stroke of her hands. Her touch coaxed his muscles into deep relaxation. The sensations were heated, the fire licking straight down to his lower body, his erection throbbing. He had to focus on controlling himself for her sake.

"You really do have magic hands," he said.

"I aim to please." Cait moved to Dan's large, splayed hand, loving his long, square fingers, the calluses on his palm. He elicited secret pleasure from her. Beneath her blue scrubs, her nipples were hard. Thank goodness they wouldn't show. Cait had wanted to do this to Dan for the longest time. He needed massage badly after what he'd been through.

She watched him carefully. He had short, thick golden-brown lashes that fell against his cheeks, and she saw that his face began to lose that hard, tight look. How badly she wanted to kiss him.

Sliding her hands across the expanse of his upper chest, sprinkled with gold-brown hair, she absorbed his masculine power. As the morphine took over his system, Dan was no longer with her in one sense, but in another Cait relished the reaction her fingertips still drew from him, his skin faintly responding to her tactile connection with him. Even unconscious, Dan responded to her. Her whole lower body felt like a slowly boiling cauldron aching for him to slide into her, give her the pleasure she so badly wanted from him.

As she worked her way down each side of his well-sprung rib cage, loosening the ribs themselves and see-ing the terrible yellow and purple of bruises that hadn't fully healed, she swallowed convulsively. Cait wanted to feel Dan's mouth beneath her lips. Just once. She felt like a coward, wanting to sneak a kiss from him. Cait was afraid to broach the subject. Right now, she felt too fragile, too broken up, but somehow, Dan just being himself, whether wounded or not, fortified her, gave her strength and made her acutely aware she was a woman with needs.

Glancing at her watch, she saw that fifteen minutes had fled. She didn't want to leave Dan. She wanted to keep running her hand over his body, appreciating him, his strength, the tenderness he always shared with her. She owed him so much. Would she ever get up the courage to tell him how she really felt about him?

Sadness filled her because when Ben and Dan had come home this time, she'd planned to sit down with her big brother and have a long, serious talk with him. She was going to let Ben know that while she appreciated his protectiveness, she had fallen in love with a military man. Cait was sure Ben would be aghast until she told him it was Dan Taylor, his best friend. And that she'd loved him almost from the moment she'd met the tall, strapping Texan. She had been prepared to fight for Dan without knowing if it was mutual or not. Cait had had to clear the decks with her brother, first. But now it wasn't necessary for the most tragic of reasons.

There was nothing to dislike about Dan. Wiping her hands on a nearby towel lying on the tray, Cait looked around. The ward was empty. The men wouldn't be back for another fifteen minutes. She moved quietly to the side of the bed, sliding her hand along Dan's jaw, feeling the beginning of stubble beneath her fingertips. She leaned forward, unable to stop herself from kissing him. Her mouth settled lightly over his parted lips. Closing her eyes, she enjoyed the feel of his mouth against hers. She felt his moist, shallow breath against her cheek as she drew back ever so slightly. He tasted of man. Of strength. Of promise. Her heart cried out for much more of him as she framed his face with her hand, luxuriating again in the touch of his chiseled mouth.

Ever so gently, Cait pulled away from his lips, caressing his jaw as she straightened. Her heart was pounding. He was a beautiful man in her eyes.

Ever so carefully, Cait lifted each of his arms, brought his blue gown upward and eased it around each of his shoulders. It took some doing to tie one of those ties, and Cait didn't want to startle him. She pushed the pillow down behind his head, tying that top tie so that when he awoke, he would find himself decently dressed once more. She smiled secretly, taking her fingers and gently moving them up and down his nape, knowing how much he'd enjoyed the massage in that area particularly. It was as if he had become putty in her hands, his thick muscles willing to be molded fully by her fingers. He trusted her.

She couldn't help herself. Cait placed her hand on Dan's shoulder, her lips taking his softly. Then she whispered, "I love you, Dan Taylor. Just know I love you..."

One more week and he could get out of this prison of a bed. Dan looked darkly around the emptied ward, damn jealous of his five ward mates. His stomach grumbled with hunger. As he looked around, he tried to manage his frustration at feeling caged. He was anxious to see Cait once more. She tried to see him every day, taking her lunch with him. It was early January now, and today, she'd promised him, she had a surprise that would rock his world.

Dan tried to resist his need to move. According to his ortho surgeon, Dr. Barker, his leg was healing spectacularly well. She was very pleased with his progress. He just wanted to get the hell out of his bed. He was dying for fresh air and sunlight. Anything to feel sun on his flesh again. Or to stand barefoot on the white sands of the beach and inhale the salty air into his lungs. With Cait at his side.

Dan slid his fingers through his recently trimmed hair in an aggravated motion. It felt odd not to have shoulder-length hair anymore. He missed his beard, too, since he hated to shave every day. The only good thing was that Cait seemed to think he was even more handsome than before and that pleased Dan.

The door opened.

"Hi," Cait said breathlessly as she pushed a wheelchair into the room. Grinning widely, she said, "Guess what, Dan Taylor?"

He couldn't help but smile at her radiant enthusiasm, her red hair down and glinting copper and burgundy highlights across her shoulders. "I give. What?"

She gave him a prim look. "How would you like to have lunch with me? Outside?"

His mouth dropped open. "Are you serious?"

"Sure am, Texas guy." She pointed to the wheelchair. "I have orders right here—" she patted her upper blue scrub pocket "—to take you outside for at least an hour so you can feel the world around you. How's that for a healing prescription?"

Dan shook his head. "You're serious?"

"Oh, am I ever." Cait laughed. She turned just as three orderlies entered the room. "These guys are going to officially untruss you."

A nurse came in with a huge, odd-looking leg brace for his thigh in her hands.

"And Abby is carrying your leg stabilizer. Once she and I get it into place, the guys are going to slowly move you and your legs off to the side of the bed. Sound good?"

Dan could hardly believe it. Cait's cheeks were flushed, her green eyes dancing with giddy happiness. "But," he stumbled, "I've only been on bed rest for five weeks."

"Dr. Barker said you're a week ahead of your bone-knitting schedule. She's the one who cut these new orders for you, Dan." Cait handed them to him to read.

God, it was true! His heart bounded wildly in his chest. "Lunch with you outdoors? Somewhere in the sun?"

"I've got the perfect spot for us," she promised, her eyes glistening with happiness.

"Then, let's get on with it," Dan told all of them. "I want out of this prison."

Cait stood back and grinned. Abby was waiting at her side, smiling. The three orderlies dismantled the tent of covers over the lower half of Dan's body. He had finally gotten rid of the catheter last week, which pleased him no end. His right leg was red and purple and there were stitches up and down it from his knee halfway up to his hip.

Cait's trained eyes saw that his once-thick leg muscles had atrophied and were now half the size of his other thigh. He'd lost a lot of muscle mass, but that was to be expected. She would help him rebuild it over time with a lot of hard work on Dan's part.

The orderlies were quick and efficient. She and Abby went around to his right thigh and placed, as gently as possible, what resembled an external cast over the leg to not only protect it, but to give it stability and strength. Dan gritted his teeth when they had to gently lift his leg with the help of the orderlies.

She hoped they could get him out of his bed and into the wheelchair without morphine. As the weeks had

gone on, Dan had begun to use less and less of it. Instead, he took more ibuprofen and had started sleeping
better. Cait tried to ignore how handsome Dan looked.
An orderly brought over a blue-and-white striped robe
and helped him into it.

Dan's leg was levered and kept in a horizontal position as the three men settled him into the large wheelchair, which had a leg platform attached to it. The
platform was covered with padding for his leg to rest
upon and to help absorb any jolts so he wouldn't nose-
dive into brutal nerve pain.

Cait smiled warmly as she gathered up the folds of
the robe and pulled them across his chest, tying the
sash.

"There," she said, pleased. "How's that leg feel?"

"Free at last," Dan growled, his hands resting on
the wheels of his chair. He looked up at the orderlies
and thanked them. Abby left with them, the door open
to freedom.

"I'll do the driving for now," she told him, standing
behind him, gripping the handles and slowly guiding
him out the door. "Just sit back and enjoy the scenery."

Dan inhaled deeply, smelling that spicy flower perfume she wore. "How long have you known about this?"

"Since this morning," Cait said, pushing him past the
nursing desk and halting at the freight elevator. Pressing the button she said, "The doctor called me in for a
consult. She's releasing you to me. You're going to start
therapy this afternoon."

He gawked. "Really?"

"Yes." The elevator doors open and she pushed him
in, taking great care that his injured leg didn't acciden-

tally brush one of the walls. "We have to be back inside in an hour, Dan. We're going to start working with you to get that knee to bend and not take off like a banshee on you every time." She flashed him a happy look. "Baby steps, I know, but that leg has been immobilized for five weeks. Ligaments stiffen up. I won't lie to you. There's going to be a lot discomfort."

The doors opened and they were on the ground floor, the green tiles waxed and shining. The place was busy with uniformed doctors and nurses as well as civilians. His spirits rose to new heights as she pushed him outside the door, took a left and moved into an empty alcove. There were two palm trees overhead, their fronds waving gracefully in the breeze. Dan saw a dark green picnic table with several chairs and benches around it. The sun felt divine and he lifted his face to it, closing his eyes, enjoying the hot rays on his pallid flesh.

"God," Dan whispered, "this is heaven..."

Chapter 5

Parked next to the picnic table, Dan worshipped the hot sunlight as if he were a man who had been kept in a dungeon all his life until just this moment. Cait sat near his wheelchair, opening the paper sack containing their lunch.

"I know you love tuna fish, Dan, so I made some." She handed it to him.

Her thoughtfulness made a fierce love for Cait sweep through Dan. "Thanks," he said as their fingers touched.

She laid out a small plastic container of sweet pickles and then placed an opened bag of potato chips in his lap, being careful to place it on his good thigh. He watched the sunlight dance through her loose hair, the gold shining against the crimson strands. Inhaling deeply, Dan could smell plumeria on the air.

"Cait," he muttered, shaking his head, "it just feels so damn good to be outside again."

He held her gaze, saw her eyes grow moist and saw her swallow several times. Why hadn't he realized Cait was so easily touched? Dan ate the sandwich slowly, savoring every bite. "No one outdoes you when it comes to making a tuna sandwich."

She smiled a little. "Gotta keep my reputation intact."

Dan waffled. When should he talk to her about *them*? He knew the Moore family would grieve for a long time over Ben's death. There was no such thing as a "good" time to broach his personal needs with Cait. Right now, she looked happy. "I must have dozed off when you were giving me that massage last night."

"You did. It was the morphine."

He bit back a curse. "I'll be glad to get rid of that friggin' medication."

"It's just something you have to do, Dan. Your leg is doing wonderfully and I think someday you'll look back on this period of incarceration and be glad that you toughed it out."

He glanced at her. "I know you're right. I look at the other five guys in my ward and none them have a leg. I feel lucky. There are just some days when this struggle eats me raw."

She reached over and touched his arm, which was resting on the wheelchair. "I know… I'll keep trying to find ways to get you out of the hospital. I know how much you love being outdoors and back into nature."

He caught her hand, holding her luminous gaze. "I dream of us running down the beach, surfboards under our arms, heading for the ocean."

She sighed. "It's been so long since I went to the beach, Dan." Cait stared at their hands. Dan's was roughened and yet, he held hers gently. Her skin was pale from being indoors too much. "This past year while you and Ben were deployed, my workload increased substantially and I haven't had the time off I've wanted anymore."

"That's because there are so many men getting their legs blown off by those friggin' IEDs."

She heard the barely veiled anger in his growl. "For you, Dan, the war is over."

His gut clenched. "Since I turned eighteen, all I ever wanted was to be in Army Special Forces, Cait. Me and five other Texas boys who lived in Rush City, a small town in the panhandle. The six of us were football champs for the state. They called us the Sidewinders." He pointed to his upper biceps, hidden by the blue gown. "We all had a sidewinder tattooed there to remind us that for four years we dominated Texas high school football. We were a no-name town, but we played our hearts out and we became champs."

"I saw the tat the first time I massaged you." She tilted her head, studying him. "Do you miss Texas? Do you want to go back there?"

Shrugging, he chewed on his sandwich, watching the palm fronds move gracefully in the sporadic breeze above them. The sky was a light blue, the humidity high because Tripler sat on the ocean. But, damn, the sun… it felt so life-giving to him, as if it was feeding his depressed soul and bringing him back to life.

He saw concern in Cait's green eyes. "I was born there, Cait. Both sides of my family are still back there. It was my father who up and tore our roots out of Texas to come here. He was following some crazy dream of living in the islands."

"I remember you said he was an alcoholic. That Joyce and you didn't want to leave."

"Yeah," he said with some bitterness. "My old man was one stubborn bastard. Good thing he's gone. At least my mother thinks that about him. I still miss him in some ways. In other ways, I don't. He was hard on everyone."

"But you joined the Army in Rush City?"

"Yes. And little did I know I'd end up here on Oahu." He smiled a little. "Kismet for me, but hell for my mother who still misses her family to this day."

"Do you think she'll move back?"

"I don't know. She's got a good paying job here. There's no work in Rush City. It's a poor, struggling farm and cattle community." He stared down at his right thigh, which ached like a banshee. Just gently handling his wounded leg had set it off again. He frowned. "Can I level with you, Cait?"

"You always have before," she answered, smiling a little. "What's bothering you?"

"What if my leg doesn't shape up, and I can't go back into Special Forces?"

Her mouth quirked. "I'll do everything in my power to help you get to the point where you'll have a chance to make it back into the teams." Cait saw the anxiety in his eyes even though he said nothing. "Dan? You have to try to take it one day at a time right now. It does no good to fly into what-if mode. The guys in the hospital—" she gestured toward the coral-pink medical complex "—who do the best focus intensely on each day as it arrives. They don't think about the future. They know the time they spend here at Tripler in physical therapy is a make or break for them. The ones who are successful? It's those guys. The ones who try to ferret out the future often fall into depression." Her voice fell. "They usually do less well here in rehab. It's just a state of mind and focus. You're black ops. You, more than most of these men, know about mental attitude and focus, Dan. I feel once we can get you mobile, get you into a steady, reliable program to bring your leg back, you're going to do well." She knew it wasn't the surefire positive answer what he wanted to hear, but it was the truth.

"I'm not going to get kicked out of the Army because of this." Dan jabbed his finger down at his trussed-up leg.

"I wish I could promise you that, but I wouldn't be doing you a favor if I did," Cait offered him quietly.

"I like you just the way you are, Cait. I rely on your honesty. I can always count on it."

"Not very romantic." She sighed, shrugging.

Dan's eyes narrowed on her. "What about you, Cait? What's going on in your life?" He might as well ask. He needed to know.

"Since you and Ben left on that last deployment, I got that second bedroom finished. I painted it a light green color. It's really beautiful." She smiled a little. "Now I can have company come and visit. I planted an avocado tree and replaced a failing grapefruit tree with a new one."

Dan knew she loved getting her hands into the soil. "Do you still have your garden?"

"Oh, always. Vegetables and fruit are 30 percent more expensive to buy over here in the islands than on the mainland. I even made myself three more raised beds. You'd be proud of me." She held up both her hands. "You showed me how to make them the last time you were home. Remember?"

He'd never forget. "I do," he said drily, watching her eyes flare with surprise for a moment. And then Dan saw yearning in her expression. Clearly. No mistake this time. He was off the morphine and his mind was working just fine. "Can I come over someday and see what you've done to your place?"

His heart started to race over the possibility that she might say no. Cait had always treated him like an older brother. Never a lover. This time he saw a light come to her eyes and he saw it was hope. Hope for what?

"I'd love that."

"When do you think I can do it?" He pointed at his wounded leg.

"Your body is responding fast, but right now we need to get you to be able to bend that knee so I can fold your big, tall body into my itty-bitty Toyota Prius."

He groaned. "I'm a big guy, Cait. You think you're going to squeeze me into that little hybrid?"

Laughing a little, she nodded. "We'll make it happen," she promised him warmly, finishing off her sandwich. All the pickles had been eaten and she placed the lid on the plastic box, sliding it back into the paper sack.

"That's one of the many things I love about you, Cait. You hold out hope for the hopeless. You work with men who have lost so much. I know they look to you, and you're always there for them." Dan didn't realize until after he'd spoken that he'd used the word *love*. And he'd seen the instant change in Cait's expression when he'd said it. First, she'd gone pale, and then her cheeks had flooded with pink. As if she couldn't believe her ears, maybe? Couldn't believe that big, tough, old Texan Dan Taylor would use that off-limits word with her—*love*.

Dan recalled a number of nighttime conversations out on the beach as they barbecued hamburgers after surfing all day. Cait had asked him if he'd ever been in love. What was it like? Dan had scoffed and told her he wasn't interested in love. Only sex with a willing woman. She'd rolled her eyes, snorted and shaken her head, giving him a disappointed glance. Ben had sided enthusiastically with him.

It was just one of the spirited conversations the three of them had gotten into about love versus sex. Ben and he had contended you didn't need to love a woman to bed her. Cait had argued most woman needed an emotional relationship before they would commit to going as far as having sex with a man.

"You just used the *L* word, Taylor."

He heard the teasing in her low voice as she watched him intently.

"I did, didn't I?" He rubbed his jaw and gave her a lazy smile. "Maybe I've changed, Cait. I'm older. Maybe a little wiser?"

"You know how to shock me, Dan." She stuffed the wrappers from the sandwiches into the paper sack.

"A good kind of shock, I hope?" he inquired, feigning innocence. He'd damn well used the right word. And Cait was confused, staring at him, bewildered by a seeming monumental change in how he saw women, sex and relationships.

"I—really don't know, Dan. You've been very clear about women in the past."

"Guilty," he muttered. "But five weeks in that damned bed have had me reviewing my life. I'm not eighteen anymore, Cait. I'm twenty-nine."

Her eyes darkened and she licked her lower lip, sending his lower body into instant spasms. She had no idea how much she turned him on.

"Your priorities are shifting?"

"Some are, for sure." He stared pointedly in her direction. How badly he just wanted to come out with it. But she was laboring from the shock of losing Ben. Dan couldn't selfishly lay what he wanted at her feet right now.

"Oh...I see..."

"I don't think you do."

She lifted her chin, holding his stare. "What does that mean, Dan?"

He dragged in a deep breath. "Help me get this knee bent and working again, okay? I need to start walking on my own, and stop being pushed around in this wheelchair." He saw her full lips curve faintly.

"Maybe it's your Texas-sized personality, Taylor, but you aren't asking for much, are you?"

An unwilling grin tugged at his mouth. "We have a saying in Texas, sweetheart—Go Big Or Go Home."

Sweetheart. Cait's heart spun with sudden joy. Dan had never called her by an endearment. Not ever. She dug into his narrowed gray eyes, which held so many unspoken secrets. Her fingers suddenly became cold and she looked away, trying to understand what was happening between them. Because something *was* happening. She felt as if Dan were tiptoeing around something important. Something life changing, but he wasn't ready to divulge it to her yet.

"I like that saying. That's what every guy I work with has to do: give 110 percent effort every day. Day in and day out."

"Yeah," he chortled, relaxing a little, "I hear they call you a slave driver down there in the PT department. That you're really tough on them. The five guys in the ward come back every afternoon bitching about how hard you are on them."

"That's true," Cait admitted ruefully, pushing her damp palms against her thighs. "It's because I care, Dan. Just like I'll care about you when you start down there." Her voice was firm. Passionate. Stubborn.

"Well, then," he drawled, "I'm just going to have to find some special way to reward you for all your hard work when this is over."

Suddenly Cait remembered kissing him all those weeks ago. The look in Dan's face was unreadable but she wondered for a split second if he remembered her kissing him goodbye that day. *Oh, God... What if he did?* Panic thrummed deep within her and her mind spun with anxiety. Except for a sisterly peck on his cheek, she had never kissed Dan. And he was holding secrets—she could feel it. But wasn't she holding secrets, too?

With a hissed curse beneath his breath, Dan tensed as Cait slowly bent his knee. He had endured four weeks of physiotherapy, it was late February and still the damned joint acted as if it was encased in concrete. He sat in a gym chair as she knelt down on one knee, one hand beneath his calf, the other around his large foot. Sweat was running off his temples, his breathing fast and shallow as she continued to slowly apply more pressure.

The muscles in his thigh had atrophied and now were being asked to stretch so that his knee could bend. He was gripping the seat where he sat, his knuckles white as she began the painful process once more. Every day, he did this. Every day it was a painful hell. His knee was so damned locked up.

"Good," Cait soothed, holding his limb, not allowing him to relax it. "This is good. It's moved another inch, Dan."

"Like I can tell," he grunted, pushing back against the chair, his teeth clenched, eyes closed. He'd given up pretending to be a tough guy four weeks ago. All around him physical therapists and nurses were helping men like himself. Some were walking. Some were exercising. Others were grunting and groaning just like him. The bright morning sunlight filtered through the large windows into the gymnasium-like area. There was all kinds of weight-lifting equipment and an Olympic-sized pool where he tried to swim and move that wounded leg of his.

He felt his leg burning as though a raging fire was built within it as Cait gently eased his knee a little more.

"Son of a bitch!" he exploded, rearing back, the sizzling pain like a knife being jammed violently up into his thigh. Dan wore loose gray gym pants and a dark green Army T-shirt. It was darkened by sweat in patches down the center and beneath his armpits. His back stuck to the plastic of the chair.

"Okay," Cait soothed, easing his limb and allowing it

to rest. She placed his foot on the floor. She smiled up at him. "Good progress, Taylor. Not bad." She remained where she was, watching the pain swirl in his gray eyes, his face glistening with sweat. He was breathing hard, a sign of how much he was enduring to get that knee to work once more. Cait wanted to hold him but resisted, as always. To coddle Dan at this stage would set him back in his progress.

"Damn," he hissed, sitting up, wiping his brow with the back of his forearm. "This is hurting more and more."

"Yes, as we ask the muscles in your thigh to start re-building muscle, the slow pumping action that I'm doing with your leg is actually sending more blood into the area. More blood means more oxygen and the muscles start rebuilding. Repetition does it."

He lifted his upper lip. "I know, I know…don't tell me the rest. I can quote you verbatim. More blood flow into the muscles helps rebuild the muscle."

She picked up a bottle of water nearby, handing it to him. Their fingers met and Cait secretly reveled in his contact. As Dan drank deeply, she began to gently move her fingers just above his knee, massaging those tight, screaming muscles, trying to get them to relax. Her touch was light, not heavy. There was always plea-sure in touching Dan, and Cait was glad her job gave her leeway in doing just that.

"God, that feels so good," he grunted, capping the emptied water bottle, tipping his head back against the chair.

She smiled a little as her hands drifted beneath his

knee, engaging those taut ligaments. "Every day, an inch of progress," she praised.

"It's hell," Dan muttered darkly. His whole body was arching and enjoying her soft touch, making the pain ease considerably. "I didn't feel this much pain after I got shot. Seems unfair that I have to go through it *twice* and the second time around is a hundred times worse than the first time."

"You can't come over and see my home until we can bend this knee a little more," she teased, resting her hand on his large calf. Cait knew the amount of pain Dan was in. She wouldn't pamper him or give him an excuse to feel sorry for himself. So many men, when the pain was constant, day in and day out, wanted to give up. He hadn't. It seemed like the more his knee refused to work for him, the more concentrated and stubborn he became about forcing it to work, or else. She was proud of his work ethic. Dan had taken her words to heart about just looking at the day in front of him. Nothing more, nothing less and it was helping him make good progress whether he believed her or not.

"Tell you what," she said lightly, giving him a warm look. She moved her hand across his resting knee. "You're this close," and she held up her thumb and index finger about one inch apart, "to getting your knee bent enough so you can to get into my Prius. What I want you to do when I begin to flex your knee again is visualize being at my place. You know what the kitchen and living room look like. See yourself at my bamboo table eating a stir-fry dinner I'll prepare for us. Are you game?"

Cait knew the value of placing something her patient

wanted just out of their reach to give them the impetus
to go for it because it was important to them. They'd
just talked last night over a game of Monopoly in his
ward about her cooking skills. She was a darned good
cook and took pride in it. Dan admitted he had dreamed
about eating chicken and vegetables straight from her
wok. He was a big vegetable eater, so she'd use that
carrot and dangle it before him. Cait knew how badly
he wanted to see her small home. She wanted him out
of this hospital complex and anywhere else that would
help him relax. He was beginning to hate being in the
hospital and she didn't blame him.

"You're serious, right? If I can get that knee bent a
little more, you'll take me to your house for dinner tonight?"

Her lips lifted and she drowned in the flaring desire
she saw in Dan's eyes. She could feel the shock rolling through him at her offer, but it was a good kind of
shock. "I'm a woman of my word, Taylor." She luxuri-
ated in his gaze, feeling his need for her. Cait had slowly
begun to realize that Dan liked her on more than just
a casual friendship level. Oh, it was subtle, but it was
there. All the time.

He grinned wickedly and set the plastic bottle on the
floor. "Okay, let's go for it."

Nodding she positioned herself once more, lifting
his leg and slowly asking his knee to bend. "Just remember the wok-seared chicken and veggies I'll make
for us," she murmured, watching him begin to tense
as she brought the knee to the angle where it was still
frozen. "Close your eyes. See your knee relaxing. See
those muscles in your thigh stretching." Because visual

pictures did, indeed, help the physical body respond. She saw him grip the edges of the chair he sat on, his mouth tightening. "Smell the scents coming from the kitchen," she said, moving the knee slowly, holding the pressure so that his muscles would begin to relax and loosen. "The scent of ginger and nutmeg in the air…"

Cait felt his whole body stiffen with pain as she pushed gently, asking that knee to flex a bit more. He was grunting with pain, explosions of air tearing out of his twisted mouth, his powerful back arched against the chair. Beads of sweat gathered in his deeply furrowed brow, his eyes scrunched shut, lips lifting away from clenched teeth. He was a black ops soldier. He knew the value of controlling his body, demanding more of it when necessary. And Cait could feel him struggling to force his wounded body to do exactly that. As she applied gentle, constant pressure to that knee, she felt him force himself to relax. His knee moved another inch.

"Great," she praised. "Keep it up! Keep allowing that leg to relax. Right now the pain is stopping you from reaching that final inch I need your knee to bend, Dan. Give it to me?"

It took five more minutes, but Dan did it. Cait praised him in a husky voice, holding his knee in that needed and necessary position. He was sweating heavily, breathing hard as if running a marathon, when in reality, he was trying to control the pain enough to allow his body to relax as best he could. Cait knew the pain these vets went through, and she felt pride for his monumental efforts. "Good job!" she called, smiling up into his barely open eyes. His face glistened with sweat, his gray eyes slits of agony. "You did it, Dan. You did it!"

Chest heaving with exertion, he groaned as she gently eased his knee outward, relieving the pressure. Dan was barely aware of anything for the next few minutes, his right leg feeling as if it was being scalded by a stream of hot water continuously poured into it. His muscles were learning to stretch all over again. Releasing his fists from around the edges of the metal chair, sweat dripped into his eyes, blurring his vision. With a couple of swipes of his hands, he focused back on Cait.

She was crouched at his feet, the biggest, proudest smile on that luscious mouth of hers. He'd give anything to kiss her. To tell her in some damn way, that he was interested in her as a woman.

"Nice work," Cait praised, placing her hand on his good knee, squeezing it gently.

"Damn, my leg is killing me," he muttered while trying to soothe it by rubbing the scarred, puckered flesh up and down its length.

"Here…let me." And Cait rose. She went to the rear of the room and brought back a huge white towel. "This should help," she said, easing his leg into an L shape and gently laying the wet, warm towel across it.

Groaning, Dan collapsed against the chair, eyes closed, head back, feeling the instant relief of heat on the screamingly taut muscles in that thigh. "God," he rasped, "you can do that any time you want."

"A warm, moist towel will do it every time. You need to remember that when you're not here anymore, Dan. It's always going to stiffen up on you, and a quick way to relax it is either a hot shower, a bath or a towel like this across the area."

The agonizing scalding sensation eased and the

agony dissolved within five minutes. Dan opened his eyes and sat up. Cait stood there, hands on hips, watching him critically. Her green eyes held an emotion he couldn't translate. Desire? For him? Dan had seen her work with a number of guys from his ward, but she never looked at them like she was looking at him right now. Dammit, he had to find out if there was anything between them. Or if it was his "head over heels in love with her" imagination wishing it was so.

Chapter 6

Dan was the last patient of Cait's day. The gym was empty. He knew that she was staying late to work him into her schedule so she could continue to get that knee of his to bend. Last week, she'd been true to her word— she'd driven him to her house and made him dinner.

He hadn't gotten up the courage to ask her how she felt toward him. In the end, Dan felt like the world's biggest coward. He could face a Taliban firefight, but he couldn't face her. He was afraid of what Cait's answer might be and it stopped him cold. He'd had all week to feel his way through his fear. He'd never let it stop him before and he'd finally, grimly, made the decision he was going to do something to show her exactly how he felt about her. It was time.

As Cait helped him stand, placing his left arm around her shoulders, he hobbled badly, leaning heavily on her to get to the torture chair, as he called it. Once there, he released her and slowly sank down into it. There was a thick blue plastic pad all around the chair. He'd fallen out of it once already. Others did, too, when stubborn joints were asked to flex more than they wanted to. Maybe the damned chair should have a seat belt on it, Dan thought with wry humor.

He watched as Cait came around to his right thigh. This was a favorite part for him, her hands on that angry-looking scar across his thigh. It was red and purple, the leather-like skin stretched and shiny. A thing of beauty it wasn't, but he relaxed, allowing his arms to hang at his sides. She crouched down, her small, cool hands lightly positioned at the top of his thigh, above the surgery scar. He wore loose, almost knee-length swim trunks and just her touching him like she was doing right now aroused him.

"Mmm, this is not feeling as tight," she murmured, pleased as she gently slid her hands on either side of the scar. "Does it feel a little more relaxed to you, Dan?"

"Hmm?"

Her hands halted on his thigh and she gave him a flat look. "Don't drift off."

"How can I help it?" he teased. "You touch me and I think I'm in heaven, Cait."

"Well," she grumbled good-naturedly, "in a minute you're going to feel like you're in hell."

He managed a crooked grin, holding her shining green gaze. Today, her hair was in a long ponytail down between her shoulder blades. Those blue scrubs she was required to wear hid her assets from his eyes, unfortunately. "I always feel better when you're touching me, sweetheart." He'd decided to keep calling her that when it felt right, get her used to his personal attention.

Cait colored, feeling heat rush to her cheeks as she continued to assess the muscles of his thigh around the wound site. "You never called me that before you got wounded," she challenged, holding his amused gaze.

"I told you—I've changed, Cait."

Mouth quirking, she frowned and kept focused on feeling those muscles. It wasn't lost on her that he was aroused beneath the dark green swim trunks he wore. And it happened every time she worked with him. Cait had worked on many soldiers over the years, but never had this happened as consistently as it did between her and Dan. Sometimes, when he didn't seem to realize she was watching, Cait would catch a wistful look in his gray eyes. And she'd sense a yearning, so deep and so secret she was never able to penetrate or interpret it.

Rising to her feet, she met his eyes, which danced with humor. Dan always teased her. She used to think it was just that, but now she wasn't so sure. How to ask him? Cait felt awkward about approaching him directly about what she felt burning between them. Could there really be something there? Dan kept saying he'd changed. What did that *really* mean? Frustration thrummed through her, and she got down to the business of getting that knee of his to give a little more. She'd like to have him over for dinner again. That one night had helped him so much. And it had made her happy, too. Cait wanted him with her again, alone in a personal, relaxed atmosphere.

"Well, you're one of the strongest men I know, Dan

Taylor. And I'm not just saying that because I'm about to push you a little harder."

And push him, she did. Dan groaned deeply. For thirty minutes, Cait ruthlessly forced that knee of his to bend. The pain was always there. That scalding sensation felt as if his thigh had ruptured. But the knee moved better and even he could see the progress he'd made. Cait went to retrieve a warm, wet towel for his thigh afterward.

Glancing around as he wiped his sweaty face, Dan saw they were alone. The pool was blue and glassy smooth. It was quiet. He watched her, appreciating the graceful sway of her hips.

"Here," she murmured, laying it across his thigh, "this should help in a hurry."

He inhaled her scent along with the spicy cinnamon shampoo he was sure she'd used. As she crouched, her hands gently draping the towel around his thigh, he felt the pain leave, replaced with a fierce need of her in every way. When was he going to get up the guts to talk to her about it? It had to be now, no matter how scared he felt inside. She sat down, legs crossed, her hand moving slowly, lightly across the damp, hot towel. This was new to Dan. He looked down into Cait's face and saw her chewing on her lower lip. She only did that when something was really bothering her. Her hand felt so damned good on him, even if there was thick towel between it and him.

"When you touch me, Cait, the pain goes away," he told her. Dan saw the flash of surprise in her eyes as she tilted her head up to catch his gaze. "Don't you think that's pretty awesome?"

Her hand stilled for a moment. "It is," she admitted.

"Do other guys tell you that?"

"No, not hardly. After they've worked with me for a while, they know what's coming and it's not pleasant. You've seen that."

"The pain goes away," he told her in a low voice. Dan reached out, nestling some loose strands of her red hair behind her ear. He was taking such a risk. It was an intimate gesture. There was some shock on her face, and yet, as his fingers grazed her small ear, her eyes turned molten for a split second. No, he wasn't imagining this. He'd seen she liked his touch. Her lips parted briefly as he caressed her hair, smoothing it against her scalp. Well, if she didn't get it now, she never would. His heart was pounding as Cait studied him. Just one touch. There was so much in that touch. Would Cait get it? Would she accept his small act of intimacy with her? Dan knew it was coming out of nowhere.

"Okay," she whispered in a strained voice, "what's going on, Dan?" Cait stilled, her ear tingling wildly in the wake of Dan's unexpected touch. She licked her lower lip, trying to read his mind, trying to read the intent behind that gesture. She forced herself to continue her light, stroking touch across the hot towel.

"Did you like that, Cait?" His heart was pounding in his ears. He could barely hear anything while he waited for her answer. Throat tight, Dan waited, feeling like a man waiting for the executioner's ax to slice down on his neck.

"I'd be a liar if I said I didn't."

It was his turn to look surprised. His heart bounced hard. Dan had to be honest with her. Cait deserved nothing less. "What if…what if I told you that when I first met you, I instantly fell in love with you?"

Cait's lips parted, shock in her eyes and then, something else…something Dan didn't dare believe.

"What if I told you that when we were introduced, I thought you were the most handsome man I'd ever met, Dan? That I felt my heart opening to you in such a way that it scared the hell out of me?"

Dan frowned. "I scared you?"

"In a good way," Cait corrected. "You looked like a warrior, maybe a throwback to the time of knights and ladies."

Dan wanted to so badly lean over, cup Cait's chin, lean down and kiss her senseless. To taste those naturally pink lips just once. Just once. "I knew feeling like I did toward you, Cait, was wrong." He swallowed, looking away for a moment, trying to find the right words. "I was eighteen. You were slightly younger. I was so full of myself. But I thought you were the most beautiful girl I'd ever seen." He grimaced and added, "When I was on the football team in high school, I had my pick of any girl I wanted. The six of us, the Sidewinders, were heroes and champs to everyone in Rush City. Especially to the girls at the high school."

She smiled, moving her hand a little more firmly against his thigh. Excitement thrummed through her as she tried to maintain a neutral expression, but her heart was doing backflips over what he'd just said. She loved Dan. It was that simple and that complicated. Her throat ached with wanting to say those words: *I love you. I've always loved you. I never stopped loving you.* "I imagine you were a very, very popular boy," she deadpanned.

"Let's put it this way—by the time I left and joined the Army, Cait, I knew my way around a woman. Which is why, when I met you, I felt like the floor had fallen out from beneath me. But you were seventeen. I couldn't do anything except appreciate you from a distance."

"Well," she drawled, "there was Ben. He was fierce about making sure I never looked at a soldier. Even then he was drilling into me to stay away from military types."

"Yeah." Dan sighed, looking up at the ceiling for a moment. "At the time, I was okay with that because you were so young, beautiful and mature for your age."

"I was always the serious one in our family," she admitted with a half smile. "Ben was the joker, like you."

"Yeah, we played a lot of jokes on one another over the years, that's for sure."

"When I turned eighteen, Ben made me promise to never date a soldier and I didn't. I began to date civilian guys from the university as I worked to get my degree in physical therapy."

Dan saw the sadness in her eyes and heard it in her voice. "I don't think the quality of a man is predicated on whether he's a civilian or in the military."

"I didn't, either, but I wasn't about to go back on my word to Ben." Cait got to her knees and positioned herself so that her hands could gently knead his thick thigh muscles through the warm towel. "I found out real quick, like Ben had told me, that too many guys were after one thing—sex. I hated being used and caught on quick. After I graduated with my degree, I got a job here at Tripler. I dated an ortho doctor…"

"Tim, as I recall?"

"Yes." She shot him a look. "You've got a good memory."

"Well," Dan said, "I remember coming off deployment to spend thirty days' leave here in Honolulu with you and Ben. You'd just broken up with Tim after being with him a year."

She frowned. "And I remember when I broke down crying there on the beach about it, you were the one who came over and held me." She couldn't help but look up at him, see his sadness for her.

"You were hurt, Cait. I wanted to help you any way I could."

"You did. More than you could ever know, Dan." Because she'd had a crush on him for so long. *Look but don't touch.* Dan was off-limits. Ben would not have forgiven her if she'd been honest and told Dan the truth.

"If memory serves, you had three serious relationships," Dan said. "Ben and I thought for sure you'd marry one of the two docs."

Shrugging, Cait moved her fingers down below the towel, slowly kneading the heavy hamstring muscles in his leg. "I guess I didn't love either of them. I tried, but it didn't work."

"They were both good men, Cait. I know. Ben showed me one of your emails one time when we were at our FOB—he was all excited about Wes asking you to marry him."

"I couldn't go through with it, Dan. I just couldn't. I know Ben was thrilled. My mother was doing a dance. She wants grandchildren."

"Were you getting pressure to settle down?"

"Yes. My parents felt I should seriously be thinking

about marrying and having lots of children. My mother, in particular, but my father is old-fashioned, too. You know the type—marry for security and all that stuff. I couldn't do that, Dan. I'm just not built that way. I never was, but it took me until my midtwenties to mature enough to realize it."

"It seemed like every time Ben and I got home, you were going through some kind of emotional breakup with another man."

Giving him a wry look, she said, "You're right. And you were always there for me, Dan. Ben would chew me out in private for dumping another guy. He didn't understand me or why I couldn't marry the guy. But you—" her voice grew low with rich feeling "—you'd catch me looking sad. Or maybe when the three of us were surfing together, you'd sense I wasn't happy."

"I've always been sensitive to your moods, Cait. But you're easy to read, sweetheart." He reached out, barely grazing her flushed cheek.

Her breath caught. Her lower body tightened. The pad of his thumb was calloused, her skin skittering with fire, the pleasure like sweet honey drizzling into her clenched lower body. She lifted her lashes, holding his stormy gaze, noticing the way his mouth pursed as he stared intently down at her.

"W-why are you calling me sweetheart now, Dan? You've never done that before." Her voice sounded wobbly even to her. Her heart was pounding and fear pressed down on her chest—she was afraid of what he might say. Searching his open expression, she didn't feel him putting on his game face, which is what he did most of the time when it came to deeply personal questions. Dan would always avoid answering them by joking and teasing with her, instead. This time the seriousness in his eyes seared her from her heart down to her aching center.

"I told you—I've changed, Cait. Maybe because I'm older. I've done a lot, seen a lot. I think I know what's really important in my life now."

Her breath hitched and her eyes widened slightly at the growl in his tone. She watched as he slowly sat up, his hand slipping beneath her chin, angling her face upward. Dan was going to kiss her! Suddenly, her emotions went wild with a fierceness that made her lean forward to eagerly meet his descending mouth. He was really going to kiss her! How long had she waited for this moment, thinking it would never come? Her fingers stilled and came to rest on his thigh, being careful to put no weight upon it.

Cait felt the moistness of Dan's breath as it washed across her nose and cheek. Her lashes closed as she strained toward his descending mouth. His other hand came to rest against her other cheek, guiding her, holding her tenderly as his mouth barely brushed hers.

His kiss was so light, and yet devastating to her that her heart threw open the doors, wild with joy over their contact. Cait wanted more. Much more. She moved another inch forward, meeting his mouth again. This time, she slid her lips shyly against his. Instantly, she heard Dan groan, felt his fingers grip her chin a little more firmly. He tasted so male. He felt so powerful and yet Cait could feel him watching for her every reaction. When his tongue moved against her lower lip, she whimpered softly, her hand lifting and coming to rest against his expansive chest, the T-shirt damp beneath her fingertips as she dug them into the fabric.

He deepened the kiss slowly, artfully and absorbed every sound that rose from her throat. His mouth created need and set a fire within her as he moved his lips from one corner of her mouth to the other, worshipping her. And when he slid his tongue between her parting lips, she froze with pleasure, drowning in his heat, the sensations stabbing downward into her taut lower body. Dampness collected between her thighs as he adored her mouth, his tongue gently engaging hers, inviting her to join him in the sensual foreplay.

Her breathing became choppy, shallow, her fingers digging insistently into his T-shirt, the muscles of his chest reacting to each touch. He smelled male, he smelled of perspiration and the Ivory soap he used. It was an aphrodisiac to Cait and she hungrily returned Dan's kiss, wanting so much more.

Cait was trembling as Dan slowly eased his mouth from hers. As she opened her eyes, she was lost in the stormy gray of his, which were focused only on her. He released her chin, his hands framing her face as he seemed to drink her into his heart and memory. The feeling was so profound, so life changing, that all Cait could do was stare up into his eyes. She'd never wanted a man more than she did Dan. How many dreams had she had of him? Of her loving him? Pleasing him? And him pleasing her.

Because now, at her age and experience, Cait could tell just by the way Dan caressed her, was tender in his advances, that he would be a consummate lover, interested in pleasing her first, not last. Not like the other men from her past who were more interested in climaxing first and then, maybe, pleasing her if they weren't too tired afterward. It didn't always happen, and often Cait had gone away frustrated and dissatisfied. All her screamingly alive senses told her that Dan would make her pleasure a priority, bring her along, engage her fire, understand that she was slower to come alive than a male. Dan had always been patient with her, sometimes the student, sometimes the teacher. But now, as always, he was her equal, introducing himself to her. Her heart thrilled at his bold move to let her know he wanted her.

"That was a nice hello kiss," he rasped. He released her and sat up, but he was unwilling to break the connection with Cait. He saw clearly the arousal burning in her eyes. Even though she wore a bra and those ugly blue scrubs, Dan could see that her nipples had hardened. His hands itched to curve around her breasts, expose them. He wanted to suckle her awaiting nipples, hear her crying out with pleasure, wanted to give her so much more. He moved his fingers lightly through her hair, taming the strands into place here and there. Cait's eyes were clouded with arousal and he saw her struggling to come back from that wet, torrid kiss they'd just shared.

"That was…" she whispered, touching her wet lower lip, "so nice…"

Dan studied her in the silence around them. Cait's cheeks were flushed, her eyes radiant with yearning for him, so much unspoken between them still. "Let me come over to your house, Cait. The kind of food I want to share with you, though, isn't coming off a stove. Do you understand?"

She nodded. "Because things have changed between us."

"We need privacy to really talk about this...about us," Dan pressed.

Cait looked around. "This isn't the place to do it," she agreed quietly. Pushing her fingers through her tamed hair, she took a deep breath. "I didn't know, Dan. I didn't know until just now how you felt toward me."

"Sweetheart, I've been trying to tell you this for a while. I wasn't sure my subtle signals were reaching you."

"Oh, they did, Dan, but I thought I was making them up. Because I wanted you so much, I thought I was reading what I wanted to read into it. I didn't trust myself to read you accurately."

Wry humor sparkled in her eyes. "Funny," he rumbled, "I saw things in your eyes, felt hints in your touch, and I thought I was making it up, too, Cait."

"Because we were taught we could never want one another," she whispered rawly, sliding her hand into his. "I was so afraid, Dan...afraid that if I showed you how I really felt toward you, you'd say no..."

He gripped her hand in his, wanting so badly to kiss her again. Kiss her and take her down on the blue mat and love her until she melted into his arms. "I was thinking the same thing, sweetheart." He squeezed her fingers gently. "Let's talk more when we're at your house."

She looked up, giving him a brushing kiss on his cheek before she rose to her full height. "There's so much to say...to explore with one another," she promised in a husky voice. "Tomorrow evening, I want you to come over for dinner."

* * *

The next day Dan sat in a pale green contemporary lounge chair. Everything in Cait's home reflected her minimalist style. She had moved the chair around so that he could see from the living room where she worked in her U-shaped kitchen. It was an open-concept home and, although small, it appeared large and airy. The lounge chair was modern and S-shaped so that as he sat in it, his legs were propped up, allowing him to fully relax.

It felt damn good to be dressed in his own clothes— a black-and-white Hawaiian flower shirt, a pair of tan loose-fitting cargo pants and sandals. He was back into his surfer-dude Hawaiian gear and Dan couldn't begin to tell Cait how grateful he was to her. After his PT session, he'd gone into the heated whirlpool to help his aching leg.

Afterward she had driven over to his small apartment. He lived near the Army base and he'd given her the key. Cait had brought some of his civilian clothes to Tripler. Then, behind closed curtains, she'd helped him dress in them instead of that damned blue gown with the loose-fitting cotton pants everyone wore at the hospital.

This time, she was not embarrassed as she pulled the covers off the frame above his legs. He wore nothing beneath those covers and it was clear he was partially erect. Her heated smile as she'd carefully pulled the loose-fitting cargo pants over his lower body, told him all he needed to know.

Cait had taken him home with her at five that evening. Trussed up in that special external support system, his thigh screamed at him like a banshee, but he'd been able to slowly fold his tall frame and get into her Prius. The comfortable lounge chair at her home was wide enough for him to sit in without feeling as though he might tip over one side of it or the other. He was a big man and didn't always fit in normal-sized furniture, but it was as if this lounge chair were made especially for him and his wounded leg.

Cait had already changed out of her medical uniform, trading it in for a dark blue, green and purple sarong that damn near made him leap out of that chair and take her right then and there on the highly polished blond bamboo floor.

She had taken her red hair and piled it up into a loose topknot with two gold combs. His heart leaped when he saw she'd tucked three white plumeria blossoms above her right ear. It wasn't lost on him that when a woman in the islands did that, it was a signal to young males that she was single and open to a relationship with the right man. He'd never seen Cait wear flowers on the right side of her head before. She looked beautiful, alluring and incredibly open to him. Had their kiss from yesterday evening opened the door of possibility? He'd barely slept last night, his mind and body in utter turmoil, pitching from hell to heaven and back. Cait had returned his kiss. What did that mean? How far was she willing to go with him?

Dan forgot about the pain drifting up and down his thigh. That silk sarong was gathered between her breasts with a tortoiseshell buckle, and it was his undoing. His imagination ran hot and wild. The ends of the sarong were pulled through the two openings, hanging there, tempting him. All he had to do was pull those ends through that buckle and the sarong would open, revealing Cait's small, beautiful breasts and the rest of her body. Of course, most women who wore sarongs in the tropics usually had a sports bra and panties on beneath. Sometimes…they didn't. It just depended. He couldn't discern an outline of bra or panties beneath that sarong. His imagination burned hot with the idea that she might not be wearing anything beneath that knee-length sarong. His erection pressed tightly against the zipper of his cargo pants.

Dan tried to keep his mind off sex with Cait, but he couldn't do it. The scent of nutmeg and ginger in the air couldn't keep his mind on dinner as she began to mix ingredients in a wok. From his vantage point, he could see her move, her bare, slender arms, a peek every now and then of how the silk flowed across her breasts. Dan swore he could see her nipples pushing up against the material. She was barefoot, her toenails painted red. Cait looked like a young college-aged woman so ripe and willing that he was in a constant ache to take her. When was he going to get up the courage to honestly talk to her about his feelings for her? It seemed impossible that Cait would willingly allow him to love her.

Would she?

That kiss of hers had melted him in a split second. She had kissed him passionately, without any reservation. Cait had not been shy. Her kiss had been bold and direct, and Dan wanted her so badly. In every possible way.

Chapter 7

Cait felt her heart pound as they finished off a dessert of sliced mango, papaya and pineapple. She'd pulled a chair next to the green lounger and sat facing Dan as they ate. He wasn't able to sit at a table or on a regular chair yet. Tonight was the night when she was going to find out if there was something lasting between them. There was no question he was aroused. For her, that was a sign but not the ultimate answer.

Rising, she took their empty bowls and spoons to the sink and rinsed them off. The winter sunset had been a watercolor palette of reds, oranges and yellows before it disappeared into the Pacific Ocean. Now, from where her small house sat in a cul-de-sac, the jungle behind it, she could see the stars wink and twinkle through the large picture window in the living room.

She felt Dan's gaze on her back, as if he were soaking

up each of her movements. It made her feel good. Hopeful, maybe. Throughout the dinner, she had occasionally seen an unknown emotion banked in his expression as their eyes met. It made her lower body yearn.

He'd never made a sexual advance on her. Ever. She was haunted by what he'd told her a month ago—that he'd changed. He'd repeated it yesterday and then made the first move and kissed her. Tonight, she would get her answers. Gathering her courage she walked toward Dan, holding his hooded gaze, seeing the arousal in his eyes. She sat down, gathering the silken folds of her sarong in her lap.

"You said you wanted to talk," she said shyly.

Dan watched her sit down gracefully, her long, slender fingers gathering the excess sarong material so that it remained closed. Now he knew without a doubt that Cait was wearing nothing beneath that sarong. *Nothing.* He was aching for her, wanting to love her senseless.

"We need to talk about that kiss, Cait. What it meant to both of us." His voice was low, strained. She became very serious, her gaze sharpening on him. Her hands were folded in her lap and Dan saw them tighten just a little more. "I have a confession I need to make to you." A lump started to form in his throat.

Tilting her head, she said, "Oh?"

Dan looked away for a moment. "Yesterday I told you I fell for you when we met." He gave her a wry glance. "I liked you…way too much." He opened his hands. "When you turned eighteen, Ben made me swear that I'd be your big, bad Texas guard dog and keep military guys from chasing you down. He saw how beautiful you were. He knew most of the guys would hit on you and that they might not be interested in a long-term relationship with you."

She smiled a little. "Ben guarded me from my thirteenth birthday until he went into the Army. Believe me, I can repeat his concerns verbatim, Dan."

"Yeah, he was a crusader in that area," Dan muttered, frowning. "Cait...all those years I've kept a secret. Even from Ben...and especially from you." Dan held her moist gaze and reached out, covering her clasped hands in her lap. "All along, I wanted you. All of you. I fell in love with *you*." Her expression brightened. "I tried my damnedest to ignore you, to do what was right, to do what Ben had asked of me..."

"When did you know, Dan?"

He heard the emotion in her low voice. "When did I know I loved you? Forever, Cait. I knew it was wrong of me to fall in love with you. At first, I tried to tell myself it was lust, not love. The thing was, I never fell out of love for you. How I felt about you just deepened and widened across time and distance. Every time we came home on leave, I looked so forward to seeing you."

"You never let me know. Not even once, Dan."

"With Ben there? Yeah. I didn't want to lose his friendship. I didn't know if you had any interest in me, Cait." He focused on the white plumeria flowers in her hair. "Until I saw those flowers in your hair tonight, I wasn't sure of anything." His large hand squeezed hers gently. "I've never seen you wear flowers in your hair, much less on the right side of your head. I was hoping like hell it meant what I thought it meant. That you were open to a relationship with me."

"I have a secret to share with you, too, Dan." Cait

nervously cleared her throat and bravely lifted her chin. "I told you yesterday that, from the beginning, you were like a knight in shining armor to mc. I kncw you were off-limits, and that you were Ben's best friend. He needed someone like you in his life and I was happy for both of you. As time went on, and you two came home, I knew I was falling in love with you, Dan. But I couldn't speak of it. If I did, I knew Ben would be shocked and so disappointed in me. I couldn't do that to him. And I was never sure you liked me at all, except as a little sister."

Dan released the breath he'd been holding as he searched her calm face, those green eyes of hers pools of shadow and light. "You fell in love with me, then?"

"Yes." Cait managed a shy look in his direction. "You have no idea how tough it was to be around you, Dan. So close, and I couldn't do anything. I couldn't say anything…touch you…kiss you…"

"Damn," he muttered, shaking his head. Dan lifted one of her hands, pressing a soft kiss to the center of her small, opened palm. His hand was nearly twice the size of Cait's.

Tiny ringlets of fire radiated from where he'd pressed his strong, well-shaped mouth against her opened palm. There was another kind of fire Cait saw in his eyes—clearly this time. There was no mistaking Dan wanted her. Coals came to life at the core of her. Cait wanted to match his courage with her own.

"I think we both loved Ben so much that we held off admitting anything to one another. We knew he wouldn't be happy to hear we were helplessly drawn to one another. I know he wanted only the best for me,

Dan, but I can't begin to tell you how often, especially during your last two leaves, I wanted to pull you aside and confess how I really felt about you. I was just too chicken to do it."

"But you didn't know I was interested. I get it, Cait. We were both on our best behavior because we loved Ben. And neither of us wanted to hurt him."

"No," she whispered, wiping her eyes, "we loved him so much… We still do…"

Dan swallowed against a constriction in his throat, hearing the tremble in her voice. "I've had ten weeks of lying in that friggin' bed at Tripler, Cait, to think about us. Ben's not with us any longer. I wrestled with what he'd think if I came to you and told you the truth of how I feel toward you. And, hell, I wasn't sure if I could trust that the signals you've been sending me since I got moved to Tripler were real. Sometimes, I thought I saw your feelings for me in your eyes." His mouth pulled. "And then I'd tell myself it was because I'd been wanting you for so long, that it was my imagination fueled by the morphine."

"I understand," Cait whispered, turning her hand, her fingers gently grazing his calloused palm. "I was torn between my grief for Ben and loving you, knowing you'd nearly died, too. There were so many times I just wanted to let it rip out of my mouth, to tell you that I loved you, Dan. It was so difficult in those first few weeks. I felt like I was living in agony one moment and then heaven the next because you were there. I could touch you, hear your voice, look into your eyes, and I knew you were going to survive your wound."

The tears glimmering in her eyes conveyed such

need. His body was hard, throbbing and ready. "That was when I started picking up little signals from you, two weeks after I arrived," he said roughly. "And I kept telling myself it was a dream that would never come true. I dreamed of loving you, Cait. Holding you in my arms. Sleeping at your side. I wanted it so damn much. I like the long talks we always had, walks on the beach and surfing together."

"What do you want from me, Dan?"

Dan could see Cait trying to prepare herself in case he had bad news. "I want the right to get to know you, Cait. If I can hold a love for you all these years, we both deserve a chance to explore it in every possible way. How do you feel about us?" Now, it was his turn to feel scared.

Cait brought her chair closer to his lounger, close enough for her to frame his face and lean down, gently placing her mouth against the line of his. "Kiss me again, Dan? Make this real for both of us. Because I want the same thing from you..."

Her sweet, moist breath flowed across him as her soft lips barely grazed his mouth. A groan rolled through him and he took her lips just as gently, tasting her, welcoming her, wanting her, but smart enough, old enough, to let Cait take the lead. Dan had no idea where this would go tonight. None. Except now, he knew Cait loved him as much as he loved her. And they both wanted the same thing: time to explore what was really between them. It felt as if his heart would explode out of his chest as her lips, wet and hungry, deepened their kiss. Her fingers slid up along his jaw, framing his face again, holding him in place as she slid her tongue into his mouth. Dan stiffened, gripping her bare shoulders, feeling her fire, feeling her warmth flow hotly down through him like sweet, delicious chocolate.

Dan didn't want the kiss to end, but his erection throbbed with painful urgency. As Cait drew a few inches away from his mouth, her green eyes dark with arousal, he knew. Dan knew she wanted him. Right now. Right here. His mind spun in shock.

"How are we going to do this?" he asked thickly, moving his hand with appreciation over her slender shoulders, her flesh warm and velvety beneath his fingers.

"Well, I've given this a great deal of thought." She kissed his nose, his cheek and then his mouth. "This lounger is perfect for us. It will support that leg of yours and keep it at an angle so that you won't be in pain."

"Sweetheart, I'm in such pain right now and it's not from that leg," he confided wryly, watching her lazy smile.

Turning, Cait laid her hand across his thick arousal. She caressed him. "I know…hold on, let me give you some relief…"

Dan couldn't believe his eyes as she turned in the chair, unsnapping and then unzipping his cargo pants, opening them. His breath jammed as her warm fingers glided down the length of him, gently enclosing him, squeezing him just enough to make him groan and close his eyes. The sweet, scalding sensations blotted out his mind. Dan couldn't think, only feel. Her hand shifted, fingers gently manipulating him, and all he could do was grip her sarong-covered thigh, barely able to hang on.

"Cait," he rasped, opening his eyes. "Don't… I'll come." He captured her hand, stopping her from pleasing him. The last thing Dan wanted was to come like this. He met her half-closed eyes, those red lashes framing green eyes that burned with arousal, and he growled, "I want to be inside you, sweetheart. Inside…now…"

"Yes," she whispered unsteadily, taking his hand and guiding it to the teak buckle held the sarong closed. "Here. Open it up, Dan. I'll do the rest."

He was barely putting two thoughts together. Fumbling with the buckle, he heard Cait give him a breathy laugh.

"We have time, Dan. There's no hurry. Relax…"

He snorted and stared up at her. "I've waited eleven years for this. I'm in a hurry."

Her laughter was husky and she leaned forward, making it easier for him. "Okay, you've got a point, but you're staying here with me all night. I'm not taking you back to Tripler until tomorrow morning."

Never had he heard sweeter words than those. "I like your plan." He eased the material through the first hole and then the second. The fabric parted and his breath jammed in his throat as he stared at her small, beautifully formed breasts. The silky sarong fell away, pooling around her hips with a whisper. Her nipples were pink and taut, the rest of her naked body a soft glow as moonlight flowed through the living room. Dan placed the buckle on the floor next to the lounger. Cait moved closer, within easy range of his hands, her fingers skimming his shoulders.

"Touch me, Dan? Please…I can't tell you how often I've fantasized about you touching me…"

Her feminine scent combined with the perfume of the plumeria in her hair surrounded him. She was so small in comparison to him. Her breasts were perfect for him as she leaned forward, fitting them into his palms. Cait rested her brow against his. The sudden intake of her breath as he grazed her curves with his fingers, feeling her warmth, her nipples responding to his caress, told him so much.

Groaning her name, he leaned forward, capturing one of those taut nipples, drawing it into his mouth. He heard a low cry and her fingers dug frantically into his shoulders, telling him how much she enjoyed it. So did he. The world tilted, all the sounds, everything around him…disappeared…and in its place, only Cait's sweet, trembling body, her feminine scent filling his nostrils, the warmth of her skin tasting so good, the little cries of pleasure filling her throat as he suckled and laved each of her nipples, became his whole world. All Dan wanted to do was please this woman. She moved against him, surrendering herself to him, her taut breasts in his palms, her breath fast and shallow.

He wanted to explore every inch of Cait but he was at an odd position and so was she. Dan heard her give a breathy laugh near his ear as she eased out of his hands.

"Let's get comfortable, shall we?" she suggested, rising and pulling the sarong away from her naked body. She placed it on the chair. The moonlight lovingly silhouetted her form as she stood there.

Dan's entire being homed in on her slender form. Cait was like a willow. He took in her form from head to toe as she stood before him. Her cheeks were flushed and he could see she felt no shame in standing naked to be appreciated and devoured by his gaze. It was one thing to see her surfing in a bikini, quite another to see her standing like a goddess before him. He lifted his hand toward her, wanting her close once again. He saw a wicked look come to her eyes.

"First things first. I'm undressing you." She approached the lounger. "Your shirt first," she whispered, leaning over him.

Dan helped her quickly get rid of the shirt, dropping it to the floor. The cargo pants were a challenge. He watched as Cait walked around the lounger and bent down, her breasts gorgeous as she opened up the device around his leg and carefully removed it. Setting it aside, she gave him a smile of encouragement. "Cargo pants next. Just take it slow and follow my directions."

His desire was there for her to see, no question about it. And even struggling to get the loose pants off him, the pain it caused, didn't dim his arousal one iota. He liked the way Cait watched him as he lay naked before her. She shared a heated look with him after she hung his pants on the back of the chair.

"See? Not as tough as you thought. Right?"

"I've got a feeling you've gone over this scenario a hundred times in your head. Am I wrong?"

Cait's mouth twitched and she shook her head, meeting his dark, hooded stare. As she approached him, she said, "More like a thousand times. I knew you had to heal up to a certain point before we could do this."

"I like a woman with a plan," Dan growled, tugging on her hand, pulling her closer. He saw that sphinx-like smile on those lips of hers, that burning hunger in her eyes.

Cait lifted her leg and straddled him, her body hovering close to his. Settling her hands on his shoulders, stroking them in appreciation, Cait slowly lowered herself over his hips and slid wetly across his erection.

Dan wasn't prepared for how good Cait would feel against him. How wet, warm and wonderful feeling it was as she cautiously eased her weight down upon him a little at a time. She was careful, no doubt wanting to make sure her weight wouldn't stress that healing leg of his. It didn't, but in the state he was in, he could be dying from pain and he would ignore it. Cait sure felt good. Dan couldn't think, couldn't talk, as she slowly leaned forward, inviting him to cup her breasts. The look in her eyes was that of a huntress knowing she was stalking him for all the right reasons. Dan liked her courage and he growled in pleasure as she slowly slid along the length of his erection. The sounds coming out of her slender throat, the sheer sound of joy, hardened him even more.

They both froze, the pleasure so intense, so unexpected, that all they could do was absorb these moments spun with fire and heat. Her eyes had closed, her lips parting, fingers digging into his chest as she repeated that same slow, sinuous movement down his shaft. He wanted to arch his hips, but knew he didn't dare risk the pain in his leg. "It's tough to lie still," he gritted out, caressing her breasts.

"You have to, Dan, or believe me, the pain that results is going to erase how good it feels in other parts of your body right now."

He looked up into her green eyes, which glimmered with heat and need. He knew that nerve pain could bring him down in an instant, and Dan was going to try his best not to react to her body sliding teasingly along his own. "This is a special hell," he griped, watching her lips curve ruefully.

"It's not going to keep a good man like you down," she whispered, taking his mouth.

He didn't even have time to reply, her wet, hungry mouth closing over his. And as she lifted her hips, capturing him, sliding him into her, he groaned, gripping her shoulders, frozen with the delicious sensations wrapping powerfully around him.

"Cait..." he rasped.

"Ohhhh," she whispered, sitting very still over him, "I know...I know...oh, you feel so good in me, Dan... so good..."

Her words turned him molten and he gritted his teeth. "Cait...I can't—"

"Yes, you can..." she urged him, caressing him with her body, moving him deeper, back and forth within her. "It's all right...I need you...now..."

That was all she had to whisper and he stiffened, her body wrapped hot and tight around him. He heard Cait's sharp intake of breath, felt her freeze as he released deep within her. She moved coaxingly, and he felt nearly a decade of waiting for her tunnel violently through him, erasing his mind, erasing any pain as he unthinkingly thrust his hips upward. The pain couldn't take away the scorching pleasure racing through him as he spilled hotly into her. Cait's breath was moist against his cheek, her lips seeking, finding his mouth as she moved like a cat around him, milking him, taking everything he had and then giving him even more pleasure.

For however long it was, Dan drowned in her body, the wetness, the heat, the boiling sensations surrounding him as she deliberately moved and made the experience even more profound for him. Weakly, he sagged against the lounger, barely opening his eyes, staring up at her in wonder. Cait's mouth was curved, her eyes half-closed and he could see the need in her.

"I want to please you," he said. "This isn't just about me, Cait." He lifted his hands, skimming her shoulders and arms.

Giving him a breathy laugh, Cait nodded. "Oh, don't worry, I'm going to take what I want from you, too." Her fingers moved through his short hair and she caressed his nape. "Just lie there and enjoy the sensations, Dan. We have all night. There's no hurry. Believe me. Consider this a night of exploration between us."

He pinned her with a dark look, caressing her breasts, hearing that exquisite sound catch in her exposed throat. "I'd give anything to take you to bed… love you properly…"

"You are doing that right now, Dan," she whispered unsteadily as she began to move slowly, engaging him once more. "It's not going to take much more for me to orgasm—believe me. I've been waiting for this moment for a long, long time, too…"

Her words were dark and husky as she moved her hands across his chest, savoring him. Dan could see the pleasure of just touching him in her gleaming eyes, see the intense satisfaction come to her lips as she allowed all her weight to fully meet his hips.

"You're a feather," he said. "Don't be worried you're going to hurt me. You can't, sweetheart."

Cait pressed down more firmly upon him, her hips grinding against his. Closing her eyes, she hummed and her fingers grew taut against his chest.

"You're so close," Dan rasped, feeling her body begin to tighten around him. He responded, growing harder. The woman knew how to move sinuously, engage and create fire within him. Dan gripped her hips, watching her closely, feeling her body begin to clench. The sweetness of her, the boldness of her actions, stunned him. He'd never seen Cait in this mode, but then, how could he have? They'd both hidden how they'd felt about one another for so long…so long…

A fierce love for Cait swept through Dan as he brought her down firmly against him. She'd been right about trying to raise his hips; it was a painful hell that made him gasp. He learned quickly to lie still although every cell in his body wanted to move with the rhythm she had established for them. Dan hated that he couldn't move his lower body at all, but Cait knew how to compensate, and within moments, a small, sharp cry tore out of her. The fierce little cries continued and he helped her by keeping her firmly seated against his hardened length. A flush began in her upper body, sweeping upward and nothing had looked so good to Dan as hearing those little satisfied sounds spilling from her parted lips.

His emotions were fully engaged with hers. His mind wouldn't work, surrounded by the heat, light and satisfaction of knowing he could still please Cait regardless of his condition. He felt her begin to sag, and he eased her forward so that she could lie fully against his upper body. Guiding her head to his right shoulder, he felt her hand move to his left shoulder, holding herself as close as she could get to him afterward. Dan inhaled her scent, felt the dampness of her body pressed against his, the rise and fall of her breasts against his chest. This was heaven on earth.

Dan didn't know how long they lay with one another; time ceased. He undid that topknot of red hair later and slid his fingers through that silken mass, guiding it around her shoulders. He cupped her breast and heard her mewl with pleasure as he moved his thumb against her hardening nipple. She felt so good—the slickness, the heat that still bubbled and simmered where they were joined. Cait had quieted, her brow against his jaw, her small hand lightly caressing his neck and shoulder.

"I'm in heaven," he growled against her ear, the strands tickling his nose. Dan heard her laugh softly.

"We both are…"

There was such a wispy, faraway quality to her voice. He could still feel her body contracting every once in a while and he smiled, knowing he'd pleasured her.

"Do you know how damned nice it is to lie here with you? To not only love you, but tell you that I love you?" He pulled away just enough to look into her drowsy, fulfilled eyes. His heart expanded with joy because he saw that she loved him as much as he did her. Her eyes grew moist, her lower lip trembling as she slowly eased away from him, pushing herself upright, hands against his shoulders.

"Mmm," she purred, leaning forward, kissing him slowly. As Cait eased from his mouth, she whispered, "Do you know how nice it is to finally be able to say I love you, Dan?"

In the darkness that surrounded them, the shadows

were deep and moonlight from outside the window highlighted the flowing curves of her body for Dan's hungry gaze. Cait was beautiful and now Dan could appreciate what a sculptor saw as he carved beauty from marble with his hands. Only, his hands moved and ranged across her slender, giving body, and he inhaled her, her spirit, her smile, that radiant look in her green eyes meant for him alone.

Dan gave a nod of his head, drowning in the rapture he saw in Cait's eyes. Never had he felt as satisfied, as happy, as he did in this instant. Her body was small against his—he felt her liquid warmth embracing him and nothing had ever felt so right. Nothing. Burying his face into her scented hair, the silky strands cool against his damp face, he inhaled her fragrance deeply into his lungs.

Dan couldn't get enough of Cait. They dozed against one another. When he awoke, she was moving against him once more, her sweet body in perfect alignment with his. And it wasn't long at all before he released himself deep within her a second time. The way she remained over him, capturing him, felt dreamlike. Dan rallied a little later, pleasuring her again. Her cries filled the room. There wasn't anything else in this world he'd ever want but Cait. And as she languished against him, weak and satiated, the slickness of her flesh against his, her breath coming in sobs, he closed his eyes and held her tightly against him, never wanting to let Cait go ever again.

Chapter 8

The mid-March sunlight was strong as Dan hobbled along on a set of crutches. He hated having to rely on them, though it was better than being imprisoned in a damned wheelchair. He moved around Cait's kitchen, feeling happiness threading through his chest. That green lounge chair of hers had been given a hell of a workout. His body was sated and he could hardly wait until Cait got home tonight from work. He'd had the day off because last week, he'd made a breakthrough with his wounded leg and Cait wanted him to take some time off to rest.

He grinned to himself as he carefully took the bright red ceramic plates to the small, round kitchen table. Tonight he was fixing her dinner. And then…God… then they could actually go to her bed, make love and sleep together for the first time. His heart was more than ready for that milestone. Up to now, he'd slept out in the lounge chair each night where Cait tucked him in with a sheet and light blanket. They'd made light of their situation because every day Dan was getting stronger, his leg responding to the brutal physical regime. He had the best reason in the world to get that knee and leg of his healed. He had Cait and he wanted to love her without constraint.

Tonight, he could lie with Cait in her bed. He'd missed holding her against him. That was so important to Dan his arms literally ached to hold Cait after loving her all night long.

He frowned as he placed the plates on the bright gold bamboo placemats. Her parents had been less than thrilled that he was living with Cait. They were still grieving deeply over Ben's death, and they hadn't been ready for him to move in with their daughter so soon afterward. They didn't understand that they'd waited eleven years for this moment. It wasn't overnight. It was over a decade of waiting.

Cait had cautioned him to back off from her parents, give them the room they needed. Someday, she counseled, they would sit down with her parents and explain it all to them. Cait felt that, once her parents were past their initial grief, they would understand. Right now, they weren't ready and Dan agreed it was best to wait before discussing the sensitive issue.

Standing straighter, he placed the crutch aside and tried to stand with even weight on both feet. Even though he felt tightness in his right thigh, there was no pain. Just a discomfort that was easy for Dan to ignore. He shifted his weight back and forth. And then he slowly bent his right knee, which had once been all but immobilized. Now it wasn't—it was a game changer. It would allow him to kneel beside Cait, open her, enter her. She wouldn't have to use that one position on the lounger every time. He smiled, his whole body humming with anticipation.

He heard the front door open and close. Turning, he saw Cait in her blue scrubs and white nursing shoes, her red hair in a top knot, walk into the kitchen. Her green eyes danced with devilry as she saw him and smiled a hello. She looked at the table as she walked over to him and slid her arms around his shoulders.

"You've been a busy guy, huh?" Cait smiled at him, pushing up on her toes as he leaned down to capture her lips. It felt so good for him to haul her up against him, squeezing the air out of her lungs as his mouth hungrily took hers. He slid a hand suggestively down her spine, cupping her derriere and pressing her belly wantonly against his thick erection.

A soft, pleasurable moan vibrated in her throat and she thrust her belly against him, moving slowly, letting him know just how much she wanted him, too.

Dan eased his mouth from hers and loosened her hair, pulling the two gold combs out of the strands and allowing it to become a crimson cascade around her shoulders. "I love you," he rasped, drowning in her aroused green eyes. His heart swelled fiercely as he saw her eyes grow soft with love for him alone, her fingers drifting through his long hair. He'd decided to let it grow out again. For him, it was a symbol every day that he was going to get better and start surfing again. He'd always worn shoulder-length hair before he'd joined the Army.

Cait leaned upward, kissing him once more, whispering against his mouth. "I love you with my heart and soul, Dan Taylor..."

He studied her in the silence that wrapped around them. "Do you know how good it feels to be able to stand here with you leaning against me? And me taking your full weight?"

"You'll never take the small things in life for granted ever again," Cait agreed gently, brushing his sun-streaked brown hair away from his jaw. "Something smells good. What did you make us tonight?"

He tucked her beneath his arm and brought her toward the stove. "Chicken with pineapple. Threw in some lemon, garlic, honey and mustard." He gestured toward the pan on the top of the stove. "White rice."

"Dessert?"

He gave her a wicked look. "You."

Cait grinned. "Do I smell a cake baking?"

"Actually, pineapple pound cake." Dan looked at his watch. "It should be coming out in about ten minutes."

"That gives me time to change. Need any help out here?"

"Nope, I've got it under control. I have some news to share with you when you come back out."

Cait brought the steaming food to the table for Dan as he took his time sitting down in the wooden chair. "That knee is doing well," she praised, picking up the bowl of rice from the counter. She'd changed into a white tank top, no bra and a pair of blue denim shorts that kept Dan's undivided interest. She'd deliberately dressed provocatively tonight, knowing they would finally be together in a real bed. Cait was more than ready to say goodbye to that lounge chair, too.

Dan leaned over, pulling the chair back for her. "I've been exercising the hell out of it today, keeping it warm and limbered up."

She sat down. "Ah, for tonight?" She saw his eyes turn predator-like and she felt her lower body simmer with heat and anticipation.

"I'm not so sure we'll last until tonight." Dan waved his fork toward the east-facing window. It would be another two hours before dark settled over the island this time of year.

She handed him the rice. "Whatever feels right for us," she agreed. The food smelled wonderful and she took a spoonful, ladling it across the rice on the plate. "What news do you have? Did you hear from your Sidewinder buddies yet?" Cait knew he'd been calling his good friends, but sometimes they were out on an op somewhere in the world and he couldn't touch base with all of them. She was glad Dan had these male friends he'd grown up with because sometimes, she saw the sadness and loss of Ben in his eyes. He never said anything, but he didn't have to. She knew how to read Dan so well.

"I got a call from Josh Patterson, one of my Sidewinder brothers, about two hours ago. He's a Marine Force Recon. He's getting hitched. Surprised the hell out of me. I always thought he'd be the last of us to go down."

She grinned. "All bachelors by nature?"

Shaking his head, he said, "It started out that way. Now I'm going down. Jack Halliday is married, and so is Travis. Josh asked if we could come to their wedding. I'd like you to come along if you can. It's going to be held April 4 in Texas."

Cait frowned. "That's the week I'm taking credit courses in new PT instruction here at Tripler. I won't be able to go, Dan. I'm sorry." She saw his disappointment. She knew he was happy for Josh. "And I don't think the Army is going to look kindly on your leaving, either. You're right in middle of rehab."

Shrugging, he hungrily dug into the tasty rice and pineapple chicken. "Can you rig it up for me to be gone with four days leave? Now that I can bend this knee, I can fly in an airplane. I don't want to miss his wedding."

Cait knew how much this meant to Dan. She blew out a breath and said, "Okay, but I'm going to have to do some fancy footwork to get your orders cut to go out there, Dan."

"I knew you could do that," he said smugly, giving her a teasing look. "Thank you."

The thickening of his voice washed over her and Cait smiled a little. "Who is he marrying?"

"A gal by the name of Allison Landon. She's an RN. Her father is a Marine Corps general and Josh just happened to know him. Aly was working for a charity down in Brazil when she got kidnapped by drug dealers."

Eyes widening, Cait whispered, "Oh, my God. Is she okay?"

"She is now," Dan said with a pleased look. "The general asked Josh to go down there to find and rescue her. He did. Along the way, he told me on the phone earlier, they fell in love. Then he got hauled out on another black op just days after bringing her stateside from Brazil. He got back three months later, bought a ring and proposed to Aly." His smile widened. "She said yes. So, he's the fourth Sidewinder to bite the dust."

"Are the others happily married?"

Nodding, Dan said, "Yeah, they all picked good, strong women."

"Is that a Texas thing? You guys go looking for a woman to complement you?"

"As a football team, we were all strong in various ways. There wasn't a weak one among us," Dan said. "And I think the women they fell in love with are all equally strong in an emotional and mental sense."

"Do you see me as strong?" Cait asked, falling into his warm gray gaze. She could literally feel the invisible embrace from Dan surrounding her. They ate at one another's elbow, but she could still feel that warmth wrapping around her shoulders. It was an incredible feeling. A sense of protection woven with fierce love coming from Dan.

He reached over, his thumb grazing her cheek. "I'd call you Texas strong in a heartbeat, Cait. You've been there for me when I needed someone. When I was coming out of anesthesia, hearing your voice near my ear and feeling your hand on mine gave me hope. You've helped me fight back to get well." His voice lowered with feeling. "I couldn't have done this without you, sweetheart…"

"We've waited so long for one another," Cait whispered unsteadily, blinking back tears. "Over a decade."

Mouth quirking, Dan held her gaze, lost in the shades

of green in her eyes, from dark to light. She was a complex woman, a woman who always challenged him in the best of ways. Cait didn't see herself at all, he realized. She saw only the nature of her patients' personality, saw what was weak and strong with them and then worked to help them recover. She honestly didn't see how incredibly strong she really was. Tonight, Dan would show her. Tonight was theirs.

To be able to lie beside Cait, to feel her velvet-soft, curved body against his, was a dream come true for Dan. As they languished in one another's arms after making love to one another, he held her close. "Even just feeling your breath on my chest is incredible," he growled, moving his head to the right, kissing her hair.

Cait stirred, satiated and feeling lazy for the moment, her body radiating and glowing from the orgasms he'd given her. "Better than that lounger, huh?" There was amusement in her husky tone. "That lounger is going to hold a special place in our lives. We'll never forget it."

Laughter rumbled through his chest. "Better believe it." Dan threaded his fingers through her loose, silky hair, watching the weak moonlight catch the strands. Skating his hand down the curves of her back and hip before coming to rest on her thigh, he added, "The lounger was a lifesaver for both of us."

"Well," Cait whispered, nuzzling his jaw, stretching her arm across his narrow waist, "this is so much better. We'll actually be able to sleep together tonight. That is what I'm looking forward to."

Dan guided Cait onto her back, propped himself up on his elbow and drank in her shadowed face, those luminous dark green eyes filled with love for him. "Who said we're getting any sleep tonight?"

Cait's lips lifted and she ran her hand slowly down his chest, his gold-brown hair tangling between her exploring fingers. "Touché."

"Lucky for us, it's Saturday tomorrow."

"Do you think we'll even leave this bed over the next few days?"

Dan basked in her smile, his heart swelling with so many emotions for Cait. "Probably not. Just to get up every once in a while, shower, grab some food to give us renewed strength and then get back in here."

"You have a plan. You always do, Dan Taylor."

Eyeing her wryly, he leaned over, his mouth hovering over hers. "I'm black ops, sweetheart. What else did you expect?"

He captured her smiling mouth beneath his, feeling her woman's warmth, a musical sound caught in her throat as he stroked her firm breast, feeling her nipple tighten beneath his teasing. He couldn't get enough of Cait. He never would. They'd waited so long for one another. Dan found it nearly impossible to realize how strong they'd been in denying themselves one another. And now they were making up for it in the best of ways.

"Hey," he whispered against her wet lips, "there are some things we actually need to discuss."

Cait laughed and opened her eyes. "Like what? I thought everything we needed was right here. Right now."

"That's true." Dan leaned across her, opening the bedside table drawer, fumbling around to find something in it. He glanced down at Cait. "Found it."

"What?"

He pulled his arm from beneath her neck and with some effort, sat up and leaned against the bamboo headboard. "Come here." He took her hand, coaxing her up beside him. Cait's hair was nearly to her breasts and as she moved, he watched the gleaming strands slide gracefully around her. She snuggled beneath his proffered left arm, pressing herself fully against his left side.

"You've got a crafty look on your face," she accused. "What are you up to?"

"Can't fool you, can I?" Dan showed her a small dark blue velvet box. "Here, this is for you. Open it." He searched her widening eyes as Cait realized what it was. A small gasp tore from her. She looked at the ring box and then stared in disbelief up at him.

"Dan!"

"Open it. Please?" He nudged the box near her hand, which was still resting on his chest.

She shook her head. Dan slid his arm behind her back, curving it around her waist, keeping her close as she cupped the box into her hands. "I—I never expected this, Dan."

"I did." He watched with trepidation as she opened it. Never had he wanted anything more than this moment with Cait. "Do you like them?" His voice was a little strained.

"Oh, Dan..." Cait pressed her hand against her lips, giving him a teary look.

"Are they okay?"

She looked down at the set of rings. "They're beautiful." She held the box up so that the moonlight washed over it. "Is that a green diamond, Dan?"

"It is." He gave her a concerned look. "I know it's not the exact color of your eyes, but when I saw it, I wanted it for you."

Cait gently touched the small diamond glittering fiercely in the gold setting. "I love it." She looked at him, whispering, "I love you…" She leaned forward, her hand against his jaw, giving him a long, slow kiss.

Dan caressed her nape as they eased apart. "Marry me, Cait? We've waited a hell of a long time for one another. I don't want to spend another day apart from you if I can help it." He lost his smile, seeing distress come into her large, readable eyes.

"I'll marry you, Dan," she whispered unsteadily. "But…not right now. My parents are in deep mourning for Ben. Could we wait a bit? Give them the time they need to get over his loss?"

Dan tucked her beneath his arm, drawing her against him. "Of course. We don't even have to say anything about this to them until you think the timing is right. This is just between you and me, Cait." He pulled back enough to meet her darkened eyes, wanting to reassure her. "Okay?"

Cait nodded, pressed her cheek against his chest, giving him a squeeze. "Yes, thank you for understanding."

"Your parents are hurting," Dan said gruffly, kissing her hair. "I get that. But, Cait, I love you. I'm not going to let any more time slip by before I tell you what I want to share with you. I want to wake up every morning in this bed with you in my arms." He caressed her warm, soft shoulder, watching hope and love come to her eyes as she studied him. "And if that means waiting a year before we marry, I'm fine with that. What I need is you. And now I have you." His voice deepened with emotion. "I'm not ever letting you go."

Sighing, Cait whispered, "I feel the same way. And it may take a year before my parents emerge from that tunnel of grief. I mean…I still cry suddenly, out of the blue, and when I do, I know it's grief working its way through me."

"I know," Dan rasped, sliding his hand against her hair, holding her tighter for a moment.

"You, too?"

"Yes. He was like a brother to me, Cait. Ben will be in our hearts and our memories from now on. I'll never forget him, but your parents have a different path to take to mourn the loss of their only son." Dan knew Cait's grief would last a long time, as well. She and Ben had been so damned close.

"Thank you for understanding," she wobbled, sniffing.

"I want you to be happy, Cait," he growled. "I'll do everything I can to always see that smile in your eyes."

"You do, believe me, you do," Cait whispered, kissing his chest.

Dan knew that Cait had choices to make. She could opt to wear the green diamond engagement ring. Or not. Her mother would spot it immediately, and that could turn into an upsetting situation for Cait and her. And them. Dan didn't want to put Cait in that kind of a position. He gently eased the box from her hand. "Tell you what. We'll just put the rings in the bedside table for now until you feel it's the right time to tell your parents. Then, when it's right, you can let me slip that engagement ring on your finger." Because Dan could feel Cait being torn over this very issue. And he didn't want her to feel guilty. She still had a lot of grieving to do first.

It wasn't his intent to pressure her, rather, to let her know unequivocally that he loved her and he wanted her as his wife. They'd waited so long for one another. The fact that they were living together and would continue to do so, sent a very clear, nonverbal signal to her parents, anyway. They knew what was coming sooner or later, but to push it too soon on the three of them would be a bad move. Dan could feel the tension in Cait dissolve beneath his words. "That an okay plan, sweetheart?"

"Yes, wonderful. Thank you…"

Dan slid her hair aside, nibbling on her nape, feeling the goose bumps rise in the wake of his tender kisses and gentle nips. She moved her breasts against him. She was so sensual. So sexual. And so in love with him. He gave her flesh a nip and then soothed the area with his tongue.

"We have one more thing to talk about," he told her.

Cait lifted her chin, melting beneath his dark, burning look. "What else could there possibly be to talk about?"

"I've been busy since I started living here with you," Dan said, his thumb sliding across the warm slope of her cheek. Looking deeply into her aroused eyes, her lashes framing their deep green color, he said, "I'm not going to stay in the Army, Cait."

Stunned, she sat up, staring openmouthed at him. "What? I mean, why? You love the Army, Dan! And your leg is healing wonderfully. There's every chance that you could meet all the physical qualifications to remain in Special Forces."

He heard the stunned quality in her voice and saw it

in her eyes. He smiled gently at her. "Would it bother you if I left the Army? Start a real life here with you instead?" Cait's face crumpled with emotions and tears leaped to her eyes. Yeah, he had his answer all right. And Dan had known all along that Cait was trying to steel herself against his leaving once he was well enough to go back into Special Forces. She would wait and worry. He'd be gone on deployments for six months to a year at a time. She'd be alone. Again. Like always. They'd be separated. Like always.

"A-are you serious, Dan?" Cait wiped the tears from her eyes, her heart beating with hope over the possibility.

He caressed her cheek and leaned over, giving her a quick kiss on the mouth. "I've already got a job lined up for when my enlistment is up. That's eight months from now, Cait. I'll be the head of security for a shipping company here in Honolulu. It'll be a nine-to-five job, five days a week." He smiled a little, emotion thick in his voice. "It means I'll be coming home to you every night. We can have a life, Cait. A *real* life."

"Oh, God." Her voice trembled and more tears fell. "I—I never expected this, Dan."

"I know you didn't," he soothed, kissing her wrinkled brow, her cheek, and tasting her salty tears as they fell. "Are you okay with it?"

"More than okay with it."

Dan searched her radiant expression, saw relief shining in her eyes. "I've lost so many years away from you, Cait. I don't want any more separations. I don't want you worrying about whether I'm going to get killed or not. You've lost Ben. That's enough…"

With a moan of joy, Cait threw herself into his arms, clinging to him, holding him as tight as she could. "Oh, Dan! I love you so much! So much!" She sobbed, burying her face in the crook of his shoulder.

Closing his eyes, Dan relaxed against the headboard, the woman he loved more than life itself in his arms. She'd been so brave, so strong, for so long by herself. He swept his fingers through her hair, caressing her graceful back, holding her close while she cried out her relief. And he fully understood her tears this time. Dan knew Cait had been dreading his going back and being deployed once more. He would catch her at odd moments when they were together when he could almost hear her thoughts. Cait would have worried herself endlessly if he'd gone back into Special Forces.

He loved her, and this was about more than what he wanted out of life from now on. It was what they needed in order to make a go at their relationship. And he knew, in order for them to have a fair chance at success, it meant giving up something he loved because he loved Cait more. It was that simple. Dan had no regrets about the decision.

Her sobs lessened and he could feel her warm tears running down his chest. Cait's sense of relief was palpable. Dan knew she'd never have asked him to leave the Army. She, of all people, understood it—what he did and how much he loved what he did. Now, as he kissed her hair, caressed her small shoulder, she knew that he loved her more than anything. They would have to wait to break the news of their engagement to her parents. In the meantime, they would have a chance to really live together. Loving one another. Making the compromises he knew would have to be made so they could work as the good team that they were. They were already, automatically, doing that precisely because they did love one another. Nuzzling into her hair, kissing the top of her ear and angling her head, he captured her soft, willing mouth. Just the simple act of kissing Cait was enough to make Dan happy to turn his life inside out for her. He'd found love a long time ago, nursed it, nurtured it and finally been brave enough to act upon it.

Cait deserved a man like him, who was loyal and true. Dan knew he could be all that and so much more to this healer who'd mended so many people's lives. She had a world of patience, of kindness and compassion for those who were suffering. She brought out the goodness in him, and he wanted to spend the rest of his life returning all that she had selflessly given to him. Knowing how much Cait loved children, Dan knew that once they were officially married with her parents' blessing, it probably wouldn't be too long before she became pregnant.

Heat rolled through him as he splayed his large hand out across her soft belly. Someday, she would carry his son or daughter within her. It only made Dan love Cait more fiercely than before. She would be such a good mother, and he would be sure not to emulate the broken, dysfunctional home life of his childhood with her or their children. Life was too short and Dan knew every day counted. And he would relish each one with this woman who loved him against all odds. Forever.

* * * * *

DESERT HEAT

Merline Lovelace

Chapter 1

"Majan one, this is Majan one-five."

"Go ahead, one-five."

Master Sergeant Pete Winborne kneeled beside the injured crewman, shielding him with his body. Two other pararescuemen, known in the military as PJs, worked frantically to staunch the blood spurting from a femoral artery. The remaining three PJs on Pete's team stood with weapons ready, their faces grim and their eyes on the figures that had just topped a distant dune. Squinting through the shimmering desert heat, he radioed the heavily armed Pave Hawk helicopter circling overhead.

"Enemy at one-two-zero degrees. Four hundred meters. Target description, troops in the open."

"Roger, one-five, we see 'em."

The Royal Air Force chopper broke hard right and

acquired the target. Pete kept one eye on the deadly tracers that arced from the side-mounted 50-caliber machine gun, the other on the PJs now transferring their Code Alpha to the rescue litter.

Part combat troops, part emergency ER docs, these pararescuemen had completed two years of brutal training to land here, in the searing desert of southern Oman, working desperately to package a critically wounded troop for the flight back to base.

"Majan one-five, target destroyed but we see a second wave of big uglies to the north."

Hell! That was all they needed. Another wave of hostiles. A quick glance at the wounded troop showed that his squad had the man stabilized enough to move. Jaw tight, Pete called for extraction.

"Majan one, ready for ex-fil."

"Roger that, one-five."

Ordinarily the Pave Hawk would set down so the PJs could slide the litter into the open bay and scramble aboard. But this area of operations contained nothing but mountainous sand dunes. Not a level patch of dirt anywhere in sight. So the Pave Hawk went into a hover, throwing up a maelstrom of whirling, biting sand, and lowered the hoist. Working with grim efficiency, the PJs attached the litter to the hoist. Once it and the PJ accompanying it had been hauled into the bay, the remainder of the squad went up.

While one of the team started an IV and another cut off their patient's uniform to check for additional wounds, the Pave Hawk banked sharply and ripped across the dunes. The powerful, much-modified Sikorsky chopper could travel at more than 220 miles per hour. In this instance, every second counted.

They touched down at Thumrait Air Base exactly seventeen minutes later. Well within the vital one-hour parameter to locate, stabilize and transport a Code Alpha to a field hospital. Pete verified the time and sat back on his heels, grinning.

"You did it, dudes."

Whoops and high fives erupted all around. Even the "patient" popped up to slap palms. A PJ himself, the Omani sergeant hadn't been very happy about playing the injured soldier in this live-fire exercise. Drenched now in fake blood and sucking saline through an IV, he was only too happy to extract the needle and swab off some of the blood.

They debriefed at the TOC—Tactical Operations Center—before breaking down and cleaning their weapons and stowing their gear. A battle-hardened team of US, UAE and Omani airmen, they'd been at Thumrait for almost two weeks now. Pete couldn't fault the facilities, the accommodations or the men he'd come to know and respect during this combined exercise arranged by Prince Malik al Said. A distant relative of Oman's ruling sultan, the prince served as Chief of Operations for the Royal Air Force and was determined to ensure his country could meet any threat in this dangerous and highly volatile region.

Pete had acted as the prince's escort during his visit to the USAF Pararescue School at Kirtland Air Force Base, New Mexico, last year. He'd also flown several training missions with Prince Malik. In his opinion, the

Omani's keen intelligence and skills as a pilot more than matched his reputation as an international jet-setter.

A very well-deserved reputation, according to the tabloids. Which was why Pete wasn't surprised to see al Said's face smiling up from the front page of one of the newspapers tossed on a table in the TOC's lounge. The face beside the prince's, however, stopped him in his tracks.

"Hey, Najjar!" He hailed one of the Omani PJs just entering the lounge. "Translate this headline for me, will you?"

Najjar's English was a whole lot better than Pete's limited Arabic. He needed only a brief glance at the headline to reel off a quick translation.

"'By special invitation from Prince Malik al Said, internationally renowned opera star Riley Fairchild will perform tomorrow evening at the Royal Opera House.'"

Christ! It *was* her.

Riley Fairchild.

Blonde, beautiful and a complete bitch.

That last was according to her mother. Meredith Fairchild's caustic commentary on her ungrateful offspring should have sent Pete running for cover when he'd encountered both mother and daughter at Josh and Aly's wedding. God knew, he'd accumulated enough scars from his own marriage to a spoiled diva.

Head cheerleader Nancy Sue Collins had starred in the wet dreams of just about every male attending high school in Rush Springs, Texas. As curvaceous as she was addicted to the adulation of her lovesick admirers, she'd picked Pete—the football team's all-state cornerback—to be her chosen mate. She'd even strutted her stuff and told everyone how proud she was when Pete and his fellow Sidewinders all enlisted the day after graduation.

Then came basic and twenty grueling months of Special Ops training. Didn't take Nancy Sue long to discover the wife of a low-ranking trainee on a big, bustling military base was a small frog in a *very* large pond. She hightailed it back to Texas before Pete finished Phase One of PJ training. He got served with divorce papers halfway through Phase Two. Six months later, Nancy Sue married the wealthiest man in Rush Springs. The new-and-used car dealer was twice her age, a fact she dismissed with a defiant toss of her hair when she bumped into Pete at Josh and Aly's reception.

She'd shown up uninvited, he'd learned later. But since she'd been part of their crowd way back when, no one said anything. Pete would be the first to admit she'd looked as lush and sensual as ever. But her brittle smile and the champagne she'd guzzled nonstop suggested her second marriage wasn't working out any better than the first.

Which was probably why Pete had tried to ignore his ex-wife and zero in instead on the delectable Riley Fairchild. Despite her mother's bitter comment, the gorgeous singer had a tumble of honey-blond hair and the serene, almost ethereal face of a Madonna. Ha! Some Madonna! She'd cut off Pete at the knees with an icy stare and about six well-chosen words. He was still licking his wounds when she got up to serenade the bride and groom at their reception.

Pete wasn't into opera. Didn't know Puccini from Pink Floyd. And he didn't find out until later that Riley

Fairchild had made a phenomenally successful cross-over into pop. At the time, all he knew was that her incredible rendition of "I Will Always Love You" brought tears to Aly's eyes and a fist-sized lump to everyone else's throat.

Now she was here. In Oman. Performing tomorrow night at the Royal Opera House in Muscat. Helluva small world, Pete thought wryly as he departed the TOC.

The desert heat hit him like a balled fist. He should be used to it after almost two weeks in Oman. He wasn't. Squinting through his Ray-Ban sunglasses, he started across the compound. Originally an oil depot, Thumrait had been converted to a busy military base. Oman's ruling sultan had allowed the US, UK and Allied air forces to stage out of Thumrait during Desert Shield, Desert Storm and the on-going global war on terror. In support of those operations, the US had established a major war reserve matériel depot here. Row after row of sand-colored storage facilities were filled to the rafters with medical supplies, munitions, fuels, vehicles, rations and a whole host of other consumables.

Angling between two rows of rectangular warehouses, Pete made for the Containerized Housing Units that served as housing for transient personnel. The boxcar-like CHUs came equipped with air-conditioning, phone and data links, and hot and cold running water. All the comforts of home—if your home was a six-by-twenty-foot box. Rows of CHUs stretched almost to the razor-wire-topped fence protecting the perimeter. The fence kept out the locals but not the wind-driven sand. Mountains of it piled up every day, obscuring walkways and obstructing runways that had to be swept continuously by the army of locals employed at the base.

Pete shared a two-man CHU with the ranking Omani noncom for the duration of their combined Special Operations exercise. Faisal was at the Tactical Ops Center, preparing for a night exercise, so Pete treated himself to a long, cool shower before padding naked to the mini-fridge and popping the top of an ice-cold beer. Although Oman was a Muslim country and alcohol forbidden to its natives, visitors were permitted to indulge in the privacy of their homes, hotel rooms or on-base quarters.

The Heineken went a long way to washing the sand from his throat and gullet, but the call from the TOC some moments later almost made him choke on it.

"Sergeant Winborne, we're patching through a call for you."

"From?"

"Prince Malik al Said. Hold, please."

Hell! Nothing like standing stark naked, beer in hand and taking a call from royalty. Trying to ignore the air-conditioning that was now shrinking certain parts of his anatomy to minuscule proportions, Pete set aside his beer.

"I just received a report on the exercise this morning," the prince said in flawless English when he came on line. Educated at the École Spéciale Militaire de Saint-Cyr in France, with follow-on flight training in the United States and Great Britain, Malik al Said was fluent in a half dozen languages. "I'm pleased, Pete. Very pleased."

"So am I, Your Highness. Our guys did good."

"But pararescue... Only the best of the best are worthy to become PJs."

Pete wouldn't argue with that. Every PJ worth his salt trained every day to make their creed—That Others May Live—more than just a slogan. Like the air commandos before them, they would do whatever it took to rescue stranded troops or downed crew members. They could enter hostile territory by parachute, scuba, motorcycles, snowmobiles or skis. Climb up or rappel down sheer mountain precipices. Fight their way out of deadly ambushes and firefights. They were also fully qualified EMTs. Their brutal training regimen resulted in the highest washout rate among any of the military branches, including Army Rangers and Navy SEALs. Less than fifteen percent of all personnel who entered PJ school earned the right to wear the coveted maroon beret.

"You must convey my congratulations to the men," the prince continued.

"I will, sir."

"And to celebrate, I'm ordering a two-day stand-down. Rest, my friend, and enjoy this well-deserved break."

"Thank you, I will. Or..."

The idea that popped into Pete's head was so crazy he decided later it had to have been the beer talking.

"Yes?" the prince asked.

"I saw in the papers that Riley Fairchild is performing in Muscat tomorrow evening. I met her once, back in the States. Briefly."

"Did you? Then you must come and hear her perform. I shall tell my people to have a ticket waiting for you at the box office. And," the prince added after a brief pause, "I will have them arrange an appointment with my tailor. The event tomorrow evening is white-tie, as I'm sure you must know."

Hell, no, he didn't know!

"You cannot wear your dress uniform," al Said cautioned. "Not in such a setting."

Translation: Not with Oman walking a delicate tightrope between East and West. There were sure to be high-powered diplomats there from both sides of the power struggle. No need to flash a US uniform loaded with combat badges and campaign ribbons in their faces.

Pete started to tell the prince to forget the whole thing, but al Said didn't give him a chance. "My people will attend to the details and call you," he said briskly. "Go with God, my friend."

"Your Highness…"

Too late. The prince had cut the connection.

Smart, Winborne! Real smart! Talk yourself *out* of a couple lazy-ass days and *into* a fancy dress function up in Muscat!

Shaking his head, Pete finished his beer, tossed the can into the trash and stretched out on his rack. The mental and physical stress of the past few hours should have seeped out of his pores the way it always did, slowly and with a detailed, step-by-step review of each phase of the rescue operation just completed.

Instead, he found himself prey to a different kind of tension. This one settled low in his belly and knotted just a little tighter each time his thoughts drifted to Riley Fairchild.

What the hell! So she had the personality of a she-wolf with a thorn in her paw, she could still sing like nothing Pete had ever heard. It would almost be worth it to make the trip up to Muscat and gussy up in white tie and tails.

Almost.

Thumrait Air Base was a little over 900 kilometers southwest of Oman's capital city. Ten-plus hours by truck or four-wheel drive. Even longer if you climbed aboard a camel and followed the ancient frankincense trading route through the desert.

Pete might have used the arduous journey as an excuse to bow out if a Royal Air Force C-130 Hercules didn't made regular runs between the base and Muscat. So he hauled his butt aboard the cargo plane a little after eight the next morning and was in the capital by eleven.

The ride in from the airport took him through the near blinding sunshine along spotless new highways. Muscat wasn't as flashy as Dubai or Abu Dhabi, its glitzy neighbors to the north. No world's tallest buildings or monster shopping malls with indoor ski slopes. Although modern and more progressive, Oman incorporated its past into its present.

The capital city formed a crescent fronting the cobalt waters of the Arabian Sea. Red, barren mountains ringed its perimeter, holding the desert at bay. The old section of the city was a jumble of narrow streets and busy souks fronting the harbor, where dhows laden with silks and spices from all over the world once found anchorage. Oil tankers, cargo ships, the royal yachts and the occasional cruise ship now rode the turquoise waters.

Muscat's newer environs spread out from the old. The disciplined sprawl of gleaming white adobe structures constructed in Arabic style included the sultan's palace, the Royal Opera House and the blue-domed Grand Mosque that could accommodate more than twenty thousand worshippers. International hotels catering to companies hoping to tap Oman's rich oil reserves were low-rise and also conformed to traditional architecture. So did the embassies set amid compounds filled with palms and flowering bushes.

The sights and scents of the city filled Pete's senses at every turn. The souks, where men in traditional Omani embroidered skullcaps and flowing white robes sat cross-legged in stalls. The mud-and-adobe homes of old Arabia, their arched windows shaded by tall palms. The scent of spicy kebabs roasting on charcoal braziers.

Pete caught the tantalizing aroma when he climbed out of the taxi at the address provided by one of the prince's underlings. Before hitting the tailor's shop, he claimed a rickety table at an outdoor café and treated himself to a traditional Omani meal. The barbecued lamb and grilled vegetable kebab was served over lemon rice with a side of succulent olives and dates. Suitably fortified, he entered the dim, musty tailor's shop.

He was greeted by a wizened gnome in a traditional white robe and skullcap. Wire-rimmed glasses sat on the tip of the man's nose, measuring tape dangled around his neck.

"As-salám aláykum."

"Peace be with you, too," Pete replied in passable Omani.

"I am Yassim," the tailor said, switching to English.

"And you must be the one the prince's people told me would come."

His shrewd black eyes measured Pete's body under the knit polo shirt and well-washed jeans he'd donned for the excursion to the capital.

"They said you would be well-muscled. They did not lie, I see. Come, come."

He crooked a finger and led the way into a back room bursting with color. Bolts of fabric jammed shelves that reached from floor to ceiling. Giant spools spilled lengths of gold rope, silver tassels, sequined trim and metallic braid in a dozen different sizes and colors. Tailor's dummies in various stages of dress stood like sentinels guarding these bright treasures.

Pete was eyeing the tassels and sequins with serious doubt when Yassim whisked aside a curtain to display another tailor's dummy. This one was dressed in Western attire. White tie, white shirt, low-cut white vest, black pants and black cutaway jacket. With tails, for God's sake!

"It was made for the English Ambassador," Yassim explained, "but he does not return to Muscat until next month. He is a big man, as big as you in the upper body. The jacket and shirt will fit, I think, but I shall have to take in the pants. Please, try them on."

He gestured to a curtained area, where Pete traded his jeans and knit shirt for full dress regalia. The tailor had a good eye. The shirt, vest and cutaway jacket fit almost perfectly, but the pants were too large in the waist and a good inch too short.

That didn't seem to present much of a problem. Yassim produced a wedge of chalk from a pocket of his voluminous robe and made a few quick slashes.

"There! This will be easy to fix, thanks be to God. I shall deliver them to your hotel by six."

Nodding, Pete changed back into his jeans and polo shirt. "How much do I owe you?"

"There is no charge."

"Sure there is."

"Prince al Said's man said all costs would taken care of. Now for shoes. My associate Faquir is but two shops over and he—"

"I'll pay for this," Pete interjected politely but firmly. "How much?"

Tonight would most likely be the only time he would ever rig himself out in white tie and tails. Once he rotated back to his home base in Florida, these fancy duds would gather dust in his closet. Right along with the service and mess dress uniforms he dragged out for those rare instances when PJs gathered for formal military functions. Still, he wasn't about to abuse the prince's friendship or violate Air Force regulations by accepting such an expensive gift.

Shrugging, the tailor named a price. It was probably one tenth what Pete would pay for formal attire in the United States, but it still made him gulp. In normal circumstances he would have countered with a figure half that amount and enjoyed the subsequent bargaining. These circumstances were hardly normal.

As he reminded himself *again* while he mounted the steps to the Royal Opera House later that evening.

Constructed in 2011, the white marble temple to the arts gleamed in the evening sun. Clean lines and soaring arches celebrated the best of traditional Omani architecture. Within its deceptively simple walls, the massive complex housed landscaped gardens, an upscale cultural market, luxury restaurants and separate auditoriums for orchestral, theatrical and operatic productions.

Since this was a royal performance, guards checked Pete's ID and performed a quick search of his taxi before allowing it to join the queue of other vehicles discharging elegantly dressed patrons. The chandelier-lit foyer was crammed with what looked like dozens of different nationalities. The Omani men wore black outer robes decorated with glittering gold ropes and tassels over their ankle-length, long-sleeved white robes. Instead of their everyday skullcaps, the bright colors and intricate designs of their turbans designated their tribe and rank. And each sported a curved dagger in jeweled sheaths tucked into their robe at the waist.

Their spouses were almost as colorful. Omani women had more rights and freedom than women in some other Arab Gulf states. Many chose to follow strict Muslim dress codes and dressed in black from head to toe. But a good number of those present wore elaborately embroidered robes over loose-fitting trousers and jeweled slippers, although modesty dictated that they cover their hair with decorative shawls. As with the men, their bright plumage identified their tribe and area of origin.

The locals mingled in the vast foyer with individuals in Western dress. The men sported the same ultraformal attire as Pete. The women were rigged out in every color of the spectrum while still attempting to respect local customs. Their shoulders and arms were discreetly covered. Some had draped filmy scarves over their hair.

Pete collected the ticket he'd been told would be waiting for him at the box office and stood in line to get through security. It was decent, he noted with a critical eye, but not impenetrable. Guards were posted at regular intervals, their presence felt but not intrusive. He was making mental adjustments to their disposition as he followed the crowd through the lobby to the main auditorium. An attendant scanned his ticket and directed him up a half level. Another attendant escorted him to what he realized too late was the royal box.

"I think this is a mistake."

"No, sir." The attendant waved him to an ornate armchair padded in purple velvet. "Your seat is just here. The prince and his party will arrive shortly."

Okay. All right. So he'd be sitting one row behind the prince and directly under the Omani coat of arms. The best seats in the house, close enough to the stage to see the shimmer of gold thread woven into the red curtain. Pete just hoped to hell some enterprising newshound didn't snap a picture of the box once the prince arrived. If the picture should hit the news media, his fellow Sidewinders would never let him live down being caught in a monkey suit, hobnobbing with royalty.

When he took his seat, curious stares came zinging at him from all directions. He avoided them by burying his nose in the program. Printed in both Arabic and English, the playbill informed him that the Royal Opera House had opened with performances by Placido Domingo, Andrea Bocelli and world-renowned cellist Yo-Yo Ma.

It also imparted the interesting information that tonight's performance was the next to last in a series of concerts given by Riley Fairchild to benefit the United Nations Children's Emergency Fund. All proceeds from the two-month, twelve-country concert tour, Pete read, went to UNICEF's programs to alleviate starvation and reduce infant mortality in sub-Saharan Africa. He was trying to fit this information with the less-than-flattering mental construct he'd formed of the opera singer at Aly and Josh's wedding when the prince and his party arrived.

"Sergeant Winborne!" Al Said's teeth gleamed white under his inky black mustache. "I would not have recognized you, my friend."

"I hardly recognize myself," Pete admitted ruefully.

The prince's arrival brought the audience to their feet. As soon as the applause died down, the lights dimmed. Then the curtain parted and the Royal Philharmonic Orchestra struck the opening notes.

Riley Fairchild walked on stage a moment later to a thunderous ovation.

Regal and as willowy as a reed in a gown of flowing red silk, she was even more stunning than Pete remembered. A gauzy scarf shielded her honey-colored hair, but her skin was luminous and the bright stage lights put stars in the brown eyes she turned toward the royal box. Her gaze swept over the prince's entourage. Pete saw it flick past him. Stop. Kick back for a second before moving on.

She'd recognized him, Pete thought with a wry inner grin, but couldn't place him. No surprise there. He'd been wearing his dress uniform when they'd met back in Texas. And the glamorous Ms. Fairchild had barely glanced at him before letting him know she was *not* interested. He was still remembering the acid put-down when the prince stood and kissed his hand to her. She acknowledged the extravagant gesture with a smile and a bow before turning to the conductor.

Ten seconds into her opening aria, Pete was thinking he'd never heard anything as pure as the liquid silver notes she poured into the air.

Three minutes later, he decided opera might just rank up there with hot, mindless sex and juicy T-bones in his list of personal favorites.

Five minutes after that, all hell broke loose.

Chapter 2

The first warning was a short, stuttering rattle.

With two monster timpani drums booming out a dramatic crescendo, not everyone in the audience immediately picked up on it, but Pete recognized the sound of automatic gunfire instantly. So did the battle-trained prince. He and Pete sprang out of their seats at the same instant the doors at the rear of the auditorium burst open. Men in black ski masks charged down the aisles, shouting and spraying gunfire above the heads of the audience.

Terrified patrons screamed, dove out of their seats and tried frantically to wedge between the rows. On stage, chairs and music stands crashed over. Abandoning their instruments, the musicians scrambled for cover. Their guest performer stood paralyzed with fright for a moment before dropping facedown on the stage and covering her head with both arms.

The prince's personal bodyguard grabbed his arms and rushed him toward the rear of the royal box. The other members of his party tumbled out of their chairs to the floor. All except Pete. Acting on pure instinct, he vaulted over the front rail, dropped the half story and leaped onto the stage. Bullets stitched a deadly arc just inches over his head as he kicked two overturned chairs together to form a fragile shield before covering Riley's body with his own. She twisted under him, panting at the combined impact of his weight and her terror, until he snarled a warning.

"Be still!"

She went rigid with shock. Or maybe surprise at the terse command. The gunmen were still firing, still shouting in a dialect Pete didn't understand. Despite the pandemonium, his training never deserted him. He recorded every sound, every sensation. The rat-a-tat of short-barreled AK-47s. The high-pitched, adrenaline-charged shout of a female among the attackers. The sobs of sheer terror as the firing subsided and a voice vibrating with nerves issued orders in Arabic, then French, then English.

"Everyone! Get up! Get up! Now!"

The audience rose slowly, cautiously, with a chorus of grunts and gasps and more sobs.

"You people! On the stage! On your feet!"

There was a clang of overturned music stands, the tinny sound of brass instruments banging together, a slow shuffle of hands and knees and feet. Pete levered himself into a crouch and wrapped a hand around the warm skin of Riley Fairchild's arm.

"Best to do what they say."

He helped her up. She'd lost the gauzy head scarf. Also the combs holding back her hair. The honey-blond mass tumbled in wild abandon, covering her face and the terror Pete knew filled her eyes.

She had to be thinking the same thing he was. If this was a hostage situation, the attackers had their choice of any number of high-value targets. The most obvious was Prince Malik al Said, a member of the Omani ruling family. But the glittering audience probably included a good number of foreign dignitaries—ambassadors, consuls, chargés d'affaires. Then, of course, there was an international opera star who reportedly commanded upward of a hundred thousand dollars for every performance.

If it wasn't a hostage situation, chances were damned good it was a suicide mission. Pete couldn't ignore that all-too-real possibility but kept the grim thought from his face as Riley shoved back her hair. Her head came up and recognition cut through the fear flooding her brown eyes.

"I—I know you from somewhere."

"We met at—"

"No talking!"

The command was screamed at them from the AK-47–toting attacker, who'd leaped onto the stage. He jerked from side to side, gesturing with his weapon, shouting at the terrified orchestra members, herding them into a tight huddle. Pete hooked an arm around Riley's waist and started toward the others.

"Not you!" His eyes wild in the slits of his mask, the gunman stabbed the barrel at Riley. "You will go there!"

He gestured toward the wings, where another figure had just emerged.

"You," he snarled at Pete. "Release her and join the others."

Pete shook his head. The attacker leveled his weapon.

"Release her, I say!"

The nervous gunman couldn't fire without hitting Riley. He knew it. Pete knew it. They played a deadly game of chicken for three seconds. Five. Too hyped and nervous to let the game spin out any longer, the gunman grunted and jerked the barrel.

"Go!"

As Riley walked toward the other man waiting in the wings, she pressed against the wall of a hard, ridged rib cage. Not that she had a choice in the matter. The arm locked around her was like a steel belt, carving into her waist, cutting off her breath. Desperately, her frantic mind tried to sort through the terror and shouts and cries and sobs.

What did these men want?

Why are they separating her from the others?

And who was this American defying them?

She knew him. She knew she knew him, but she had no clue from where or when. She must have shaken a thousand hands on this sellout concert tour. The tour her mother had gone to court in a futile attempt to get canceled, she remembered on a short, strangled laugh.

No! She wouldn't give in to the hysteria almost choking her. If she'd learned nothing else during her turbulent childhood, she'd learned to hide her true feelings behind a cool, impenetrable mask. She'd refused to show her confusion and hurt and growing anger then. She was damned if she'd show her terror now.

Lifting her chin, she pulled on her stoic mask and looked the second gunman square in the eyes. "What do you want with me?"

His gun barrel made a short, choppy swipe to the left. "Come."

Not *his* gun barrel, she realized. *Hers.* Despite the fear still churning like acid in her stomach, that one muttered syllable was enough for her trained ear to pick up a break in the *zona di passaggio*, the point where the human voice has reached the end of a certain register and hasn't made the necessary adjustment to the next.

The woman was attempting to sound gruff and harsh but couldn't pull off the lower end of the middle register. That told Riley she was not just female, but young. Very young. For some reason the possibility a teenager was aiming that vicious-looking gun at her midsection made the weapon seem even more frightening.

"Come!" the girl commanded again, her eyes darting nervously from the stage to the auditorium and back again. The break in her voice was even more evident this time and gave Riley the impetus she needed to smooth the fear-sharpened edges from her own voice.

"All right," she responded coolly, calmly. "We'll come with you."

She didn't realize she'd used the plural until the stranger shifted his bruising grip from her waist to her arm. As he matched his step to hers, she tried to think of a way to get him out of whatever was happening. The people obviously wanted her, not him.

Or did they?

She shot the man a desperate sideways glance. Who *was* he? Where had she met him? How could she have forgotten someone with those wide shoulders and penetrating blue eyes?

"Dear Lord!" She almost tripped over the hem of her gown. "You're that friend of Aly's husband! The... what did they call you? The PJ. You're the PJ who hit on me at the wedding!"

Those lightning blue eyes cut to her. "Ixnay."

"What?"

"I'm a civilian," he said out of the side of his mouth, his lips not moving. "Like you."

"I, uh..."

His fingers pressed brutally into her elbow. "Got that?"

"Yes!"

Her head whirling, Riley hiked up her gown and stumbled alongside him. She remembered him now. Like the other groomsmen at the wedding, he'd worn a fancy uniform decorated with more ribbons and medals and badges than she could count. She'd been impressed. Who wouldn't be? She'd also been *very* tempted to respond to his wicked, come-hither grin. Right up until a sultry 44-D strolled into the reception and draped herself all over the man. A former Rush Springs High School cheerleader, someone whispered, and one-time Mrs. Winborne.

Winborne! That was his name. Pete Winborne. *Sergeant* Pete Winborne. So what was he doing in Oman? At the Royal Opera House? Wearing white tie and tails?

"In there!"

Their gun-toting teenager herded them into one of

the backstage dressing rooms. She sidled halfway in, keeping one eye on them and the other on the corridor.

Riley skimmed a frantic glance around the dressing room, searching for a phone or iPad or *any* way to signal for help. The sergeant searched, too. A swift, narrow-eyed scan that swept from one side of the room to the other. Riley caught a flicker of frustration cross his face, then watched him lean casually against the dressing table and palm a comb with a needle-pointed hair pick for a handle.

Good God! Surely he didn't intend to use a comb to combat a machine gun! Or maybe he did. Riley had only managed a few private moments with Aly at the wedding. Just long enough for her childhood friend to go all starry-eyed and rhapsodize about her groom and his best pals from high school. According to the glowing bride, Josh and his five friends joined the military the day after graduation. What's more, she'd proclaimed proudly, they'd all gone Special Ops.

Riley had made vague approval noises, but Special Operations was pretty much a remote concept to her. The closest she'd come to any kind of covert military activity was watching the movie *Zero Dark Thirty*, where a CIA operative and a Navy SEAL team took down Osama bin Laden.

The movie in mind, she shot another glance at Winborne. Okay, so maybe he *could* disable a teenaged terrorist with a comb. God help them, he looked as though he intended to. His gaze was locked on the girl. His white-knuckled fist gripped the comb.

He took an infinitesimal step toward the door. Another. Riley couldn't breathe. Couldn't move. Then a clatter of feet in the corridor almost brought her heart leaping out of her chest.

Their guard went rigid and cried a question. The answer had her sagging against the doorjamb in obvious relief. Sergeant Winborne muttered a curse and without seeming to move a muscle, slid the comb into his cummerbund at the small of his back.

Two seconds later Prince al Said was shoved into the dressing room. Two masked gunmen crowded in behind him. Blood ran in a wide rivulet from a cut on the prince's cheek, staining his neck and robes.

"Ms. Fairchild! Are you all right?"

She mustered a shaky smile. "I'm not hurt, but hardly all right."

"And you, Pete?"

"I'm good. As good as any *civilian* can be in this kind of a situation."

There it was again. That emphasis on the word *civilian*. It was so slight Riley might have missed it if Winborne hadn't crunched her elbow a few moments earlier. The prince picked up the nuance, though, and gave a barely perceptible nod.

The masked gunmen showed no sign they'd caught the signal. They exchanged some nervous, excited words and sent the female back to the main auditorium. Riley's heart seemed to stop when she noticed Winborne taking advantage of their brief distraction. Angling away from them, he palmed the comb again. The prince's glance dropped to the thin steel pick at its end. His nostrils quivered and his chin squared in a way that set every one of Riley's nerves screaming.

Then he tipped his chin slightly, so slightly, toward the gunman on the right. Winborne tipped his to the left.

Both men eased away from her. A small sidestep, a seemingly innocent shuffle. The gun barrels followed, one tracking the prince, one aimed at Winborne's mid-section.

Oh, God, oh, God, oh, God! They were clearing her from the line of fire! And they were going to jump the two men toting machine guns! Riley knew it as sure as she knew every trill, every glissando, in the famous aria from Bellini's *Norma*. Critics had rhapsodized over Riley's recording of the particular tune and raved about her ability to dazzle with the high notes.

Those same critics would have winced at the squawk that issued from her throat the next instant. It came from deep in her chest, a primal cry made sharp and grating by real terror. She barely heard the graceless sound, didn't stop to think as she lurched forward. All she knew, all that drove her, was the blind, instinctive need to draw the gunmen's attention to her for two or three precious seconds.

That was all Winborne and the prince needed. Al Said flew by in a blur of black robes and gold tassels and slammed into one attacker. The sergeant arrowed into the other.

Riley dropped to the floor and curled into a fetal ball, knees to her chin, arms around her head. She expected shouts. Screams. Ear-shattering bursts of gunfire. All she heard was a crash as something hit the dressing table and a sort of low gurgle. Then silence. Heavy, terrifying silence broken a lifetime later by a hoarse rasp.

"Christ!" Winborne wrapped a hand around her arm

and dragged her up. "What the hell were you think-ing, drawing their attention like that? You could have been killed!"

"So could you! Both of you! I saw the look that... ooooh!"

His wide-shouldered frame had blocked her view of the carnage until this moment. Now Riley could see a pair of feet. She followed them to a sprawled torso, then to the blood gushing from the comb shank imbedded in the left eyeball of one of the attackers. It was bur-ied deep, up to the hilt, and must have dug right into the man's brain.

Swallowing hard, Riley glanced from the dead man to his companion. Make that *former* companion. The second gunman was also stretched out on the floor. His head, she noted with another gulp, was at a right angle to his neck.

She swiped her tongue over dry lips, shot a disbeliev-ing look from Winborne to the prince and back again.

"We train for situations like this," Winborne said in what she assumed he intended as a reassuring voice.

"Situations like *this*?" Hysteria bubbled up. "Just how many times have you attended an opera and been attacked by armed gunmen?"

He had no answer for that. Nor could Riley articulate exactly why she fell, shaking from head to toe, into his arms. She'd long ago mastered the art of shielding every thought, every emotion. Yet the moment Winborne's arms closed around her, the mask she'd so painfully constructed over the years started to fall apart.

She wanted to cling to him. Hang on and never let go. The urge was so strong, and so unfamiliar. Her father had died while she was just a baby and from earliest memory her mother had rigidly controlled every aspect of her life. Her clothes, her schools, her friends. Meredith Fairchild had never permitted her daughter to socialize with boys her own age. Never allowed her to date until faced with an all-out rebellion and a threat to boycott all vocal training classes.

Riley had found a measure of excitement in the arms of her few dates. Sexual satisfaction with the one man she'd foolishly thought she'd spend the rest of her life with. But she'd never experience such raw emotion. Such a desperate need to shelter in a man's arms.

Those arms shouldn't have felt so strong. So absurdly comforting. Not with two dead bodies just feet away. They did, though. Without rhyme or reason or cognitive rationale, Sergeant Pete Winborne seemed to represent a safe haven in a world gone suddenly, inexplicably mad.

"Come!" The prince cut through her chaotic thoughts and swooped to snatch the gun out of his dead attacker's hands. "We must leave here."

The sergeant was already snatching up the other man's weapon. Riley recovered her tattered courage and raced past him into the corridor.

"Follow me. There's an emergency exit behind the backdrop."

For a heart-stopping two minutes, she actually thought they would make it. Throwing frightened glances over her shoulder, she darted through a maze of electrically operated acoustical curtains, hydraulic stage lifts and storage rooms. Shouts and the sound of hysterical weeping from the main auditorium pounded in her ears. A loud, tinny clatter, as though someone had kicked or stumbled over an instrument, made her jump. Then she ducked around the rear curtain and gave a sob of pure relief when she spotted the illuminated, bright red sign for the emergency exit. She shoved the crash bar and the alarm went off. The shrill scream of the Klaxon barely registered on Riley's consciousness.

When she slammed through the door, her relief turned to a strangled moan of dismay. The two black-robed figures guarding the back alley spun around and dropped into an instinctive crouch. Even in the deepening twilight, Riley could see their fingers tighten on the triggers of their automatic weapons.

She stumbled to a halt, and was thrust behind Sergeant Winborne. The ensuing scene was like something out of a movie, she thought on another bubble of hysteria. Some B-grade Western, with the good guys and bad guys facing each other in a dusty street, their hands hovering over their holsters.

She thought then she was going to die. Was sure that one of the four men would initiate a barrage of deadly fire. They exchanged shouts, frantic words, then the prince raised his arms in a slow, careful gesture of surrender. After another terse exchange, he stooped and let his weapon clatter to the ground. A moment later Sergeant Winborne did the same.

Her entire body quivering, Riley listened helplessly while Prince Malik spoke in measured tones obviously intended to calm the two masked gunmen. They weren't in the mood for calm. One swept his weapon from side to side, his movements jerky as he kept them covered. The other whipped out a cell phone and stabbed a button.

He barked something into the phone, listened a moment, uttered what sounded very much like a curse.

Eyes blazing through the slits of his ski mask, he shoved the phone in his pocket. The prince said something in that same cool, reasoning tone, then grunted in pain as a rifle stock slammed against his temple. Al Said staggered, and Sergeant Winborne caught him as his knees folded.

Riley could see the tendons in Winborne's neck cord. See his jacket stretch taut at the shoulder seams. Oh, God! He couldn't be planning to launch another attack! Not with the prince limp and half-conscious in his arms!

A sudden screech of brakes preempted whatever desperate measure Winborne had been contemplating. He and Riley both spun around as tires whined and a truck careened around the corner. Its headlights stabbed through the purple dusk. Seconds later the mud-covered, canvas-topped Range Rover squealed to a halt just feet away. The gunmen who'd been guarding the emergency exit shouted orders and gestured with their weapons.

The prince translated, his voice heavy with pain. "They want us to get in the back." His eyes locked with Riley's. "Just you and me."

Winborne snorted. "No way that's gonna happen."

The taller of the two gunmen reinforced the order in heavily accented English and a threatening jab of his weapon. "The woman, she comes with us."

"Yeah?" Winborne faced him, feet spread, shoulders squared. "Then I go, too."

Why was he doing this? Riley wondered wildly. Why put himself at risk?

"I'm her husband," he added, showing no sign that he was winging it as he went. "She's my duty, my responsibility…under your law and mine."

The gunman looked ready to settle the matter with a bullet when a third man jumped out of the truck's cab. Plastic ties dangled from his fist and his voice held an unmistakable note of command.

"Take him, too, and be done with it. Bind them, and quickly."

The plastic strip was pulled so tight it cut into Riley's wrists. Rough hands shoved her up the steps into the Range Rover's rear compartment. The sudden darkness blinded her, and the stink of hot, dusty canvas clogged her nostrils. A gunman scrambled in behind her and pushed her down onto a side-facing bench. Yanking up her bound wrists, he used another plastic tie to anchor them to one of metal struts supporting the canvas cover.

With her arms stretched above her head, she watched helplessly as Prince al Said and Sergeant Winborne were similarly secured. When the man who'd issued the orders jumped back in the cab, the driver gunned the engine. Riley clung to the metal strut with both hands as the truck sped down the alley, careened around a turn and suddenly accelerated.

When she heard the distant shriek of sirens, hope and fear clawed at her throat. Someone must have seen them being hustled aboard this truck. The police were already giving chase. The possibility that their heavily armed captors might opt to shoot it out rather than surrender sent the nauseating taste of bile into her throat.

So real was that possibility, so terrifying the consequences, that Riley sagged against her arms when the sirens seemed to move in another direction. Her heart hammered as she listened to their wail fade in the distance. They were converging on the Royal Opera House, she guessed. Rushing to the scene of the horrific chaos.

She tried to remember the drive in from the airport earlier this morning. As best she could recall, the opera house was located in the new part of the city. Just off the modern highway that cut through Muscat. The same highway that led east to the sea. And west, through the mountains ringing the city.

Into the desert beyond.

Chapter 3

Pete had completed a nine-week PJ indoctrination course at Lackland AFB, in Texas. Learned parachuting skills at the US Army Airborne School at Fort Benning in Georgia, and advanced free-fall techniques at Fort Bragg in North Carolina. He'd earned his underwater operations badge after combat-diver training in Panama City and US Navy Underwater Egress Training at Pensacola Naval Air Station.

At that point the going got really rough. He'd strained every muscle and sinew in his body during the twenty-week paramedic course and follow-up twenty-four-week pararescue recovery specialist course at Kirtland AFB in New Mexico. In between, he'd made it through the brutal USAF Survival School at Fairchild AFB in Washington State, learning to live off the land and survive regardless of climatic conditions or hostile environments.

Those months of training and his hard years of experience in uniform had honed his mind and body to a combat edge. Yet even he felt the jolt when the Range Rover turned off the paved road onto a rough desert track. He gripped the strut with white-knuckled fists as the vehicle jounced up and slammed down. Despite his tight hold, the plastic restraints cut deeper with every jarring thud. He could only imagine the agony Riley had to be experiencing with her shorter reach and less conditioned muscles. He angled toward her and focused on the pale blur of her face in the sweltering darkness. Her eyes were shut, her mouth twisted into a rictus of pain.

"Hang on," he said with as much encouragement as he could muster.

Her lids lifted, and her lips pulled back in a travesty of a smile. "Do I have a choice?"

Jesus! The woman had grit. Pete would give her that. Not many females—or males, for that matter—could take this kind of punishment without a whimper. And damned few would have risked a bullet by letting loose with that screech back at the Royal Opera House. Her shriek had distracted two gunmen just long enough for Pete and Prince Malik to take them down.

Not that the takedown had gained them much more than a fleeting—although admittedly savage—moment of satisfaction. Pete should have anticipated the attackers would post guards at the theater's rear entrance, dammit. Should have stashed Riley in a hidden alcove and held off all comers until the Omani authorities regained control of the theater.

He was still kicking himself for that screwup when the Range Rover slowed to a halt. The driver kept the engine idling and threw some instructions over his shoulder. One of the men in the back loosened the flap and climbed out. A low hiss and the sudden tilt to the vehicle told Pete that he was letting air out of the tires. Which meant they were leaving the track, as rough as it was, and taking to the dunes.

Dune bashing was a favorite sport at some of the more touristy spots in Oman and the UAE. Whole caravans of air-conditioned four-wheel-drives would set out from Muscat or Dubai or Abu Dhabi to give thrill-seekers a taste of the desert before ending up at a Bedouin camp complete with camel rides and belly dancers. Pete suspected, however, that this would be no tourist outing.

Sure enough, the Range Rover hit the windswept mountains of sand with a vengeance. The front end shot up, then slammed down. Several times the whole vehicle slid sideways down slopes so steep Pete braced for a rollover. With all the twists and turns required to follow the contours of the dunes, he gave up trying to gauge speed or distance or direction. He could see the illuminated face of the watch strapped to his wrist, however, and knew exactly how long they bounced around in the back of the damned truck before it finally stopped after two miserable, kidney-jarring hours, twenty minutes and a few seconds.

The gunman nearest the rear untied the canvas flap and rolled it aside to let in a pale wash of moonlight. Pete saw nothing but shadowy dunes beyond the truck bed, but in the sudden stillness when the engine shut off he was sure he heard a faint tinkle of bells. Goats, he thought, or camels. They had to be near some kind of a camp or desert outpost.

One of the gunmen climbed out and stood with his weapon at the ready while his pal untethered the hostages. Pete's arms had long since gone numb. When the gunman cut the plastic tie binding them to the overhead strut, they dropped like lead pipes. He knew the blood would rush back, but being prepared for the fiery rush didn't mitigate the pain. Hurting like a son of a bitch, he locked his jaw and reached for Riley as her plastic restraints were cut.

Her elbows hit her thighs. Barely conscious, she slumped sideways. Pete kept her from sliding off the bench in a boneless heap while the prince was cut free. Blood from the blow to al Said's temple had left a rusty streak on his cheek and his ceremonial headdress was tipped to one side. Gritting his teeth, Malik took time to right it before pointing to Riley and issuing what sounded like a curt command.

The thug closest to them fired back in a tone that said clearly the prince was in no position to be giving orders. He and his pal had abandoned their ski masks soon after leaving the lights of Muscat behind. Their faces had been nothing but dim blurs in the darkness inside the truck, but moonlight now illuminated the utter implacability in the men's expression. The prince shrugged and shuffled toward the truck's rear gate.

"They say you can help her," he told Pete grimly as he edged by. "Since you're her husband."

It took some doing but Pete managed to get Riley out of the truck. She was pretty well comatose by this time. Enough blood had returned to his arms for him to heft her against his chest. She made a small sound that ripped right into his heart. Not a moan or a sob. More like the mewl of an injured kitten. Vowing swift and extremely painful vengeance on their captors, Pete fell into step with the others and made for the shadowy outline of a desert fort just visible against the moon-lit dunes.

Riley fought her way through the gray mist slowly, reluctantly. She'd never hurt in so many places. Her arms, her shoulders, her neck, her back, her throbbing wrists. Even her butt, which had slammed against that damned truck bench more times than she wanted to remember. All that kept her from dissolving into a weepy puddle was the sure, steady kneading that was working on her kinks. The magic fingers moved up her forearms. Cupped her sore elbows. Massaged her screaming shoulders.

"Come on, sweetheart."

The voice that came at her out of the darkness was calm. Deep. Irritatingly insistent.

"Tell me your name."

She did her best to ignore the annoying voice. It wouldn't go away.

"Say your name, Slim. Say it. Riii-ley."

"Oh, for...!" Irritated, she blinked awake. "Riii-ley. There. Are you satisfied?"

"Pretty much." The gruff reply resonated with relief and what sounded suspiciously like a hint of laughter. "You okay?"

Who was this guy? What universe did he inhabit?

Certainly not the same, pain-racked solar system she was currently occupying.

"I'm about as far from okay as I can ever remember being."

She levered up a few inches, frowned at the strips of shiny satin knotted around her aching wrists and skimmed a glance around what looked like a small, square, dimly lit cell. She was stretched out on the dirt floor, half in and half out of Sergeant Winborne's lap while he leaned back against a rough adobe wall.

"Where are we?"

"Best I can tell, this is a small storeroom in a crumbling desert fort somewhere along one of the old spice trade routes."

"Somewhere?"

"My mental gyroscope crapped out five minutes after we hit the dunes."

A shudder rippled down her spine. "I was hoping I'd dreamed that roller-coaster ride."

She sagged against the wall of his chest. It was warm and solid and unbelievably comforting. Riley tried to remember the last time she'd gleaned such pleasure from simple human contact. Was it months? More like years. Not since her brief and ultimately humiliating engagement, at any rate.

Even now she squirmed at the memory of that fiasco. Of her mother's triumphant expression when she'd presented evidence that Riley's fiancé had traded on her name to float some questionable business loans. Of the fact that he'd talked to Riley's agent about a North American tour without so much as consulting her. That awful mess, she reminded herself, was only one of the reasons why a thick layer of ice would coat Hell—or in present circumstances, the Arabian Desert—before she trusted another smooth, handsome operator.

Speaking of which…

She angled her head back a few more inches and studied the shadowy planes and angles of the face so close to her own. It was more rugged than handsome, and one most women would not soon forget. Riley certainly hadn't. That square jaw… The nose that looked as though it had taken a fist or two… The white squint lines carved deep into the corners of those electric blue eyes… The combination made for one *very* potent package of masculinity.

Although she hadn't been able to put a name to the face when she'd spotted it in the royal box, Riley had known instantly she'd met this man before. The white tie and tails had thrown her, though.

His sophisticated civilian attire was certainly looking worse for the wear now. The tortuous drive through the desert had done a number on his black cutaway jacket. One shoulder seam was split, the other showed serious signs of giving way any moment. His white bow tie, she now realized, had been torn in half to bandage her wrists. His pleated shirt, open at the neck, carried several dark splotches. Blood, she realized with a quick gulp.

She probably didn't look much better. She'd lost her jeweled combs when she'd dived for the stage floor. Her hair felt like a sweaty, tangled mess. One strap of her flame-red gown had torn free during the drive through the desert. The other was hanging by a thread. If she wasn't careful, she'd end up naked to the waist, her breasts crushed against this man's chest.

And why the *hell* would that thought cause her to quiver? This was without doubt the most terrifying situation of her life. That liquid pull low in her belly had to be pure nerves. A delayed reaction to being shot at, trussed up like a Thanksgiving turkey and bounced across endless miles of desert.

Except the sensation wouldn't go away. If anything, the urge to hook her arms around Winborne's muscled shoulders and hang on for dear life grew more urgent by the moment.

The need was frightening and totally foreign. One Riley had never felt. Not with her cool, manipulative mother. Not during her short-lived engagement. She'd learned self-discipline at the same tender young age she'd learned to disguise her private thoughts. She'd never shared them with anyone but Aly, and then only when they were giddy schoolgirls. Since then she'd schooled herself to bury her feelings and show an outer calm to the world.

She pulled on that invisible cloak now but curiosity made her ask. "Why did you vault onto the stage back there at the opera house? You jumped right into the line of fire."

"That's pretty much what PJs do, Slim."

She didn't buy the nonchalant reply. "Sure. They just go around charging to the rescue of damsels in distress."

Okay, that sounded as ungrateful and idiotic to her ears as it must have sounded to his. Wincing, she abandoned her lofty perch.

"Sorry. What I meant to say was thank you."

"Yeah," he returned with a hint of laughter. "I figured that's what you meant."

"Still," she said with dogged persistence, "you didn't have to let them take you along with me and Prince Malik. Or," she added after a pregnant pause, "tell them you're my husband."

"We-e-ll…"

Pete stretched the single syllable, rolling it out as slow and lazy as an armadillo ambling across a backcountry road. He guessed the prickly diva sitting with her legs folded under her tattered gown and her chin tilted to a stubborn angle wouldn't take kindly to an honest answer. The truth was the primitive instinct to protect the female of the species went bone-deep in him.

Maybe that came from the old-fashioned, down-home values he'd absorbed through his pores with the dust and heat of West Texas. Or growing up the oldest in a family of six kids, four of them girls. Or…

Oh, hell! Who was he kidding? He hadn't thought about anything or anyone except Riley Fairchild when he'd leaped onto the stage and covered her body with his.

"You're right," he agreed with a shrug. "I didn't have to tell them I was your husband. But that was the only angle I could come up with at the time to stay close to you…and to Malik al Said. The prince and I go way back," Pete explained. "He's the reason I'm in Oman right now. And why I was at the Royal Opera House for your concert. No way was I going to tuck tail and abandon a comrade in arms."

"Oh. Well. I understand."

Mostly, Riley amended silently.

Although she didn't doubt his band-of-brothers rationale, she suspected there was something more basic behind his jumping into the role of husband and protector. She'd gotten a glimpse of his machismo at Aly's wedding. It had been right there, in his swagger and cocky grin. Ironically, he'd turned her off completely then. Now...

Now Riley was secretly, fervently grateful for his protective instincts. And more than a little humbled. She'd never been exposed to that brand of selflessness. Despite the opera world's pretensions to a high art form, it was as cutthroat and competitive as any other field of entertainment. She hadn't gained the coveted title of *diva* without climbing over a number of other talented performers. In her defense, though, she'd never exercised the same degree of ruthlessness as her mother. No one could lay a shattered career or broken dreams at Riley's feet. But still...

To cover the confused emotions Winborne's seemingly selfless act stirred, she yanked at the twisted skirt of her gown and freed it enough for her to sit fully upright. She was more accustomed to the gloom now, but a second glance at their surroundings wasn't any more encouraging than the first.

The room couldn't have been more than ten or twelve feet across. The floor was dirt, the walls crumbling adobe over mud brick. There were no windows and only one wooden door. The room was dim but not completely dark, which Riley didn't understand until she tipped her head and peered up at the tall, narrow tunnel almost directly above her. The shaft was roofed but open openings on all four sides near the top let in a bright glow of moonlight…and a surprisingly cool breeze.

"It's a wind-catcher," Pete said as she craned her neck for a better look, "designed to trap the prevailing desert winds and funnel them downward."

"This one certainly works."

"Wind-catchers were a vital feature in old outposts like this one. I'm told they could keep rooms cool enough to store water at near freezing temperatures even during the hottest months."

She dropped her gaze, dragged her tongue across dry lips and glanced around the room again. "Speaking of water…"

"Our friends didn't leave any. Or any food. There's a relief bucket in the corner, though, if you need to use it."

Riley glanced at it with a moue of distaste. Although this twelve-nation tour to benefit Africa's starving children had taken her primarily to major cities with modern facilities, she'd visited a few less developed areas. At some of those spots she'd used primitive restrooms with squat toilets consisting of cement trenches or jagged holes cut in the floor. This would be her first bucket, however.

"I'm good," she replied, wondering how long she could hold it. "But if you have to…"

"I did while you were still out."

"Oh." She gestured helplessly at the wooden door. "I assume you also tried that."

"You assume right. No lock, but it's barred on the outside."

Of course it was. What was she thinking? Winborne

had no doubt checked every corner and chink in the wall. Probably wedged his body partway up the narrow wind tower to see if they could use that as an avenue of escape.

Fighting a rush of desperation, she raised a hand to push back her tumbled hair and winced at the burning ache in her shoulders. "Did I miss anything else? I mean, did you talk to any of the guys who brought us here? Did they say what they want? And where's Prince al Said?"

"I couldn't get anything out of them. Then again," he added with a wry grimace, "it wasn't a real friendly discussion. As for the prince, I though I heard his voice and some...sounds a while ago."

The brief hesitation made Riley's insides squeeze. "What kind of sounds? Shouts? Screams? Gunshots?"

"More like grunts. And moans," he added with obvious reluctance.

Okay, now she really needed to hit that bucket.

"Then I guess there's nothing else we can do now except wait."

"Actually," Winborne commented as he wrestled his way out of his torn jacket, "I can think of several interesting ways to pass the time, but we'll save them until you aren't hurting all over."

And there it was. The cocky, come-hither grin he'd sent her way at Aly's wedding. This time she couldn't help responding. "Don't get your hopes up, Cowboy."

"A man can only pray. Here, put this on."

He held the jacket up for her to slide over her arms. It hung from her shoulders like a blanket and provided surprisingly welcome warmth. The wind-catcher was doing its job.

His low-cut white vest was as grimy as his shirt. He removed the vest, then unfastened his cuff links and rolled up his shirt sleeves. Riley gasped at the vicious bruising and lacerations caused by the plastic ties. Her wrists no doubt sported a matching set of raw, red bracelets under their makeshift bandages.

She was still examining his awful bruises when he hefted the cuff links in a palm. Testing their size and weight and, she realized with a lurch, their potential as a weapon. The face of each link was a small square of burnished silver. A metal stem connected the face to a movable tab. She couldn't imagine what Winborne could do with them until he planted both squares against a palm and closed his fist. The stems protruded through his fingers like small silver spikes.

She looked from his fist to his face in disbelief. "You're not really planning to go on the attack with cuff links, are you?"

"Not unless I have to." He glanced up, saw the dismay in her expression and hooked a brow. "What, you've never heard of brass knuckles?"

"Yes, but..."

She broke off, suddenly remembering the lethal damage he'd inflicted with the pointy end of a comb.

Her shoulders sagged as a feeling of complete unreality gripped her. She couldn't believe she was locked in a dim storeroom in some crumbling fort in the middle of the desert, at the mercy of armed men. All the stress of her career, all the years of strife and turmoil with her mother, faded into insignificance. This was real, this was now and this was scary as hell.

More scary for her, apparently, than for Pete Winborne. He eased down the wall and stretched out. Crossing his ankles, he wadded up the discarded vest and stuffed it under his head as a pillow. "First rule of any op," he said in response to her incredulous expression. "Rest when you can and conserve your energy. No saying when you'll need it."

Riley just stared at him.

'Here…" He patted the dirt beside him. "You might as well get comfortable."

"Don't we need to…to…?" She circled a hand in the air. "I don't know. Figure out an escape plan?"

"As I see it, we have two possible options. One, we shimmy up the wind tunnel, cross the roof, drop down, overcome any guard posted outside and take off across the desert."

She glanced at the narrow shaft and shook her head incredulously. "You seriously think you can get up that?"

"Only if necessary."

"What's option two?"

"The door opens. One or more men come in. Or they order us out. I assess the situation and take appropriate action."

"*Appropriate action?* That's it? That's your Plan B?"

"Can you think of something better?"

He wasn't being sarcastic. He looked genuinely interested in her response. Riley opened her mouth. Sucked dusty air for several seconds. Let it out on a slow whoosh.

"No."

"If you do, let me know. In the meantime—" he patted the dirt beside him again "—we should sleep."

She hesitated long moments, then gathered the tattered shreds of her dignity. "Turn your face to the other wall. I need to take care of business first."

Chapter 4

With Riley curled into his side, Pete knew he wouldn't get much rest. No way he could force his spring-tight body to relax with her breasts flattened against his ribs. Or release his coiled tension when she burrowed closer and her breath painted a warm, moist patch on his neck.

He lay unmoving for most of what remained of the night so as not to disturb her restless sleep and reviewed the intel he'd gathered so far.

Despite Riley's look of near shock when he'd said his main escape plan at this point consisted of assessing the situation and taking appropriate action, he'd been dead serious. Gathering and assessing intel formed the first and probably most critical phase of any operations plan. No Special Forces team would launch without assimilating as much information about the target area as possible. The more data points a team put together, the better its chances of success.

"Uhnnn."

The little moan slipped through Riley's lips as she stirred and snuggled closer. Pete gritted his teeth and forced himself to focus on what he knew so far.

One, their kidnappers weren't wild-eyed fanatics looking for a path to glory by blowing up themselves and as many innocents as possible. They'd come in heavily armed and conducted a well-orchestrated raid.

Two, they'd zeroed right in on Riley and the prince—arguably the two highest value targets in the theater. Their appearance had been well publicized. Hell, it had made the front page of the papers. Although there'd been a good number of diplomats and wealthy patrons at the theater as well, Pete doubted the attackers could have ID'd them in advance. They certainly hadn't tried to sort them out on-scene. That told him they'd come in with the specific intent of taking Riley and al Said, with Riley's pesky "husband" tossed into the bag at the last minute.

Three, they'd chosen their base camp, if this was it, well. There had to be thousands of these old forts strung along the old trade routes crisscrossing the desert or guarding against attack by sea. Oman itself boasted more than five hundred ancient fortifications along its thousand-mile coastline. Some, like the mighty crusader-era Nizwa Fort, were huge castles bristling with watchtowers and ramparts and cannon. Others, like this one, were small strongholds, unrestored but still intact enough that their thick walls would prevent penetration by satellites or drones searching for infrared heat signatures.

Pete's final piece of intel left him distinctly uneasy. The attackers were disciplined. Prince Malik had tried to engage the men in the truck in a dialogue several times during the grueling drive across the desert. They'd responded only with grunts and, once, with an obvious threat to shut him up with another rifle butt to the temple.

The fact that they *were* so disciplined added considerably to the pucker factor, Pete thought grimly as he stared up at the thin moonlight filtering down the wind-catcher's shaft. It made them less likely to get all jumpy and trigger-happy. But it also meant they were *more* prepared to follow orders…including, if it came to that, torturing or killing their hostages. Pete guessed the chances of getting close to one of them, playing on his or her sympathy, were slim at best. Still, he intended to try.

He made the first attempt several hours later when the sound of wood scraping against wood broke the dusty stillness.

"Riley. Wake up."

"Huh?" Groggy and disoriented, she started to push upright, jerked to a stop, grimaced and put up a hand to rub shoulders that obviously still ached like hell. "Wh—"

That was all she got out before the door to their windowless room swung open. Pete rolled swiftly to his feet, recording details with the speed of a Nikon camera. The door opened onto another room, bigger and swept with the soft light of a desert dawn. He didn't see any sign of the prince but did note the bare essentials—a low table with cushions stacked around it, an oil lamp hung on a chain, a frayed prayer rug—before the two figures silhouetted in the doorway blocked his view.

They were too savvy to come into the small room, where Pete might have been able to jump them. One was thin and wiry, in his late twenties and carrying a bulging cloth sack. The other was taller, heavier and sported a scar that cut across his left cheek and pulled his upper lip into what looked like a permanent sneer. Since neither seemed inclined to speak, Pete broke the ice.

"As-salám aláykum."

The traditional "peace be with you" sure as hell didn't fit the circumstances, but it was the best he could do given his limited Arabic. He wasn't surprised when neither of the two men returned a response.

"Teh ki ingleezi?"

"Yes," Scarface sneered. "I speak English. You and the woman, move back. Against the far wall."

"My wife's wrists are raw and bleeding," Pete said, reaching a hand down to help Riley up. "We need—"

"Save your lies! We know she is not your wife."

His black eyes shifted from Pete to Riley. Disdain filled them as they made a slow sweep from her tangled hair to her bare shoulders and back again.

"We have studied you." His deformed lip curled even higher. "Google is a most useful tool, yes? We know all there is to know about you. Your singing debut at the age of nine, your dislike of chocolate, your schedule, how much you earned last year. But nowhere in all this information was there mention of a husband."

Pete scrambled for an answer, but Riley beat him to it. Her chin lifting, she oozed a frigid confidence he knew was sheer bravado. "What you read on Google is exactly what I allow my publicists to put out. I don't share my personal life."

"You are much in the spotlight," Scarface argued. "There would be mention of a marriage."

"Not if it took place at a private estate in Switzerland," she countered icily, "with only two witnesses."

"And no paparazzi," Pete added, hooking a protective arm around Riley's shoulders. "The bastards have hounded my wife since her first performance at the Met. They still nip at her heels like jackals, but we refuse to let them into our bedroom. As far as the world knows, I'm her business manager."

"Her business manager? Then perhaps it was meant for us to take you, too. You will not waste our time with useless hostage negotiations."

"Is that what this is about? You're holding us for ransom?"

"Ransom? No."

The twisted smile fell off their captor's face, and the malevolence that flooded his black eyes raised the hairs on the back of Pete's neck.

"This is blood money we speak of. Which you will see is paid with all speed or you will watch your *wife* fed to the vultures, piece by piece."

He barked a curt command to his pal, who tossed the cloth sack onto the dirt floor. Both men then backed up and the younger reached for the door.

"Wait! What about Prince Malik? Is he...?"

The door slammed on Pete's questions. He heard the scrape of wood on wood, then the thud of a heavy bar dropping into place.

Riley broke the stark silence that followed with a small, hoarse laugh. "That went well."

"Yeah, it did." He dredged up a shrug. No way he was going to let her see how hard Scarface's last threat had hit. "At least we know they're after money, not on some extremist jihad. C'mon, let's check out our goodie bag."

There was water, thank God. Two quart-size plastic bottles. A half-dozen rounds of doughy flatbread. A wedge of cheese so ripe Pete's nose wrinkled when he unwrapped it. Goat, he figured, or camel. Plus a small sack of dates, the main source of protein for desert dwellers.

The clothing stuffed in the bottom of the sack spoke to their captors' cultural bias. Muttering thanks for male chauvinists around the world, Riley snatched up the slippers, baggy trousers and loose tunic. Its colors were too faded to provide a clue to the original owner's tribe. Not that the information would have helped, necessarily, but Pete was still digging for every scrap of intel.

"Face the wall," Riley ordered briskly.

Marveling at her resilience, he watched her march to the darkest corner of the room to shed his tuxedo jacket and her tattered gown. Then—reluctantly, manfully— he turned his face to the adobe-pocked wall.

She gave him the all clear a few moments later. He turned back and saw the pointed toes of the slippers peeking out from under the baggy trousers, which billowed around her slender thighs. She'd used a strip of red silk torn from her gown to belt the faded tunic. Covered now from neck to toes, she folded her legs and sank gracefully to the dirt floor.

Her first order of business was to guzzle half a bottle of water. Her second, to pin Pete with a puzzled frown. "What did he mean, 'blood money?'"

He'd asked himself the same thing. Several times. And didn't have an answer. "I don't know."

"Well, what do you think? Have we landed in the middle of some kind of tribal feud?"

"I don't know, Slim."

Riley mulled that over while she tore off a piece of flatbread and wrapped it around a chunk of cheese. Her eyes were thoughtful, her expression distant as she took a bite and chewed slowly.

Pete guessed their captors wouldn't let too much time pass before they returned with a specific demand and some means of communicating it to the outside world. So he used the interval to prep Riley as best he could.

"They'll probably use a cell phone or digital camera to take a photo or record a video. If they go with a video, they'll have a script prepared. I'll try to convince them to let me deliver it. They don't know my real identity— yet—but you can bet my Special Forces unit at Thumrait has been notified that I went missing during the raid on the opera house. All I need is a few seconds of screen time to communicate a few essentials to them."

"Like what?"

"The approximate number of hostiles, their type of weaponry, our location, although they'll get that quick enough if these guys aren't smart enough to strip the metadata from any photo or video they transmit."

"You can communicate all that in a few seconds?"

"We establish codes before every op. Also hand and

eye signals to pass information silently when necessary."

He hated to douse the hope that sprang into her face but needed to level with her.

"Odds are they won't put me on display, though. You're the star, the internationally renowned celebrity. Plus you're a woman, weak and helpless and terrified. In their eyes," he added quickly. "And the fact that you're so damned gorgeous only adds to the sympathy factor."

"Thank you. I think."

Pete ignored the touch of sarcasm and stuck to his brief. "If they go with a video, it's okay to play the frightened hostage. In fact, the more nervous you act, the better. Stammer. Fidget. Tug on your hair, touch your neck. Lose your place in the script." His eyes held hers. "Then swat the air in front of your face, whine a little and complain that this place is swarming with a dozen bugs. Got that? A dozen…"

"Bugs. Got it. I assume that's a Special Ops code word?"

"Stands for *big ugly guys*. One of our more polite terms for hostiles," he confirmed. "I think we borrowed it from some movie or video game. If you can, work the word *saw* into the same or a second sentence with *bugs*."

"And *saw* stands for?"

"Squad automatic weapon. It'll tell our guys what kind of return fire to expect. You could throw out something like 'Ick, I just saw another bug!'"

She gave him a pained look. "I'm sure I can do better than *ick*."

"Yeah, I'll bet you can. Just don't overplay it," he

cautioned. "You don't want Scarface and friends to pick up on your signals."

Another pained look, this one accompanied by a distinct huff. "I hate to be the one to break it to you, Sergeant, but opera isn't all lung power. I studied piano and the cello to better appreciate orchestration. I had to learn French, German and Italian, with a smattering of Russian and Czech thrown in for good measure. I also spent almost a year with a coach from the Actors Studio in New York, so I could not just sing my character, but *become* her."

"Whoa." Pete held up his hands in mock surrender. "Didn't mean to step on your professional toes. Sorry."

"You should be," his honey-haired diva sniffed. "An audience has to feel my character's passion, her genuineness, her pain."

"I understand. But this isn't the Met or the Royal Opera House, and I doubt you've ever given a performance while staring into the barrel of a gun. A real gun," he amended when she arched a brow. "Loaded with real bullets."

"True." She conceded the point with a regal nod. "I'll just have to ignore both."

Easier said than done, Riley discovered as the hours dragged by. She had nothing to do but worry while Pete tried to work out her remaining kinks. In the process, she got a little better acquainted with her self-appointed husband.

He told her about his family, about growing up in Texas, about the other Sidewinders, most of whom she'd met at Aly's wedding. All the while his strong hands and clever, clever fingers massaged her shoulders, her arms, her lower back.

"What about you?" he asked when he had her almost melting with pleasure. "I talked to your mother briefly at the wedding. Got the impression relations between you two are a bit choppy right now."

"That's one way to describe them, although downright hostile might be a more accurate assessment."

"What about your father? Isn't he in the picture?"

"He died when I was a baby. So it's always been just…"

"Shhh!"

His hands went still, his body rigid. The next moment he was on his belly, his ear pressed to the crack at the bottom of the door.

"What is it?" Riley hissed. "What do you hear?"

He sliced a hand through the air to silence her and kept his ear pressed to the crack. Straining, she picked up a muffled shout, then what sounded like a dull thud.

Pete muttered a vicious curse and rolled into a crouch. Reaching out, he wrapped his hands around her upper arms.

"Listen to me, Slim. Don't try to pass any signals. Don't act anything but natural. Do whatever they say, when they say it."

"Why? What did you just hear?"

He didn't want to give details. She could see it in his eyes, feel it in his hard, bruising grip.

"Tell me! What just happened out there?"

"Scarface and one of his pals were talking to…" He stopped, shook his head, made a quick correction. "Were arguing with Prince Malik. I couldn't understand their words, but I recognized their voices."

"And?"

"And whatever Scarface wanted the prince to do, I'm guessing he refused to play ball."

"Why? You said you couldn't understand their words."

His jaw worked. "I heard a whack—"

"I heard it, too. Sort of a dull thud."

"Yeah," he said grimly. "Like the sound a knife blade makes when it slams into wood. Followed by a long, low groan."

"Oh, God!"

"So if they want to take your picture or have you read a script, just do it. Straight. No code words. No hidden signals. Got that?"

A chaotic mental kaleidoscope of knife blades, chopping blocks and a groaning prince pinwheeled through her mind. For the first time in more years than she could remember, she actually wished she was home with her mother. Or at the barre, sweating off the three pounds her sadistic trainer insisted she had to lose. Or even in Milan, where she'd been so nervous before her La Scala debut she'd thrown up in her dressing room. Twice.

"Riley!" Pete gave her a hard shake. "Listen to me. No heroics. Understand?"

"Yes."

She broke off, gulping as she heard the same scrape of wood on wood that had heralded the kidnappers' entry earlier. She and Pete were on their feet when the door opened. They stood well back, him with his arm around her shoulders, her with her heart jackhammering against her ribs.

The light that burst through the opening was brighter

than before, the room beyond bathed in the fierce wash of the desert sun. Riley threw up an arm to shield her eyes from the sudden glare, lowering it only when Scarface hooked a finger.

"You. Woman. Come with me."

"Why?" Pete took a step sideways and put himself between her and the man framed in the open door. "What do you want with her?"

The kidnapper studied him for long moments, as if trying to decide whether to respond with a bullet.

"She will speak into a camera," he said finally. "If she says what we tell her to, she'll come to no harm."

Pete's outstretched arm kept her behind him. "I'm the money man in the family. I know how much we have in which accounts. Tell me what you want and I'll tell you how to get it."

"Yes, you will. But first the woman will speak into the camera. They must know how we will use her blood money."

"They who? And what the hell is this about blood money? In case you don't know it, my wife is donating the entire proceeds of this tour to—"

"Enough!" Scarface's eyes flashed. "Al Said just tested my patience. A mistake I'm sure he now regrets. Don't make the same one."

Riley's stomach rolled. She knew she had to act in the next two or three seconds or she'd pull another La Scala.

"I can talk into a camera." She gave a brittle laugh and ducked under Pete's arm. "God knows I've done it hundreds of times before."

"Riley, wait."

"No, I can do this."

"Then I go with you. I go with her," he repeated stubbornly to the gunman silhouetted against the bright sunlight.

Scarface was done with being nice. "You move," he spit out, "and you die."

"Pete! Darling! Please, please don't be stupid! Let me do this."

"Your woman is wiser than you are," the kidnapper sneered. "Come."

Her insides iced over with fear, Riley edged past him. As soon as she'd cleared the door, he kicked it shut and nodded. His cohort hefted a thick wooden bar and wedged it into two rusted iron slots on either side of the door. The bar fell into place with a now-familiar scrape of wood against wood. Like the dungeon in some medieval fortress, Riley thought on a note of near hysteria.

A quick glance around the room she now stood in suggested it had once served as the main living area. It smelled of old burlap and dead ashes. Dust motes floated thick and heavy on the air. A wide sleeping platform topped with a tattered blanket hugged the back wall. A charcoal brazier lay tipped on its side in one corner. A brass lamp, its colored glass face broken and coated with dust, hung suspended from a brass hook. Thick shutters were open to let in the morning light, but the tall shaft of another wind-catcher funneled down a breeze that kept the heat at bay.

The digital camcorder mounted on a tripod introduced the only modern note into a setting right out of *One Thousand and One Nights*. It was positioned a few feet from a low, square table that...

Riley's quick inventory came to a full stop. Choking, she stared at the glistening red stain on both the surface of the table and the worn carpet below it.

"Is that...? Is that...?"

Scarface hesitated a few beats, then obviously decided brutal honesty would ensure more cooperation than lies. "Yes, it is blood. As I told you, al Said tried my patience. You will not be so stupid, will you?"

Terror ripped at her throat with razor claws. "No."

"I thought not. Sit there, facing the camera, and read the document on the table."

She stumbled across the room and sank onto the stacked cushions. Her stomach heaved again when she saw bright red splotches on the single sheet of paper. Swallowing hard, she picked it up and skimmed the double-spaced paragraph.

Disbelief fought its way through her incipient nausea. "You've got to be kidding! You want fifty million dollars? For me?"

"And..." he prompted, his eyes flat and cold.

She wrenched her attention back to the paragraph. "And the release of Abdul Haddad." The paper shook in her hands. "Who's Abdul Haddad?"

"Such ignorance." Scarface gave a disgusted snort and said something to his cohort. "But then," he added with his ugly sneer, "you are a woman, and a Westerner. It is to be expected."

A thread of anger wormed its way past Riley's fear. Slow and reedy at first, but steady enough to spark a sizzle. She nursed the heat like an ancient vestal virgin tending the sacred flame while the second kidnapper moved into position behind the video camera and fiddled with the settings. When he looked up and nodded, Scarface issued a curt command.

"Read the words written on the paper. Only those words."

She obeyed, her voice wooden. "My name is Riley Fairchild. The men holding me hostage demand fifty million dollars for my safe return. They also demand the release of Abdul Haddad. If these demands are not met within the next forty-eight hours, they will do to me what was done to Haddad's wife. You will receive instructions for delivery of the money and...ugh!"

She jerked back, swatting at the brown specks drifting on the breeze generated by the wind-catcher. "Bugs! A dozen tiny, stinging bugs. I *saw* them," she insisted when Scarface growled at her from off camera. "*Saw* at least a dozen of them!"

She swatted the air again, turned her head and hacked, as if spitting something out. When she faced the camera again, tears flooded her eyes.

"Please! Whoever's listening! Give these men whatever they want and get me out of here."

Chapter 5

"Abdul Haddad!"

The name hit Pete with the percussive impact of an IED. He rocked back on his heels, knowing their situation had just gone from dangerous to deadly.

"Dammit all to hell."

Riley had returned to the storeroom, the kidnappers apparently satisfied with her performance in front of the camera. Pete's reaction to her recital of the kidnapper's demands promptly shredded her relief at putting that ordeal behind her.

"Who's Haddad?"

"A third-rate thug masquerading as a tribal chieftain in Yemen. The bastard lets his troops murder and rape at will. Or did, until he made the mistake of slipping across the border to raid an Omani village a few months back. Massacred the men and carried off most of the women to sell into slavery. Prince Malik led the Special Ops assault that took him down."

"Do you think that's where we are now? In Yemen?"

Pete pulled up an area map in his head, picturing the wide swath of desert that constituted Yemen at the bottom of the Arabian Peninsula, with Saudi Arabia to its north and Oman to its east.

"No, Muscat is too far from the border with Yemen for the kidnappers to have driven us there in just a few hours. My guess is we're either still in Oman or we crossed into Rub' al Khali—the Empty Quarter of Saudi Arabia. In either case," he added grimly, "we can't hang around and wait for the Sultan of Oman to order Haddad's release. He ain't gonna do it."

"Even if Prince Malik begs him to?"

"Which the prince ain't gonna do, either. He saw firsthand the carnage Haddad left behind in that village."

Pete paced the small room, his steps short, his muscles taut. It took a lot to turn the stomachs of Special Forces troops. The Omani PJs he'd trained with for the past two weeks were as tough as any of the breed, but reports of Haddad's brutality had sickened even them.

Pete spun on his heel. Started back across the small cell. Stopped dead center. Angling his head back, he stared up the funnel that provided both light and a cooling breeze.

"Dammit," he muttered. "I shouldn't have waited to see what their agenda was. I should've hauled us up and out of here last night."

Riley crowded next to him and craned her neck.

"Pete, it's too narrow! You won't get your shoulders halfway up."

"It'll be a tight fit," he admitted.

"You'll get stuck."

"Then I'll just have to hack free."

"With what?"

"Well, we've got the brass knuckles. And..."

His eyes swept the room, zeroed in on the wooden bucket in the far corner. He'd already decided the rope handle was too short to use as anything other than a garrote. The rusted metal bands ringing the wood offered considerably more potential.

"Sorry, kid. We'll have to sacrifice our honey bucket."

She followed his gaze and wrinkled her nose but didn't protest any further. "Okay, tell me what to do."

"First, we make a rope. We'll start by tearing the remnants of your gown into strips and braiding them together. We'll do the same with the lining from my tux jacket. We'll save the rest of the jacket and our pants for later, when Scarface and company think we're settled for the night."

"And the bucket?"

"That will have to wait, too, until after they bring us more food and water."

"*If* they bring more food and water."

"They will," Pete predicted confidently. "You're too valuable to lose to dehydration."

He settled on the dirt floor, his back to the wall, his legs outstretched. Riley plopped down beside him and worried her lower lip while he stripped the lining from the jacket. He kept the denuded black shell close in case they needed to use it to cover their rope-in-progress, then set to work reducing the skirt of Riley's gown to long, usable strips.

Tearing the red silk took more muscle power than Pete had anticipated, which was good. Braided together, the strips of tensile fabric should do the trick. It had to. Hauling Riley up behind him was the main weakness in this escape plan. It was also the primary reason he waited this long to attempt it. Even with him taking most of her weight, there was no way she could have shimmied up the wind tower last night. Not after those agonizing hours in the Range Rover.

The odds weren't all that great they'd make it tonight, either. They couldn't risk another delay, though. Riley's account of the bloodstained table showed Scarface was every bit as ruthless as Haddad. Pete didn't know if they'd killed or just maimed Prince Malik, but he didn't intend to wait around for them to start on Riley.

And he knew damned well Scarface or his pals had someone—or several someones—monitoring news coverage of the raid and the kidnappings. The Special Ops unit at Thumrait would try to keep Pete's real identity under wraps but some enterprising newshound would dig it out, probably sooner rather than later. When it became known, Pete would lose the advantage he had now with Scarface and friends being ignorant of his background and training.

They'd woven and knotted together a good four feet of rope when Pete picked up the sounds signaling the kidnappers' return. He draped the tux shell over the coiled rope, then rolled to his feet and moved far enough away from the seemingly careless pile of discarded clothing so as not to draw Scarface's attention to it.

Riley fit herself readily within the circle of his arm. He could feel the tension in her rigid spine, the taut muscles, but she kept her chin high and barely flinched when the door opened.

As before, the two kidnappers remained outside the room. One was the younger man from earlier this morning. The second Pete recognized from the dressing room at the opera house. Barely more than a girl, she refused to look at either of the hostages as she tossed another sack into the room.

"Wait!" Riley stretched out a hand to the girl, trying to make contact, establish at least a tenuous rapport. "Are these your clothes? This tunic and the pants? If they are, thank you for the kindness."

The girl threw a nervous look over her shoulder and didn't respond. She scuttled back a step and barely cleared the door before her companion slammed it shut. The thud of the bar dropping into place echoed like dull thunder.

Pete broke the silence that followed with a small grunt. "Scarface must have gone to deliver the ransom video to someplace that has cell towers and/or internet access. With any luck, he'll be away for the rest of the night."

The sack contained more water, flatbread, cheese and dates. Pete cautioned Riley to eat and drink sparingly, though, as he intended to take what was left with them. She tried her damnedest to share his confidence that they would escape, but her nerves stretched thinner and tighter as the light funneling down through the wind-catcher slowly faded. After what seemed like several lifetimes, all that was left was a dim glow of moonlight.

Still they waited, until Pete finally decided it was safe to proceed. His first task was to scrape a shallow hole in the corner and empty the bucket. He scoured it with dirt and sand, then went to work on the rusty iron bands. Several bruised knuckles and the same number of muttered oaths later he pried off the upper band. Riley watched in mingled suspense and admiration as he twisted the metal into a sharp point. When he did the same with the second band, she had to ask.

"What do you plan to do with those?" she asked, keeping her voice soft and low.

"First we'll use 'em to gouge hand- and toe-holds. Then as cams. Pitons. Anchors," he said in answer to her blank look. "Haven't done much mountain climbing, have you?"

"Have you?"

"Remind me to tell you sometime about the Special Forces Advanced Mountain Operations School at Fort Carson. You complete that course, you could give a mountain goat lessons in scrambling up a sheer precipice."

That reassured her. Some.

"Okay," he said as he tested the point he'd made of the second band, "that's the best I can do. Time to strip off and add to our rope."

He had Riley sacrifice her baggy pants but not the thigh-length tunic. Pete, however, donated both shirt and trousers to their cause. She tried her best not to goggle at the acre or so of sculpted chest that came into view when he peeled off the blood-stained white shirt.

Or the muscled thighs and the trim, tight butt displayed to perfection by a pair of thigh-hugging briefs.

"Didn't have time to buy shorts to go with my spiffy new tux," he said with a quick grin when he caught her sneaking a peek. "We call these Ranger panties. They're the latest in tactical hot weather gear. Moisture-wicking and heat-signature-reducing."

"If you say so."

The grin widened. "They're functional, but sure not as enticing as that scrap of red lace you're wearing under that tunic."

"Ha! I should have known you wouldn't keep your face to the wall."

"I tried. I really did."

She was about to give that another "Ha!" when he angled toward her and she caught sight of the tattoo banding his right bicep.

"Is that a snake?"

"Sure is. A sidewinder. Fastest, meanest rattler west of the Pecos."

He flexed his arm, and the snake's mouth widened to display a nasty set of fangs. Riley grimaced, but Pete gazed down at the vicious reptile with the same fondness a dog lover might display for his pet schnauzer.

"We all have the same tat," he told her. "Travis, Duke, Jack, Josh, Dan and me. Like our mascot here, we were fast and mean. Best football players ever to come out of Rush Springs, if I do say so myself."

"I'll take your word for that."

"It's a fact," he assured her as he set to work tearing his shirt and their trousers into useable strips. Riley settled beside him, helping to weave the pieces together and add them to what they'd done earlier.

"Looks like about fifteen feet," Pete murmured some time later, snaking out the long braid. "Not as much as I'd hoped but we'll have to go with it."

He coiled the rope, then wrapped a leftover piece of cloth around one of the pieces of bent metal. He kept his voice easy, but his eyes were dark rounds of utter seriousness as he passed Riley the makeshift tool.

"Here's the drill. I'm going to put you on my shoulders so you can reach inside the tower. You'll have to dig two handholds. Three, if you can stretch a little higher. Then I'll set you down, jump up and take it from there."

Disbelieving, Riley looked from the shaft to his shoulders and back again. The drill, as he called it, would never work. Despite that boast about being able to teach mountain goats to climb, Riley didn't see how he could leap up, get a grip on whatever shallow indentations she could hack out, and shimmy up that narrow tunnel.

"Ready?"

Swallowing her doubts, she stepped onto his bent knee. The sidewinder seemed to hiss at her, its fangs wide, as Pete's muscles bunched and he guided her into a kneeling position on his shoulders. She tottered dangerously, sure she was going to fall on her face, but he pinned her in place with a bruising grip on her thighs and slowly straightened. Just as slowly, Riley pushed upright. The shaft was within reach!

Anchored on his shoulders, she hacked at the inside of the tower. Adobe flaked off in small chunks. The hard-baked mud brick underneath proved tougher to crack until Pete told her to chink at the mortar between the bricks. Following his instructions, she dug out a shallow opening.

Dust swirled in the confined space. Sweat dripped from her forehead. Her nostrils were clogged and her eyes stung when she reached higher and started on a second cut. By the time she hacked out a third, her arms were on fire and she was wobbling dangerously on Pete's shoulders.

"That's good enough," he said.

Lowering her slowly, he supported her until her legs stopped shaking and feeling had returned to her arms. Then he looped the braided rope over her head and settled it under her arms.

"I'll give it a tug when I'm ready to pull you up." His intent gaze raked her dust-caked face. "Okay?"

"Okay."

Then it was his turn. As agile as the mountain goat he'd referenced, he leaped straight up and caught the lowest handhold on his first try. Reached for the second. Hauled himself up to the third. His taut, corded thighs dangled in midair while he used the tool he'd reclaimed from Riley to carve a fourth handhold. Then a fifth. When he pulled himself high enough up to wedge his back against one wall of the tower and get his foot in the first step, her heart was hammering so hard and fast it hurt.

He worked his way up the shaft inch by steady inch. The rough adobe had to be murder on his bare back and shoulders, but he kept going. All the while, Riley's glance darted from the tower to the door and back again. She'd almost forgotten how to breathe when the loop around her upper chest suddenly went taut. She grabbed the rope above her head with both hands to keep it from slicing into her armpits while Pete hauled her up slowly, steadily.

The tower walls closed in on her. Cloying, choking claustrophobia filled her throat. She held onto the rope with desperate hands, scrabbling for a toehold, scraping both knees against the rough surface. She almost panicked when she heard a slow, agonized creak above her. Like the sound of old wood pulling free of rusty nails.

Oh, God! The tower was coming apart around them!

She cranked her head back as far as she could and gasped in relief when she realized it was just Pete shimmying through one of the openings between the tower and its wooden roof. When he disappeared over the rim, the rope she dangled from sawed up, down, up again. Riley jerked around like a puppet, panic clawing at her again, until the pull steadied and brought her up to the top.

Any other time the symphony that greeted her eager eyes would have called to the artist in her. A treble clef of black sky spangled with a thousand twinkling notes. A bass clef of dark, undulating desert stretching to infinity. And there, far off on the horizon, the faint glow of lights that just might signal civilization!

On a rush of pure adrenaline, Riley straddled the tower's rim. Her rush took a quick dive when she looked down and discovered a twelve- or fifteen-foot drop to the flat roof below. Pete must have rappelled the tower's outer wall, using his weight to pull her up inside as he went down. *She*, he indicated with urgent hand signals, would have to drop into his arms. Sucking in a quick breath, she swung her other leg over the rim, mouthed a silent prayer and pushed off.

The catch was awkward. He took a knee to the ribs and an elbow in his face but merely grunted. When he set her on her feet and dropped into a crouch, however, Riley was the one who wanted to weep. His shoulders looked as though someone had taken a meat tenderizer to them. Blood streaked his back and thighs. But before she could say anything, he grabbed her hand and dragged her down beside him.

They crouched side by side, getting their bearings, waiting for their hearts to slow. Riley saw then he'd been right about this being an abandoned outpost. Except for the building they'd been held in, everything else was in ruins. Her gaze took in sunken rooftops. Tumbled walls. What must have once been a round guard or grain tower spearing empty arms up at the night sky. And a dark, oblong bulk hidden in the shadows of a date palm.

"Pete!" She elbowed him in the side and jabbed a finger at the palm. "The Range Rover!"

"Yeah," he whispered back, "I see it."

She knew it was asking too much to pray the kidnappers had left the keys in it. But she did! Dear God, she did! With every fiber of her being.

Her heart stuttered as she and Pete crept across the flat roof and approached the edge. But after the windcatcher climb, exiting the roof turned out to be a piece of cake. They found a low corner, dropped to the sand and made for the Range Rover.

Riley crouched in the shadows of the palm while Pete hunkered low on the running board and peered through the side window. Unable to corral her galloping nerves, she hissed at him.

"The keys? Are they there?"

"No."

She was fighting to hold back a groan when he dropped down beside her.

"But this baby is so old, any ten-year-old could hotwire it. So here's the plan."

"Plan?" Nerves bit at her like sharp little sand fleas. "Why do we need a plan? We get in, you jiggle the wires, we get out of here!"

"Close. We get in. I strip the ignition wires and show you how to cross them. Then I go back for Prince Malik."

She wasn't surprised. She'd half expected this mucho macho warrior to revert to type. Although... She bit her lip, ashamed that a cowardly corner of her mind had tried hard to blank out what must have happened to the prince. But Pete wasn't letting her blank anything out now. Wrapping a hard hand around her nape, he pulled her close.

"If you hear anything—anything!—that sounds like trouble, promise me you'll get the hell out of here."

"Oh, sure," she huffed. "Like I'm just going to drive off into the desert and leave you behind."

"Dammit, Riley. I can't do what I need to do if I'm looking over my shoulder the whole time, worrying about you. Promise me you'll make tracks."

"Okay! I promise."

His grin was a white slash in the dark. "That's my girl."

She couldn't remember the last time anyone had called her a girl. And she knew no one had ever held her collared like this. They were nose-to-nose, breath-to-breath, his fingers hard on her nape, his mouth just inches away.

"You saw the lights in the far distance?" he asked.

"Yes."

"Aim straight for them and don't stop."

"I will."

"At the first sound of trouble."

"I will, Pete."

His grip eased. His thumb stroked the soft hair at the back of her neck. Riley sensed what was coming and was ready, *so* ready, when his mouth locked on hers.

The kiss seemed to hold everything they'd gone through, every desperate moment they'd shared. It was hard. Hungry. A triumph over impossible odds. A taste of things to come. Assuming, of course, they got out of this damned desert alive.

"You have to promise me something, too." She pushed back a few inches. "You will not, I repeat, you will *not* get yourself killed!"

"Not planning on it," he muttered, crushing her mouth again.

She was still feeling the heat when he crawled into the Range Rover. The overhead light flashed on, stopping the breath in her throat, but he doused it almost instantly. Then he wedged himself under the steering column and played with the wires.

"Go around and climb in," he whispered a few moments later. "I'll show you how this works."

Riley crawled on hands and knees to the driver's side of the vehicle. Once she'd hauled herself up and into the cab, she had to swallow an ironic laugh. She'd been taking lessons for as long as she could remember. Voice. Diction. Piano. Cello. French. Italian. Drama. She'd even spent a mind-numbing week with her business manager—her *actual* business manager—after she'd finally cut her mother out of her financial affairs and needed to learn where her earnings had been invested. This was her first shot at hot-wiring a truck, however. Or driving one, for that matter. She sweated about that for several nervous seconds until a panicked glance confirmed it was an automatic.

"All you do is cross these two wires."

The terse instruction dragged her attention from the gearshift to the man sprawled beneath the steering column. He'd located two wires—one red, one yellow— and used his bucket tool to peel away an inch of the plastic coating. Holding up the exposed ends, he waved them at Riley.

"Just put the tips together and give 'em a little twist. That'll kick the engine over. Don't do it now!" He jerked the wires away from her outstretched hands. "Wait till you're ready to hit the gas."

As she watched him melt into the darkness, a tiny niggle of guilt wormed through her almost suffocating tension. She hadn't lied. Exactly. She'd promised to make tracks at the first sound of trouble, and she would. She'd simply reserved the right to categorize what trouble *sounded* like.

She held the two wires nervously, red in one hand, yellow in the other, their tips six inches apart. Hunched low in the driver's seat, she searched the structure she and Pete had escaped only moments ago. It was little more than a dark bulk against the night sky, with a few bars of light slanting through cracks in the shuttered windows. They must have lit an oil lamp. That faint glow was the only sign of life amid the tumbled ruins of what must have once been a thriving desert community.

Her gaze darted to the empty desert beyond. The sheer immensity of it sent a shiver down her spine. But there were those other lights, she reminded herself forcefully. Miles away. Maybe hours. Beacons of hope. Of safety and...

"Khalass!"

The shout shattered the stillness. Riley jumped a good inch off the seat and lost her grip on the red wire. She'd ducked sideways, scrabbling for it, and gave a sob of pure terror when gunshots rattled through the night.

Oh, God, oh, God, oh, God!

Hands shaking, heart galloping, she fished frantically under the steering column. Her groping fingers finally located the loose red wire and somehow, some way, connected it to the yellow. Bent over, she didn't move, didn't breathe, until the engine coughed, sputtered, caught.

Another burst of gunfire popped her upright. She locked one hand on the steering wheel, the other on the gearshift. Jamming her left foot on the brake, she found the gas pedal with the right and shoved the Range Rover into Drive.

All Riley had to do was release the brake. Hit the gas. Roar off into the desert like she'd promised. But she kept one foot on the brake even as she pressed the accelerator. The truck lurched like an old warhorse straining at the bit, caught between competing, compelling forces.

Her desperate gaze swept the ruins. The building

where they'd been held loomed dark and menacing, with only those faint bars of light seeping through the shuttered windows.

Suddenly, a door burst open. The figure that staggered through it cradled one of those vicious-looking automatic weapons in his hand. His black robe flapped as he spun, searching the darkness. When he zeroed in on the date palm, Riley gave a moan of terror and stomped on the gas.

The Range Rover's rear wheels spun, spitting sand for several terrifying seconds, then caught. The jerk slammed Riley against the seat back, but she put the pedal to the floorboard again and aimed for the black-robed figure. Her only thought, only plan, was to smash the bastard like a bug.

"Bug," she got out on a note of pure hysteria. "Big ugly g— Oh!"

She jammed the brake, standing almost straight up, as a second figure burst through the door. Even with the light behind him and his face nothing more than a dim blur, she couldn't mistake Pete's broad shoulders or naked chest. He caught up to the first man, grabbed his arm and hauled him toward the truck.

It was the prince, Riley saw now. She could make out the gold tassels decorating al Said's black robe. And the dark stains on the white robe underneath! Halfway to the truck he stumbled and sagged to one knee. His arm lifted and to Riley's horrified eyes, he seemed to be gesturing at Pete to go on without him.

Pete didn't bother to argue. Just stooped, hauled the man over his shoulder and raced for the Range Rover. Riley's heart stopped dead for the five or ten seconds it took for him to reach the truck. He angled past her, aiming for the rear, and hefted the prince into the back. She heard al Said land with a thud, heard Pete clamber in after him, then his shout from the back.

"Drive!"

Chapter 6

The race to those distant lights seemed to take two life-times. The dunes were treacherous enough in daylight. At night they became a shifting, sinister patchwork of shadows. Riley could barely tell what was solid earth and what was a drop into nothingness.

The two men remained in the back of the Range Rover. Prince Malik had taken a bullet, Pete shouted over the shake and rattle of the truck. He'd also lost the first two fingers of one hand. While Pete worked to staunch the blood and fought to keep the prince from going into shock, Riley strained to separate sand from shadow and repeated every prayer she knew over and over again.

When the truck finally climbed the last, treacherous dune, the once-distant lights came into sharp focus directly below. They were floodlights! Racks of bright floods mounted on tall poles, illuminating what looked like some kind of tribal enclave. Tents circled a large open space. Low tables formed a second ring inside the open area. Dozens of figures sat cross-legged or lounged on colorful pillows around the tables. Parked outside the tents, Riley saw with a sharp intake of breath, was a whole convoy of Hummers and SUVs. And camels. At least a half dozen of them tied near the vehicles.

Riley stood on the brake, terrified all over again. Was this Scarface's home base? Had she driven them right into the hornet's nest?

"Pete!"

Her cry brought him scrambling forward. Crouching over her seat back, he assessed the scene with a single glance. "It's a tourist safari!"

"A what?"

"An excursion into the desert to give visitors a taste of Bedouin life. The troops at Thumrait arranged one for us when we first arrived. Hit the gas. We're going to crash their party."

She careened down the dune and rolled past the Hummers, almost taking down a tent before she got the Range Rover under control. Pete leaped out even before she shoved it into Park. As he raced for the camp, Riley tried to imagine the tourists' reactions at the sudden appearance of a near-naked man drenched in his own, and the prince's, blood.

She shouldered open her door, her nose twitching at the tantalizing scents of charcoal braziers and roasting meats. Ignoring her stomach's leap of eager joy at aromas, she climbed into the rear and hunkered down beside Prince Malik. One glimpse of him made her stomach do another lurch. The long-sleeved white dishdasha he'd worn under his black robe was in tatters. Part of it presumably now formed the bulky, bloodstained bandage wrapped around his right hand. Another strip circled his upper torso and held a thick, equally bloody pad in place. He didn't stir when she lifted his good hand and gripped it between hers. Didn't respond when she murmured his name. She was grappling with the fear he might have slipped into a coma when Pete returned. A small army of tourists and tour guides had come with him. One of them, a short, chunky blonde in khakis and a pink flowered shirt, hoisted herself into the truck. She was carrying a black bag and elbowed Riley out of the way.

"I'm Dr. Sutterfield. I'll take over. Hey! Get some light in here."

Blinding, high-powered beams stabbed into the truck. A second person climbed in to assist the doc. Riley inched around them, scrambled out of the Range Rover and fell into Pete's waiting arms. They were sticky with blood and sweat, yet she'd never felt anything as strong and safe and welcome.

Their nightmare was over. They'd reached an outpost of civilization. One with electricity and cell-phone towers and, mercifully, real food. Only after Pete eased her out of his arms did she realize the phone towers were a mixed blessing.

"I need to borrow that."

He gestured to the iPhone held by a grim-faced tour guide. The jeans-clad Omani handed it over instantly. As Pete stabbed a series of numbers, another bystander stepped forward to offer Riley a bottle of water. A third shrugged out of his long, loose outer robe and draped it over her shoulders. She accepted both with fervent thanks and guzzled half the water while Pete waited to be connected.

"Thumrait TOC, this is Majan one-five."

He paused, was obviously asked for some identification.

"Winborne, Peter. Master Sergeant, United States Air Force. AFSC 1T2X1. Currently on detached duty as part of a US-Omani Special Ops exercise. Be advised that Ms. Riley Fairchild, Prince Malik al Said and I have escaped the cadre of Abdul Haddid's troops who raided the opera house in Muscat. Prince Malik is wounded, condition uncertain at this time. Request you advise Omani Central immediately."

He paused again. Listened intently. Broke into a savage smile.

"Roger that, TOC. I'll need a set of camis and full assault gear. Give me an ETA. Right. Right. Over and out."

He hit the disconnect button and tossed the phone back to its owner, then hooked Riley's elbow and drew her aside. "Scarface's video hit the airwaves a little over an hour ago. The metadata pinpointed our exact location. And your code words tipped our guys as to the number and firepower of the raiders."

Fierce satisfaction resonated through his voice.

"Elements from the Special Ops unit at Thumrait are already in the air. They're diverting to this location. Should be here in less than ten minutes. What's more," he added with a feral gleam in his eyes, "they think they have a satellite surveillance lock on Scarface's vehicle."

"And you're going with them to intercept it."

"Yes, ma'am." He countered her dismay with that quick, cocky cowboy grin. "It's what we PJs do."

Of course it was. She knew it wouldn't do any good to argue that he'd already done enough. That she needed him. Right here, with her. Tonight. Tomorrow. Next week. Next...

She took a step back, startled by the intensity of that need. Pete didn't notice. His attention was all on the doc climbing down from the Range Rover.

"How's Prince Malik?"

"Stable. The hand needs immediate attention, but you did a good job on the gunshot wound considering what you had to work with. Where'd you get your medical training?"

"Air Force pararescue."

"That explains it. Air ambulance on the way?"

"Ten minutes out."

"Good. Let's get over there, in the light. I need to take a look at those abrasions."

Riley huddled under her borrowed robe while Dr. Sutterfield cleaned Pete's bloody back, chest, arms and knees, and applied a liberal dose of antibiotic cream. He was then offered a white robe by one of the camp operators. The camel-tender, judging by the pungent aroma that wafted from the loose-fitting garment when Pete returned to Riley's side. He started to say something but suddenly whirled and scanned the horizon.

"There they are. Four o'clock, coming in low and fast."

She followed his pointing finger and spotted the specks zooming through the night sky. A few seconds later she heard the *whap-whap* of their rotors. Mere moments after that, one of the specks grew large enough for Riley to distinguish a white medical helicopter with its distinctive red stripes on the tail. The other two remained almost invisible except for their cockpit lights…and the high-powered searchlight that suddenly drenched the entire camp in brilliant white.

The medical chopper touched down first, generating a whirlwind that had everyone flinging up their arms against the flying sand. Two burly, gun-carrying behemoths in black jumpsuits, kevlar vests and ball caps bearing the crest of the Omani royal guards jumped out first. A medical team came next and was directed to the Range Rover. While Dr. Sutterfield briefed the medics, Pete approached the guards. Hands up, palms out, he ID'd himself and had a short, fast colloquy.

One of the guards nodded, and Pete hurried back to Riley. His borrowed robe was far too short for him but he ignored the way it flapped at his calves and rode up his forearms when he reached for her.

"You're flying back with the prince to debrief the sultan's security forces. I should be there before you're done. If not, the guards promised they'll augment the security at your hotel suite until I get back to Muscat."

"You *will* get back?"

"Count on it. And when I do…"

She was ready this time. Went up on her toes to meet him halfway. The kiss was quick and hard, but the raw promise in it sent pleasure rolling through her.

As soon as she was aboard, Pete ducked under the blades of the closest military chopper. It was rocking on its skids, ready to go. He'd barely scrambled through the open side hatch before it lifted off. The second chopper followed seconds later. The last Riley saw of him, he'd ripped off the white cotton robe and was diving into a pair of camouflage pants.

* * *

After a quick phone call to her manager to let him know she was safe, Riley spent a grueling two hours with the chief of the sultan's security forces. More than willing to help, she dug hard and deep for details. The number of attackers who'd rushed the Royal Opera House. The drive through the desert. The type of restraints they'd used, their weapons, physical descriptions, accents, every word Scarface had spoken to her.

The exhaustive debrief might have lasted even longer if a personal representative of the royal house hadn't intervened. Tall and as lean as a hawk, he wore a ceremonial black robe with a curved, silver-hilted dagger tucked into his sash.

"Peace be with you."

The traditional greeting was warm and sincere. Riley replied in kind.

"And with you."

"I am Prince Faheem al Said, cousin to Prince Malik."

"How is he? Our last report said he was in surgery."

"His wounds are grievous, but he's expected to recover, thanks be to Allah."

"And the team that went back after Haddad's men? Sergeant Winborne and the others? Have you had an update from them?"

"They encountered some resistance, but the raid was a complete success."

"*Some* resistance?" Fear iced Riley's veins. "How much is some? Was anyone hurt?"

Faheem's lips curved in a small, lethal smile. "None of our men were injured, but I believe the one they referred to as Scarface will require extensive medical attention. He and his associates will join their leader, Haddad, in our maximum-security prison. And now to more important matters."

His smile lost its predatory edge, his voice warmed.

"My uncle was at a meeting of OPEC heads of state when you were attacked and taken hostage. He's cut short his trip, however, and is even now on his way home. Both he and Prince Malik have been informed of your heroic actions tonight, Ms. Fairchild. They've each instructed me to express their *most* heartfelt gratitude and their wish that you accept the hospitality of the royal house for as long as you remain in Oman."

Pete had told Riley he'd join her either here or at her hotel. She wasn't about to change addresses until they reconnected. Before she could think of a polite way to decline the invitation, however, the prince sweetened the deal.

"The al Alam Palace itself is used primarily for ceremonial functions, but there is a guest villa within the palace grounds. You would have complete privacy to recover from your ordeal, every luxury at your command. Your own pool, walled gardens, a spa, use of a yacht should you wish it."

Although the security team had provided Riley with a clean tunic and a pair of the loose trousers favored by Omani women, she had sand in every pore and her hair felt as gritty as used tarpaper. The shimmering image of a luxury villa with its own pool and perfumed gardens was too tempting to resist.

"It sounds wonderful, but I need to wait for Sergeant Winborne's return."

"That may be hours yet. And the sultan has offered the good sergeant his hospitality, as well. Let me es-

cort you to the royal compound and get you comfort-
ably settled. We'll do the same for Sergeant Winborne
when he returns."

This, Riley thought when she emerged from the
limo a half hour later, could have been the setting for
Rimsky-Korsakov's lavishly romantic opera *Scheherazade*. They'd driven through the palace's ornate blue
and gold gate into a vast U-shaped complex of white
marble buildings. Circling these, they'd reached the
guest quarters.

Her delighted gaze roamed the bubbling fountains,
the flowering pomegranate and pear trees, the gleaming white two-story villa. She could almost hear the
opening motif of the opera's fourth movement as Prince
Faheem escorted her up the shallow steps to the villa's
brass-studded front door.

A majordomo in an embroidered skullcap and snow-
robe waited on the front steps. Bowing low, he offered
a traditional greeting and introduced himself.

Prince Faheem accompanied her inside but went only
as far as the gloriously tiled entry. "I will leave you here,
Ms. Fairchild. If you wish anything—*anything*—you
have only to tell one of the staff."

"All I wish for right now is a bath, something to eat
and an update on Sergeant Winborne's status as soon
as possible."

"You shall have all three. And once again, may I
say you have earned the gratitude of the entire al Said
family. Such a debt is not something we take lightly."
Bowing low, he saluted her with a flourish of his hand
and left.

A maid in silky black trousers and a colorful tunic denoting her tribal roots stood at the foot of a broad staircase. After the majordomo issued some brief instructions, the maid showed the way to a master suite that encompassed the entire second floor.

Once again Riley felt as though she'd wandered onto the set of *Scheherazade*. The living room was the size of a hotel lobby. Colorful spangled pillows accented low couches and chairs. Hand-loomed Persian carpets covered the marble floors, while electrically operated screens and curtains cleverly disguised every modern convenience.

The bedroom was every bit as magnificent. A canopy of sand-colored silk crowned the massive bed. Three-foot-long gold tassels anchored the gauzy material to the four posts. Tall, arched windows lined two walls. Shuttered sliding doors dominated a third. Riley slid back one of the shutters and stepped out onto the balcony, her breath catching.

The balcony overlooked a crescent-shaped pool. Its water shimmered a dark turquoise in the subdued lighting, while statues at either end of the half moon tipped constant, lulling streams into the water. A lush garden surrounded the pool, with feathery palms silhouetted against the dark sky and a riot of night-blooming jasmine perfuming the air. And beyond the walled garden was the deep, dark cobalt of the Gulf of Oman.

Thoroughly enchanted, Riley stepped back inside and smiled at the patiently waiting maid.

"The gardens are beautiful."

"Most beautiful," she agreed. "Do you wish me to draw your bath, madam?"

"Yes, please!"

"I will do so, and while the tub fills I shall fetch something for you to eat."

Propped against the sloping back of a monster marble tub, Riley thought she just might spend the night there. Rose-scented water bubbled through the jets and lapped gently at her sore, strained muscles. A platter of char-grilled kebabs, fresh fruit and cheeses sat within easy reach.

She'd unwrapped the filthy bandages on her wrists and soaked the ugly bruises before attacking the succulent kebabs. The first she'd devoured in three quick bites. The second more slowly, savoring each morsel of tender meat, roasted onions and sweet red peppers. She was washing a third down with fresh-squeezed orange juice when the maid tapped on the intricately carved teakwood screen that separated the tub from the rest of the vast bathroom.

"Madam?"

"Yes?"

"There is someone who wishes to see you," she said, peering around the screen. "I told him you were unavailable but he wanted you to know that he is here."

Riley's pulse leaped. Sloshing upright, she asked eagerly, "An American? Tall? Brown hair? Blue eyes?"

"And very handsome," the maid added, her eyes twinkling. "He says he is your husband."

Riley scrambled to her knees and reached for a towel. "Send him up!"

"He's already up," a deep voice said from just behind the screen.

The maid backed away, and Pete took her place. With something between a groan and a laugh, Riley sank back into the tub.

"I should have known you wouldn't wait."

"Yeah," he agreed with a wicked smile. "You should've."

He was filthy. Dried blood still stained his neck and wrists. Some kind of soot or camouflage paint streaked his face. Dust coated the uniform he'd dragged on aboard the chopper, and two day's worth of dark bristles sprouted on cheeks and chin. Yet his raw masculinity aroused her more than every wealthy, sophisticated George Clooney–type she'd met or been courted by in her meteoric career.

Mental images of the body under that filthy uniform aroused her even more. She lounged against the back of the tub, letting the bubbles lap over the slopes of her breasts. The sensual swirl teased her nipples. Heat gathered low in her belly. To cover her sudden, aching need she splashed the water surface with her palms.

"I heard Scarface is going to require extensive medical care."

"He's alive."

His careless shrug told Riley the man was probably on life support. She couldn't work up much sympathy.

"So…" Pete's hands went to the top button of his uniform shirt. His smile was slow and bone-melting. "Want some company?"

The heat in Riley's belly shot up another ten degrees. Her body screamed *yes* at the same time her head shouted *no, no, no!*

Despite all they'd been through, she hardly knew this man. They exchanged maybe a dozen stilted words at

Aly's wedding before fate threw them together for two terrifying nights and one long, harrowing day. They'd talked a little about his family, hers. He'd kissed her, what? Twice? Three times?

And each kiss had left her craving more. That simple fact banished every doubt. Smiling, she waggled her fingers.

"Come on in, the water's fine."

He scraped a hand across his chin. "I should shave first."

"Later."

He didn't need a second invitation. His uniform shirt hit the marble tiles. The snake coiled around his biceps held her attention only until his pants and boots came off. He shed the mud-colored, thigh-hugging boxer-briefs with the same speed she'd shed her well-worn bikini briefs earlier.

Lord, he was fine! Riley sighed with delight and sank lower, thoroughly enjoying the view. Between drafty dressing rooms and quick costume changes, she'd seen her share of barrel-chested tenors, puffed-up baritones and cleverly padded basso profundos. There was nothing puffed or padded about Pete Winborne. The man was six-one or -two of contrasting tan lines, roped muscle, washboard abs and flat stomach.

Her heart was thrumming in her throat when he settled into the bubbling water facing her and crooked a finger. Electric with need, she floated across and slithered up his thighs and his stomach.

"This," he growled, digging his hands into her hair, "is what got me through the past twenty-four hours."

"This?"

She wiggled higher and locked her arms around his neck. Her voice dropped to a throaty contralto.

"Or this?"

She dragged his head down. His mouth was hard and hungry. His tongue danced with hers. Whiskers scraped her cheeks and chin. Callous hands roamed her hips, her waist, her breasts. She could feel him growing hard against her stomach. Feel her belly clench in eager response.

Giving in to that compelling need, she pulled herself up another few inches and straddled his thighs. She rocked in the water, her hips grazing his, her mound rubbing his erection. He grunted and clamped his hands on her hips.

"We'll have to be a little creative," he warned with a crooked grin. "At least until I get my hands on some protection for you."

She could feel him probing her center, feel the hot inner gush that answered him, and gasped an urgent assurance.

"We're okay. I've always taken care of that myself."

She'd had to, since her mother had flatly refused to even discuss the possibility Riley might experience the same biological urges as any other sixteen- or seventeen-year-old. Meredith Fairchild had insisted her daughter focus entirely, exclusively, on her vocal training.

Her mother would be shocked to learn how that training was paying off now! Riley's voice coaches had stressed the importance of singing from her diaphragm. She could pull air into the very bottom of her lungs. Push it even deeper, using her abdominal muscles. Exhale slowly, deliberately.

She used every one of those techniques with Pete when she relaxed enough to let him slide slowly into her. His hot flesh stretched her, filled her, lodged deep. She could feel every hard, ridged inch of him. Then she breathed in, pushed down. Her stomach went concave. Her muscles contracted. She sheathed him, as tight as a fist.

Exhaled.

Breathed in.

Exhaled.

"Whoa!" His eyes widened. A look of astonished delight creased his whiskered cheeks. "That's some action you've got going there, Slim!"

She gave a trill of low, husky laughter. "Hang on, Cowboy. You ain't seen nothin' yet."

She damned near blew off the top of Pete's head.

Propping her hands on his shoulders, she rocked his world. Literally. Her hips and thighs and belly moved with a skill that had him groaning and straining and shooting into her *way* sooner than he'd intended. His mind mush, he sank back against the marble.

"Give me a few minutes," he begged, eyes closed.

She sat back on her haunches. He felt himself slide out of her, felt the weight of her on his thighs.

"How few is a few?"

"Ten." He opened one eye, let his gaze linger on the pinkish-brown nipples tipping her small breasts. "Make that five."

"Well," she murmured seductively, "if you're sure that's all you need."

She arched her back and lifted her wet, honey-colored mane with both arms. Pete's blood hadn't fully recirculated yet, but the glimpse of golden pubic hair just visible under the bubbling water was a call to arms.

"To hell with that! I'm good to go."

He pushed upright, catching her off balance. She had to lurch forward and throw her arms around his shoulders to keep from tumbling backward into the still bubbling water.

He took full advantage of her awkward position. Locking one arm around her waist, he used the other to push up and out of the tub. The water sluicing down his legs made the marble tiles treacherous, but he got to the bedroom without landing on his ass.

"Pete!" Riley shifted in his arms and squawked a protest as he headed for the bed. "We're soaking wet!"

"So?"

"So that coverlet is silk! And the pillows! And... Oh!"

He dumped her atop the silk and spread her legs. He still hadn't shaved. Still hadn't rid himself of all the sand embedded in his skin. But he owed this incredible woman for the wild pleasure she'd just given him and he intended to make good on that debt.

Chapter 7

Riley surfaced slowly from what felt like a dozen layers of fuzzy sleep. She had no idea what time she and Pete had finally run out of steam, but it had to have been close to dawn.

She stretched languidly, snaking her arms over her head with only a few aching protests in her shoulders, and blinked sleepily at the generous folds of sand-colored silk in the canopy above. A catlike smile tugged at her lips as she discovered a new set of aches. Most were related to the beard burn on her inner thighs.

"'Bout time you rejoined the living."

Still sleepy, she turned to the sound of Pete's amused voice. He was leaning against the bedpost, arms crossed, a fluffy white towel draped low on his hips. His scruffy bristles were gone and drops of water glistened on his shoulders and bare chest. Riley feasted on the delicious sight for a moment before arching a brow.

"Did you take another swim in the tub? Without me?"

"No, ma'am. That tub is reserved for joint operations. I've been down at the pool, doing laps."

"Where do you get your energy?" she groaned. "I can barely move."

"Which," he said with a grin as he crossed the room, "is why I let you sleep instead of rolling you over and initiating a second round of joint ops. But now that you're awake…"

"Hold it right there, Cowboy! Before you initiate anything I need to, uh, use the bucket."

"You're going to like this one. It's got twenty-four-carat gold handles."

"I seem to recall that from last night." She started to slide out of bed, remembered she was naked. "Face to the wall. And don't cheat!"

Laughter crinkled the white lines at the corners his eyes. "I think I've pretty well seen everything there is to see."

"You haven't seen it in the bright light of morning."

"It's long past morning, Slim, but if you insist…"

He angled his head away. She didn't trust him, of course, and took the precaution of swathing herself in the sheet. To her delight, she discovered her suitcases had been retrieved from her hotel and now sat on beautifully carved luggage racks.

"So what time *is* it?" she asked as she snatched up clean underwear and one of the lightweight, three-quarter-sleeved, ankle-length, no-wrinkle dresses that had served her so well during this concert tour of predominantly Muslim countries.

"Fourteen thirty," Pete replied, his face still turned away. Mostly.

"What's that in human time?"

"Two thirty."

She stopped at the arched entry to the bathroom. "I slept through breakfast *and* lunch?"

"You did. I, on the other hand, had breakfast five hours ago. The staff said to call down when you woke and they'd fix us up with lunch."

"Make the call! I'm starving."

They ate on a vine-covered terrace with an unobstructed view across the harbor to Muscat's old city. A blue-domed mosque held place of honor amid flat-roofed shops and restaurants. The pristine white buildings hugged the sea, crowded against it by the craggy mountains separating them from the desert.

Two yachts were moored in the harbor, each flying a penant with the royal insignia of a curved dagger superimposed over crossed swords. Massive oil-storage tanks, the source of so much of Oman's wealth, dotted the hills beyond the port. A dozen or more supertankers rode the waves just outside the port, waiting their turn at the pumping stations. As if in counterpoint to all the modern wealth, several traditional wooden dhows sliced through the blue-green waters.

Riley had no interest in the harbor's colorful scene, however. After her first ravenous attack on the feast provided by the villa's chef, she gave Pete all her attention while he shared the details of Scarface's capture and the takedown of the rest of his cadre.

"What about the girl?" Riley asked when he finished. "She couldn't have been more than sixteen or seventeen."

"Maybe not," he agreed grimly, "but she was hanging with the wrong crowd. I doubt the kid will see the outside of a cell before her fiftieth birthday. The Omanis aren't likely to forgive an attack on their soil anytime soon. Especially one that almost took the life of a member of the royal family."

"Did you get an update on Prince Malik's condition this morning?"

"He's no longer critical. It was touch-and-go for a while, though. He lost a lot of blood, first when Scarface chopped off his fingers, then from the bullet he took when we broke out."

"If he's able to have visitors, I'd like to go to the hospital."

"So would I."

A chauffeured limo ferried them to the gleaming white hospital in the new section of Muscat. Once inside, Riley and Pete were escorted to a suite in a private wing reserved for the royal family. Instead of the usual antiseptic hospital smell, the elegant suite was fragrant with huge masses of flowers and a delicate scent of frankincense.

Prince Malik was propped up in bed. Tubes snaked from his arm to four different bags suspended from a metal stand. His dark eyes were dull with pain but lit up when his visitors were announced.

"Pete, my friend! And Ms. Fairchild!" His mouth twisted in a rueful smile. "How good to see you without a gun or a knife being aimed in our direction."

He stretched out his uninjured arm. When Riley placed her hand in his, he brought it to his lips. "They have told me what you did. I owe you my life."

Embarrassed, she gestured toward Pete. "I only followed his instructions. He's the one who got us all back alive."

The prince nodded, his glance shifting to the man at her side. "That's what PJs do."

"So I've heard."

He grinned at the drawled comment and shared a glance with Pete.

There was that bond again, Riley thought. The one that connected comrades in arms. She marveled at its power and wondered if she would ever feel anything as strong and sure and unshakable.

She got her answer about three seconds later. All it took was an easy loop of Pete's arm around her shoulders to include her as part of his select circle.

"I'd say it was a pretty much a team effort. But speaking of PJs…"

She could hear the mingled regret and resolution in his voice. Her stomach sinking, she guessed what was coming.

"I need to get back to Thumrait. We should conduct one more hot extraction before we wind up the joint exercise."

The prince forestalled her instinctive protest. "I've already contacted the TOC. The joint exercise was terminated as of this morning."

The news didn't appear to thrill Pete. What followed pleased him even less.

"I also spoke to your commander back in the States. He's agreed to put you on indefinite detached duty so you may serve as senior adviser to the Omani Special Forces."

"What?"

The arm lying across Riley's shoulders went hard and tight. She barely controlled a flinch as the prince continued.

"You will be paid by the Omani treasury, of course. We will also provide a villa and a substantial cost of living supplement."

"I don't think so!"

Al Said hooked a brow but continued calmly. "You must allow me to do this, my friend. I owe you a debt of honor."

Riley held her breath as Pete struggled to contain his anger at this high-handed rearrangement of his life and career. The prince made an obvious effort to defuse the tension.

"But think how this will benefit both your country and mine. Your president agrees this arrangement will greatly enhance joint US-Omani operations. My uncle spoke with him," he added when Pete's brows took a quick dive. "Personally."

The effort seemed to sap al Said's strength. He blew out a breath, his face going pale, and sank back against the bed.

"I'm afraid I must rest now. Please. Take a few days to think about this, my friend. It would be to your great advantage, and to ours." His gaze drifted to Riley. "I should like to speak with you again, Ms. Fairchild. Perhaps tomorrow or the next day?"

"Of course."

Pete was quiet during the return trip. Too quiet. Waiting for them at the villa was an invitation from the sultan to join him for dinner at the palace that evening. Pete nodded when the majordomo relayed the message and wandered into the high-ceilinged living room. Arms crossed, legs spread, he stared through the arched windows at the gardens beyond.

Riley tossed her purse on one of the divans and leaned her hips against its back. "Do you want to talk about Prince Malik's offer?"

"No." With a small shake of his head, he tempered his brusque tone. "Maybe later, okay? I need to process it first."

"Okay. Soooo… We've got four hours to kill." She waited a beat. Let her voice glide down a full octave. "What would you like to do instead?"

His glance cut sideways. Surprise and the beginning of a smile filled his blue eyes. "I guess we could go upstairs."

"And?"

"Get naked."

"And?"

"Oh, I don't know." The smile was full and potent now. "See if we fit together as good dry as we did wet."

Pete vowed to take it slow this time. He was determined to explore the slopes and hollows and sweet spots he'd been too fevered to attend to properly last night. But when he advised the majordomo that they didn't want to be disturbed and joined Riley upstairs, she surprised him again.

She was standing in the middle of the sumptuous bedroom, drinking in the gauzy silk and gold tassels. "This could be the stage setting for Rimsky-Korsakov's

Scheherazade. Or Strauss's *Salome.* Have you ever seen either one performed?"

"I've never seen any opera."

"Seriously?"

"Seriously. Your concert would have been my first brush with it."

"Oh." She digested that for a long moment. "Well, I've never watched a football game, so I guess all things even out."

Pete couldn't disguise his shock. "You're kidding!"

"No, and I haven't jumped out of a plane, either," she retorted, laughing at his dumbfounded expression. "But you gave me a taste of mountain climbing, so I think it's only fair I give you a taste of opera."

"Now?" He threw a quick glance at the bed. "I sort of had other ideas."

"Go! Sit over there!" She pointed to the padded bench at the foot of the bed. "You're about to be treated to a private performance of Salome's 'Dance of the Seven Veils.'"

Okay, that sounded intriguing. Pete took a seat as instructed while Riley tested the straw-colored silk of the bed canopy.

"This will work."

Tugging down a length of the gauzy drape, she gathered an armful of spangled cushions and disappeared into the bath.

"The opera's plot is pretty complicated," she called from the other room, "but basically boils down to lust, rejection and revenge. King Herod of Jerusalem is obsessed by Salome, who's been rejected by John the Baptist. In this scene, she entices the king to have John executed and his head brought to her on a silver platter."

"Like in the Bible."

"Exactly. Salome's a tough role for mezzo-sopranos." The whir of zippers opening punctuated her comment. "The highest note is the high B5, which is within our range, but the lowest is a low G-flat 3."

"Oooh-kay."

"And the Dance of the Seven Veils is really difficult. Most divas will use a stand-in for the dance portion. Someone trained in classical ballet." She paused, then continued. "Those of us who opt to perform it ourselves wear flesh-colored body suits under our veils, although a daring few have finished naked at Herod's feet."

"This is sounding better and better."

"Yes, I thought you'd like that part."

Pete stuffed a cushion behind his back. His first foray into the operatic world was turning out to be more interesting than he would have imagined.

"Ready?" Riley called.

"Ready."

"Okay, long drumroll first. Imagine timpanis building to a sensual beat, followed by a crash of cymbals. Da-da-dum, da-da-dum, da-dummmmm!"

On the last note, she whirled in from the other room and stopped dead. She'd draped the straw-colored silk bed curtain over her head, lower face and body. A tasseled gold cord was tied around her waist. Emptied cushion covers in a rainbow of spangled colors dangled from the cord. All Pete could see were her brown eyes. Alluring. Seductive. Enticing.

Slowly, sensually, she raised her arms above her

head. Her eyes locked with his, she began to trill a
tune with a vaguely Oriental air. The notes were high
and thin, like the call of a flute. Her hips began to move.
Slowly at first, matching the rhythm that seemed to
float like a playful breeze on the air.

To his surprise, Pete found himself as mesmerized
by the incredibly graceful movement of her hands as
by the erotic sway of her hips...until the tempo kicked
up and the spangles started flicking from side to side.

Her trills were still high and clear and liquid, but
her movements quicker. She pivoted on one foot, hips
swinging, and sent him a look over her shoulder that
damned near drained every drop of blood from his head.

He didn't hesitate when she sashayed closer. Taking her up on the invitation in those twitching hips,
he caught the end of a soft, satiny cushion cover and
plucked it free.

She tossed her head. Danced away. Swayed back, offering him a second scrap of spangled silk. A third. A
fourth. Pete wasn't sure how he finally got her down to the
seventh and last layer without going into cardiac arrest.

The fat gold rope at her waist belted that final veil.
Glittering tassels dangled from its ends. His throat dry
and his blood pounding, he followed their hypnotiz-
ing sway as her hips kicked right, left, right. When her
hands dropped to the knot at her waist, he knew exactly
how King Herod must have felt. He'd never wanted any
woman as much he wanted this one.

No! Not just *any* woman. Truth was he'd never met
a woman like Riley Fairchild. So vibrant, so coura-
geous, so incredibly talented. Her voice lifted him on
silver wings. Her body made him burn. She was in his

blood, in his head. And she wanted him with a hunger that matched his own.

No surprise they didn't make it to the end of the dance. The last of her seven veils was still draped around her slender body when he caught the swaying tassels, yanked her into his lap and bent her over his arm.

Later that evening, Oman's ruling sultan sent a limo to transport Riley and Pete to his private residence. Tall, lean, white-bearded and distinguished, he was the fourteenth in a line that stretched back to the 1700s. He'd received his primary education in India, attended Britain's Royal Military Academy at Sandhurst, joined the British Army and was posted to the 1st Battalion Cameronians.

He took over the sultanate after a palace coup deposed his father in 1970. A progressive ruler, he'd introduced a modified parliamentary system that recognized tribal rights and gave women the vote without lessening any of his own power. And he'd managed the diplomatic miracle of maintaining good relations with his Arab neighbors throughout his long reign while remaining an ally of Britain, the United States and other Western nations.

Given his military background and position as commander of the Omani military, it was no surprise that the sultan and Pete conversed easily. Or that he strongly endorsed Prince Malik's hope that Sergeant Winborne would remain as senior adviser to the Omani Special Forces. Pete returned a polite but noncommittal answer, saying that he had to discuss it with his commander.

When the conversation turned to opera, however,

neither Riley nor her host was the least noncommittal. A passionate devotee of classical music, the sultan was extremely proud of his hundred-piece, all-Omani Orchestra and the marble wonder of his Royal Opera House. That Abdul Haddad's rabid dogs should have desecrated his temple to the arts and put a great artist like Riley through such an ordeal struck him to the heart.

But it wasn't until his guests were once again in the limo that Riley decided to accept the sultan's generous offer to remain his guest for as long as she wished.

"I hate to cancel the last concert of my tour, but I need another few days to recover. Or weeks. Or..."

She let that sentence hang and gave Pete a sideways glance. She knew he still chafed at the way outsiders had stepped in to rearrange his career and his life. But he was military. He'd follow orders as long as they were legal or right or in the best interests of the service.

Which meant he would stay in Oman.

And she could stay with him for another few days or weeks or...

"I know your fans will be disappointed." Smiling, he reached for her hand and brought it to his lips. "I, however, would pay major bucks for another private performance like the one you gave earlier. You might just make an opera buff out of me yet."

"I'll give it my best shot," she promised solemnly.

The next morning Pete connected with his commander back in Florida via the Thumrait Tactical Operations Center's secure link. Not known for his laid-back personality, Colonel Marsh let loose with both barrels.

"Dammit, Winborne, what the hell are you doing

jockeying around in the desert, playing hero to an Omani prince and some opera singer?"

That wasn't all Pete was doing with the opera singer, but he figured the colonel didn't need that bit of extraneous information.

"I've got General Hawkins at the Pentagon on my ass," Marsh snapped, "and he's got the State Department and the White House crawling up his. You want to tell me how the friggin' foxtrot you got into this situation?"

Pete complied, keeping it short and concise. The explanation did little to soothe the colonel's ruffled feathers.

"We need you back at Hurlburt, dammit. I've got a half dozen good men I can send to Oman as an 'adviser,' but only one I'd intended to make superintendent of the 23rd."

Pete swallowed a groan. The 23rd Special Tactics Squadron's history stretched back to WWII. Air commandos wearing its blue and yellow patch had lost blood, sweat and sleep in every major campaign from the D-Day Invasion to Desert Storm to Operation Enduring Freedom. Becoming the 23rd's superintendent meant a promotion and working with the best of the best.

"Listen up, Winborne. I'm getting a lot of pressure on this and I know it would be the best thing that could happen for joint US-Omani ops. But I'll fight it if you tell me you don't want it. No, don't answer yet. Take a few of those hundred or so days leave you've got stacked up to think about it. Hell, take a week. Two. You've earned it."

Okay! All right! The prince, the sultan and now his

CO were all insisting Pete take some time to cogitate. Damned if he wouldn't do just that.

"Roger that, sir. I'll get back to you."

The connection severed, Pete hunted for Riley. He found her on the terrace, fingering her cell phone and looking as grim as he felt.

"I talked to my manager, Jason Hepplewhite. And to my agent. They'll take care of canceling the last concert and making sure the tickets are refunded. I felt so bad about it, though, that I told Jason to make up the lost revenue to UNICEF from my personal account."

"Whoa! That must have been a nice chunk of change."

She shrugged off what had to have been a dent of a hundred thousand or more in her bank account.

"Jason said the calls and Tweets and emails are pouring in from fans and well-wishers. He's got my PR team fielding them, but wanted a personal statement. I hope you don't mind that I included you and Prince Malik in the release."

"Not a problem."

The international media had picked up the story and already gone into their usual frenzy. One enterprising reporter had even obtained a copy of Pete's official Air Force photo. He suspected he was going to get a real ration from the other Sidewinders about seeing his ugly mug splashed across papers and TV screens around the world.

"How about you?" Riley asked. "Did you get through to your commander?"

"Yeah, I did. He said accepting the advisory position is my call. But, like the prince and the sultan, he wants me to think about it."

"So are you?" She cocked her head and studied him through the screen of her lashes. "Thinking about it?"

He pulled in a breath, took the plunge. "What I'm thinking is that we should blow this place. Get away from the phones and the servants and all the royal trappings."

"And go where?"

"We could drive down the coast and find some small, quiet hotel on the beach. Not think about *anything* for a while except what and where we're going to eat in the evenings."

She jumped at it. Literally. Sprang right out of her chair into his arms.

"I'm in!"

Pete shed the weight of his decision like an eighty-pound backpack. For a week… Hell, for *two* weeks, he would just wallow in the pleasure of sharing a beach towel and a bed with this amazing woman.

Chapter 8

Pete handled all the logistics. He rented the car, drove down the coast and—most importantly—chose a small, unassuming oceanfront hotel where the elderly owner, who emerged from behind a curtain in answer to the counter bell, didn't recognize either of them.

That was no small accomplishment with Omani TV and newspapers still headlining their ordeal in the desert. What saved them, they agreed later, was that the stoop-shouldered owner squinted at them through rheumy, clouded eyes and thick glasses.

The fact that his establishment was less than half full was another factor in their favor. When Riley and Pete went down for dinner that first evening on the terrace overlooking the Arabian Sea, the only other occupants were a harassed-looking couple with three squirming, petulant kids and two British women who conversed in low murmurs.

They soon established a routine. Pete ran six miles every morning while Riley slept in. After a late breakfast, they swam, windsurfed, whale-watched, or just plain lazed in the sun. One afternoon they spent exploring the rocky outcrops and sparkling waterfalls of nearby Wadi As Suwayh. The ruins of a mighty coastal fortress consumed another full afternoon. Dinners they ate at the hotel or one of the many outdoor cafés strung along the waterfront.

And the nights…

Dear Lord, the nights!

Every hour Riley shared with Pete deepened the respect and admiration and greedy hunger he roused in her. And every hour she spent in his arms had her spinning fantasies of something more than a few stolen days or weeks. She hugged those fantasies to herself, however, until Pete himself brought up the issue of the future.

She was stretched out beside him on the beach, eyes closed and body limp from the hot sun and their vigorous workout the night before. Careful to respect local traditions, she wore a modestly cut one-piece under an airy, ankle-length cover-up. She was toying with the idea of slipping off the cover-up and going back in the water to cool off when Pete sat up and blocked the sun.

She opened one eye and squinted at him through her sunglasses. He'd bought a baseball cap embroidered with some team logo at the local souk and now wore it with the brim to the back. A T-shirt with the same logo lay beside him on the hotel's blue-striped towel. He sat with his arms crossed on his knees, looking out to sea.

The snake coiled around his biceps seemed to pin its beady eyes on Riley as she pushed up on her elbows.

"What are you thinking?"

He glanced down at her. "Just trying to figure out what happens next."

"Whether you stay in Oman, you mean?"

"That, and how you and I will connect again if I do."

She scrambled upright, her heart suddenly racing. "Do you *want* to connect again?"

"Oh, yeah." Smiling, he raised a hand to brush some sand off her cheek. "How about you?"

"Yes," she said simply. "Anytime, anyplace."

His smile slipped and a startled look crossed his face. "That's the old air-commando motto," he told her. "Anytime, Anyplace."

"Really?" Her fantasies started spinning again. "Maybe we could adopt it as *our* personal code."

"Maybe we could. The logistics might be tough to work out, though. Your career. Mine. Chances are we'd be in different quadrants of the globe half the time."

"You don't think it would be worth the effort?"

"I'm just saying it wouldn't be easy."

"I've been thinking about that, too." Drawing up her knees, she hooked her arms around them. "I've spent a good part of the past two years on tour. Recording sessions and rehearsals took up most of my life before that. And if I wasn't laying down tracks or performing, I was studying roles or at the dance studio or doing PR or making nice at dinners and cocktail parties thrown by generous donors. I don't think I've chilled, just chilled, in…well… Pretty much never."

Her mother hadn't believed in letting time slip

through the cracks. All through Riley's childhood, school vacations meant longer practice sessions, trips to New York and San Francisco and Chicago to see live performances, junkets abroad to soak up culture and expose the budding ingenue to European audiences and maestros. Her schedule during the school year was twice as intense. If music hadn't been such a passion with Riley she might have rebelled long before she finally did.

"I could get addicted to this," she said, indicating the sunlight dancing on the waves. "Learn to live life in the slow lane, or at least slower than the one I've occupied up to now."

"What are you saying?" Pete's brow furrowed. "You want to quit singing?"

"No! God, no! Just cut back on commitments. Ease up my travel schedule."

She picked up a handful of sand, let it sift through her fingers. Raising her eyes, she voiced the thought she'd been kicking around for days now.

"I was thinking I could make Muscat my home base for a year or so. When we had dinner with the sultan, he hinted that he wants to start a guest artist-in-residence program. I'm fairly certain I could get the job."

"Fairly certain? Hell, he'd sign you up in a heartbeat."

"Of course," she added with a nonchalant shrug, "I'd only consider the position if a certain individual I know checked in as senior adviser to the Omani Special Forces."

The possibility didn't exactly make him leap for joy. Still frowning, he curled a knuckle under her chin and tipped her face to his. "What would becoming an artist-in-residence for a year or two do to your career?"

"Level it off a little," she answered truthfully. "Just as I suspect this advisory position would level yours. On the upside, though, we'd be in the same quadrant of the globe."

"So we would."

His gazed roamed her face. She could see herself in his pupils. See, too, the hesitation in them.

"Before you commit to anything," he said slowly, "you should know that I'm damn close to being in love with you."

She wasn't quite sure how to take that. "Let me know when you're positive."

"The thing is, I thought I was in love before." He stopped, shook his head, started again. "You know I'm divorced, right?"

This wasn't going at all the way Riley had fantasized. "Aly pointed out your ex at the wedding."

As if anyone could have missed her. The woman had crawled all over Pete.

"What I'm trying to say…"

"And not doing a particularly good job of it," she interjected drily.

"…is that Nancy Sue and I really thought we could make a go of it. When it was just the two of us, though, away from our friends and the parties and the bright lights of the football stadium, it didn't take long to realize what we had was just a near fatal dose of lust."

"Thank you for sharing that very touching memory." Irritated now by his distinct lack of enthusiasm, Riley put some frost in the response. "And that's what you think we have? A bad case of lust?"

"No, of course not. I hope to God I've grown up some since high school. I know the real thing when it's almost within my grasp."

"But I don't?"

He hesitated, then measured out each word. "We just came through a scary situation, Slim. A whole lot scarier for you than me. I've dodged bullets before. I know how that puts emotions on high and hot."

"I see. So now I'm not just too immature to know my own feelings, I'm too stupid to distinguish between reality and an adrenaline high."

"Christ, Riley, you know that's not what I meant."

He blew out a breath and adopted a calm, patient tone that tightened her jaw.

"I'm merely suggesting you might want to take a little more time, be sure of what you feel, before you make a major career move."

"Oh, I will. I most definitely will." She didn't even *try* to pretend she wasn't angry. And hurt. And thoroughly humiliated. Scrambling to her feet, she snatched up the straw tote she'd found at the souk. "Now, if you'll excuse me, I'm going to go wash off all this sand and sunscreen."

When he made a grab for his shirt and their towels, she whirled.

"I suggest you stay right here and bake until I've had time to get over being compared to your ex-wife."

Pete started to protest that he hadn't been comparing them. There *was* no comparison, except maybe for this sudden flare of temper. A last thread of common sense clamped his mouth shut.

Hands on hips, he watched her plow up the beach and march across the road to the hotel. When she disappeared, he dropped down on the sand again. Sweet Jesus! Could he have screwed that up any worse? All he'd intended to do was warn her. Let her know he was close to the edge. So close, she needed to take a quick step back if she didn't want to get dragged over with him.

Then she'd thrown out that bit about putting her career on hold and remaining in Oman. Before Pete could let her do that, he had to make sure she understood what she'd be getting into. Long-term relationships were tough enough to sustain without throwing Special Ops into the mix. Once you did, it stacked the odds even more. Constant training, short-notice deployments, secret missions, life-and-death situations—the combination was highly stressful and not exactly conducive to a stable home environment. Three of the six Sidewinders saw their marriages bust up because of it. Pete and Travis Cooper and Josh Patterson had all commiserated with each other at various times.

Although…that hadn't kept Travis or Josh from giving it another shot. Or the other three from taking the plunge. Oh, hell. Why was he even thinking wedding bells? After the way he'd just bungled things, he'd be lucky if Riley let him back in their hotel room, never mind her life. He'd give her an hour, Pete decided grimly, then try to recover the ground he'd cut right out from under his own feet.

He waited almost two. In the process he went from kicking himself repeatedly for mishandling the situation to devising and discarding a half-dozen strategies for regaining lost ground to finally realizing that his only way out was to grovel.

Determined to do just that, he tugged on the T-shirt sporting the red-and-green emblem of the Oman national football team and shoved his feet into the leather flip-flops he'd picked up at the souk. They slapped his heels during the short trek up the beach.

Just before he reached the street, a vehicle pulled up at the hotel's front entrance. The sight of the stretch limo hit like a right cross to the jaw. Had he pissed Riley off so much she'd called for transportation back to Muscat?

He picked up speed, intending to run an intercept, when the limo driver opened the passenger door and a woman emerged. Even with oversize sunglasses and a floppy brimmed hat shielding most of her face, Pete recognized her.

"Ms. Fairchild!"

The call swung her around.

"Hold on a moment," he said as he dodged a bus and crossed the street. "I'd like to speak to you."

Tipping her sunglasses, she looked him up and down. A moue of distaste thinned her lips when her glance caught on the tat just visible below the short sleeve of his T-shirt. As he approached, she made sure to keep the limo door between them.

"Do I know you?"

"I'm Master Sergeant Pete Winborne. We met a few months back at Aly and Josh's wedding."

"I'm sorry, I don't remem— Oh!" The name suddenly clicked. "You're the one! The soldier who saved my daughter!"

He didn't bother to point out the fine distinction between soldiers and airmen. "I can't take all the credit.
Your daughter did as much to save herself as I did.
Prince Malik and I wouldn't have made it out alive without her."

Surprise and disbelief crossed the woman's sculpted
features.

"She's got grit, Ms. Fairchild. All the way through."

"Apparently."

"Why don't we go inside? Have a cool drink and I'll
share some of the details that didn't make it into the
news stories."

Nodding, she told the limo driver to wait and let
Pete escort her into the hotel's cool, dim interior. He
seated her at a table in the arched alcove that doubled
as a lounge and procured two iced pomegranate juices
from the accommodating hotel owner. He suspected
Riley's mother could have used something stronger. He
could've, too, but the hotel didn't serve alcohol.

When he returned with the tall, dew-streaked glasses,
she removed her sunglasses and hooked them in a side
pocket of her purse. The few wispy strands showing
beneath her broad-brimmed hat had a more silvery hue
than Riley's honey gold, but her eyes were the same
cinnamon brown as her daughter's. They flicked over
Pete as he removed his ball cap, dropped to his gaudy
T-shirt and focused with barely disguised disdain on
his tattoo before returning to his face.

Although Pete had conversed only briefly with this
woman at the wedding, her animosity toward her "self-
ish bitch" of a daughter had come through loud and
clear. The little that Riley had subsequently revealed

about her relationship with her mother underscored the fact they weren't close. Which begged the question…

"Does Riley know you're in Oman, Ms. Fairchild?"

"No."

When he lifted a brow, she offered a stilted explanation. "I was on a private yacht in the Caribbean. Her people didn't notify me of the kidnapping until the day after it happened. By the time we put into port and I'd made arrangements to fly to Muscat, the media was already broadcasting news of her rescue." The pale ovals of her nails tapped against the glass. "I texted my daughter and told her I would come. Several times. She didn't reply."

"Riley mentioned that her PR team was fielding an avalanche of Tweets and texts and emails," Pete said diplomatically.

"Please, Sergeant…?"

"Winborne."

"Sergeant Winborne. Don't patronize me. Since you're staying here, with my daughter, I assume you know that she and I aren't on the best of terms."

"So why did you fly over?"

"*Because* you're staying here, with my daughter."

"You want to elaborate a little on that?"

The question was easy, the steel behind it wasn't. Pursing her lips, she countered with one of her own.

"Exactly how long have you known Riley, Sergeant?"

"We met at the wedding." No need to tell her they didn't exactly hit it off that first time. "I didn't see her again until the attack on the opera house."

"I see." Her nails danced against the glass again.

"And at anytime during this long acquaintance has Riley mentioned Austin Mahler?"

"Not that I recall."

"No, I don't suppose she would."

Pete rolled his shoulders in a careless shrug. "If this Mahler character matters, she'll get around to telling me about him in her own time."

"Oh, he matters. Or did. He was engaged to my daughter until I discovered he was using her name as collateral for unsecured loans. He was also trying to arrange concert appearances without consulting her."

"And I'm guessing you couldn't wait to expose him."

The drawled response carried an unmistakable barb. When it hit, a flush tinged Meredith Fairchild's cheeks. "You're right, I couldn't. Although Riley's made it abundantly clear she doesn't want me in her life, she *is* my daughter. I couldn't allow her to be taken in by that man. Or," she added after a deliberate pause, "anyone else."

"Which is what you think I'm doing."

"Quite honestly, I'm not sure. But neither can I ignore the fact that she's an extremely wealthy woman."

And Pete was an Air Force E-7. Even with hazardous duty, flight and combat pay, he doubted he made as much as one of Riley's gofers. The unspoken comparison hung in the air, but he was damned if he'd acknowledge it.

Meredith Fairchild must have sensed the dangerous ground she was on, however. Her chin tilting, she offered a stiff apology. "I'm sorry if that offends you, Sergeant. I'm merely trying to look after my daughter's best interests."

"Here's a flash. As I told you a few minutes ago, she's

more than capable of looking after her own interests. She proved that in the desert."

He'd listened to all he intended to. Disgusted, he started to push away from the table. She stopped him with a quick hand on his arm.

"Wait! Please!" She shook her head, as if to clear it, and took another tack. "From what I heard and saw on TV, you and Riley and Prince Malik went through a terrible ordeal. But you and the prince are soldiers. You..."

"No."

"Excuse me?"

"We're not soldiers. Soldiers are ground pounders. The prince is an *air* marshal and I'm an *air*man. A pararescueman, to be precise."

"I stand corrected," she said with obvious impatience. "The point I'm trying to make is that you and the prince have been conditioned physically *and* emotionally to handle dangerous situations. My daughter has not. Isn't it possible that whatever she feels—or thinks she feels—for you now may be colored by what you went through?"

Dammit all to hell! Pete had just suggested the exact same thing to Riley out there on the beach. At the time it had sounded cautious and wise. Now it sounded like horse crap. What she said next hit home, though. And once again she echoed his thoughts.

"I know I come across as unfeeling and manipulative, Sergeant. Perhaps I am. My daughter certainly thinks so. Yet I've always—*always*—been in awe of her talent. It's a gift, one I wouldn't allow her to squander." She lifted a hand, let it drop. "I drove her unmercifully when she was young. I admit it. And I lost her because of it. I accept that as the price for bringing her incredible talent to the world stage."

She leaned forward. Her coldness fell away for a moment, leaving her face naked and vulnerable.

"She's just beginning to reach her peak. Whatever you do, please don't prevent her from achieving her full potential by derailing her career at this crucial point."

Derail…as in encourage her to accept a "guest artist-in-residence" position for a year or more, which she was prepared to do. Or *had* been prepared to do before he'd made such a mess of things.

"Wait here." Shoving back his chair, he gathered his hat and the towel. "I'll go up and let Riley know you're here."

The hotel didn't run to an elevator. The worn wooden stairs creaked under Pete's weight, adding a counterpoint to the slap of his flip-flops as he climbed the two flights to their floor. But the tightness in his chest had nothing to do with the stairs.

He knew about training. About constantly striving to achieve the next level of proficiency. More than any other branch of Special Ops, PJs had to stay on top of their game. And as a senior member of that elite fraternity, Pete worked as hard as the youngest recruit to maintain his mental and physical stamina.

Granted, combat rescue was about as far from the opera world as anyone could get. Yet he fully appreciated the blood, sweat and tears Riley had shed to reach this point in her career. What's more, he didn't need her mother to drive home the fact that she hadn't achieved her full potential yet. She was so young, so vibrant, with a voice that could bring even a combat-hardened air commando like him to his knees. The thought of being the reason she put her talent on hold, let her skills get rusty, made his chest hurt.

It was still aching when he rapped a knuckle on the door, then used his key to let himself in. The room was about a tenth the size of the bedroom at the royal villa, but its shuttered window opened to the sea during the day and the stars at night.

Riley was at the window now. Her arms folded and her eyes cool, she merely nodded when Pete said her mother had arrived.

"I saw the limo drive up. I'm surprised it took her this long to make a show of maternal concern."

"She was on a yacht in the Caribbean."

"Of course she was."

"She said she texted you. Several times."

"I know. I had Jason respond. Obviously not plainly enough. I'll go down and deal with her."

When she dropped her arms and started to brush past him, Pete caught her elbow. "Before you do, I just want to say that I've done some stupid things in my life. The pompous lecture I delivered on the beach a while ago is pretty near the top of the list."

She looked up at him, surprised and just a little wary.

"I was wrong about everything, Slim, except one issue. I'm not going to let you put your career on hold because of me."

"You're not going to *let* me?"

"No. I'm not accepting the job here in Oman."

She pulled her elbow free, but instead of the flash of temper he expected, a mask seemed to drop over her face. Her eyes went flat and her answer when it came was slow, careful and cold.

"That, of course, is your decision."

"Yeah, it is. The way I figure it, if we're going to take a shot at something real, we can't start off by compromising. We have to give it everything we've got."

"Interesting." Her small shrug cut right through him. "The way *I* figure it, we shouldn't start off by making unilateral decisions. You've made yours, however. Now I'll have to make mine."

She didn't slam the door behind her.

He wished to hell she had.

Chapter 9

When Riley entered the tiny alcove that served as the hotel's lounge, the mask she'd crafted to hide her uncertainties and loneliness during her turbulent childhood was firmly in place.

"Hello, Mother."

"There you are."

She got a half concerned, half resigned glance from beneath her mother's broad-brimmed black hat.

"I was beginning to wonder if you slipped out the back door when you heard I was here."

"I considered it. Why *are* you here?"

"Is it too difficult to believe I was worried about you?"

"Jason said he spoke with you personally and assured you I was all right."

"I prefer not to get updates on your welfare from your business manager." Irritation flickered across her flawless, unlined face. "Oh, do sit down. Can't we at least have a civil conversation?"

Riley remained standing. Their last "civil" conversation had ended with her mother snarling that she was an ungrateful bitch and threatening legal action to recoup a portion of the hundreds upon hundreds of thousands she'd spent on her daughter's professional development.

"What did you say to Pete, Mother?"

Riley watched her consider and discard several possible replies before cutting to the bone.

"I expressed my concern about where you are in your career. I also pointed out your very different backgrounds…and your disparate financial situations."

A cold fury seeped into Riley's lungs. "I suppose you also felt compelled to tell him about Austin."

"Yes, I did. Despite what you think, I have only your best interests at heart."

"So you've always maintained. Goodbye, Mother."

"All right. I'll leave you to whatever mess you're making of your life."

Hooking her purse strap over her shoulder, she slid on a pair of sunglasses. She started for the door but couldn't resist a final, parting shot.

"You've known this man, this Sergeant Winborne, how long? One emotionally charged week? If I were you, my darling daughter, I would analyze those emotions carefully before basing any major decisions on them."

Riley refused to cry. She hadn't shed tears in front of any adult in longer than she could remember. But she had to fight to get past the lump in her throat.

"That's our problem in a nutshell, isn't it, Mother? You're not me."

* * *

Her mask set, she stood unmoving in the tiny alcove until well after her mother had departed. She didn't need to analyze the emotions roiling around inside her now. The hurt, the anger and the aching sadness were all too familiar.

It took some time for the storm to subside. Even longer for Riley to recognize that both Pete and her mother seemed to think the ordeal in the desert was at the heart of what she felt for him.

But why shouldn't it be? He'd jumped onto the stage and covered her body with his. He'd deliberately let Scarface's thugs take him hostage. He'd refused to allow Riley to give in to the terror that clawed at her the entire time. He got them both up that narrow wind-catcher, then went back for Prince Malik. He was her hero, dammit, and she wouldn't let him or anyone else diminish that fact.

And yet…

She needed to accept that some hostages did in fact fixate on their rescuers. Even their kidnappers. And, although it made her back teeth hurt to admit it, her mother's parting shot had some legs.

Riley and Pete had exchanged maybe twenty words at the wedding, even less during those horrific moments at the opera house. She hadn't even remembered his name! So maybe… Maybe he *was* having trouble believing she'd progressed from clinging to him for protection to falling desperately in love in a few short days.

Recognizing the problem and knowing how to address it were two different matters, however. Riley stood in the tiny alcove so long, staring sightlessly at the wall, that the stoop-shouldered hotel owner became concerned. He rounded the ancient wooden counter, his clouded eyes worried under his embroidered skullcap.

"Are you troubled, miss?"

"I… Yes."

He nodded slowly, sympathetically. "Love Allah, and He will show you the way. Then you must follow your heart."

She stared at him while that simple truth sank in. She had to put her faith—and her fate—in the power of love. Smiling tremulously, she thanked the hotel proprietor and made for the stairs.

Pete occupied the same spot at the window she had earlier. Almost the same pose, too. Arms crossed, back stiff, he tracked her as she entered and let the door snick shut behind her.

"I saw your mother leave. She didn't stay long."

"We said all we had to say to each other." Riley refused to acknowledge the ache that caused just under her ribs. "But…"

Taking her courage in both hands, she crossed the room. Pete's arms dropped as she approached, but she could see he couldn't decide from her expression whether to reach for her or not. Sighing, she laid her palms on his chest.

"You were right. You and, as much as it kills me to admit it, my mother."

"About?"

"It's too soon. We haven't put enough distance between us and what happened in the desert to know whether this—" she patted the steely muscle over his heart "—is what we both think it may be."

Was that relief in his eyes? Or regret? God, she hoped it was regret.

"Okay," she said, "here's what I think we should do. We pack up and drive up to Muscat. Tomorrow you head home to your base in the States. Or stay in Oman if that's what you really want."

"And you?"

"I fly to New York and see what my team has lined up for me. Two…no, three months from now we'll reconnect."

"Reconnect how? Where?"

"I don't know." She slid her palms up his chest, hooked them around his neck. "Guess you'll have to trust me to make it happen, Cowboy."

The wire-tight tension went out of his body. A crooked smile tugged at his mouth. "No one I trust more, Slim."

The lopsided grin settled any lingering doubts she might have tried to ignore.

"So," she murmured, her mouth brushing his. "It's settled. We start the ninety-day countdown tomorrow."

"We start now. My clock's already ticking."

When he scooped her into his arms and carried her to their bed, he was so gentle she almost wept. At first, anyway. Then he went so hard and hot and urgent that she couldn't get enough of him. Her back arched. Her hips rose. Her breath came in fast, breathless pants. She matched his every thrust. Every bruising kiss. It was almost as if they wanted to brand each other. Leave some mark to remind them in the days and weeks ahead.

When he collapsed on top of her, crushing her into the mattress, Riley had to fight the urge to hook her legs around his calves and keep him inside her. But they untangled and she waited until her vision and her breath returned to normal to ease out of bed.

Once in the bathroom, however, the face staring back from the speckled mirror was one she'd seen too many times in the past. Nervous. Uncertain. Wracked with self-doubt.

"No!" Her fist pounded the sink rim. "Not this time!"

This time was for real. If she'd needed an affirmation, Pete had just supplied it. They couldn't want each other so completely, so compellingly, unless they were bound by more than some kind of sick hostage–rescuer transference.

That utter conviction carried her back to the bedroom. Pete was sprawled sideways across the bed. He'd dragged the sheet up to cover the essentials and Riley did her best to ignore what was still exposed. But she couldn't ignore his wry smile.

"I'm having second thoughts about going our separate ways," he admitted. "How about you?"

Yes!

"No."

"None at all?"

"None."

She had to force the lie through what felt like several layers of scratchy steel wool. When she finally got it out, she derived only a small twinge of satisfaction from his frown.

"We *are* talking only three months, right?"

"Right."

"With a reunion to follow at a mutually agreed upon time and place?"

"Correct."

He studied her for several long moments, then tossed the sheet aside and rolled to his feet. "Then I guess we'd better get packed."

Chapter 10

When a combat rescue team went in hot, their goal was an hour max to locate, stabilize and transport a Code Alpha to a field hospital. As the new superintendent of the 23rd Special Tactics Squadron, Pete counted those grim minutes numerous times during training exercises at his home base and a month-long deployment to war-ravaged Kenya.

He and his men were back in Florida just ten days when Hurricane Eloise roared into the south Caribbean and devastated the island of Dominica. Within hours, elements of the 23rd were loaded up and ready to roll. As Pete and the team filed into the belly of the MC-130 Combat Talon aircraft that would transport them to Dominica, however, he conducted a separate and very personal countdown.

Fifty-nine down.

Thirty-one to go.

Fifty-nine days since he'd departed Oman, much to the disappointment of Prince Malik and displeasure of the US State Department. Forty-six since Riley agreed to step in for an ailing diva and perform the title role in the San Francisco Opera Company's production of Richard Strauss's *Salome*. She was in California now to begin rehearsals. Pete's belly tightened every time he visualized her slinking out of those seven veils.

They'd stayed in contact these past two months. Phone calls, emails, texts. Sharing details of their separate lives and careers. Learning small details about each other by long distance. Pete kept waiting for some sign she was regretting their pact. Some indication the firestorm they'd ignited in Oman had cooled, or even died.

No cooling on her part yet. And sure as hell none on his, he thought wryly as he settled his sixty pounds of personal gear and strapped in. He'd pretty well kicked himself once a day, every day, for the past two months. He didn't even want to think about the nights.

Fifty-nine down.

Thirty-one to go.

Then the MC-130's engines revved and he put his personal deadline out of his mind and focused instead on the mission ahead.

Initial satellite reconnaissance indicated the situation on Dominica would be as grim as any Pete had ever encountered. The capital city of Roseau had taken a direct hit. Dozens of other towns, fishing villages and resorts had been flattened or washed out to sea. Mudslides and mile-wide debris fields blocked roads. All forms of communication were down. An estimated thirty to forty thousand desperate islanders and tourists were cut off from food, water and any kind of medical care.

International agencies were already mobilizing to provide disaster relief. They couldn't get in, however, until the airport reopened and port facilities were cleared of overturned ships and storm-twisted docks. US Southern Command had dispatched two US Coast Guard cutters to assess damage to the ports. A hospital ship and two navy frigates were also on their way. The 23rd STS, however, would be the first unit to put boots on the ground. The next hours, days and weeks, Pete knew, would be a bitch.

They were even worse than he'd anticipated.

The island's infrastructure was completely destroyed. Bridges had collapsed, roads were washed out, hospitals sat roofless and without power, vehicles had been tossed around like matchboxes.

Working with local first responders, the 23rd's PJs helped organize triage and trauma centers in the hard-hit capital, Roseau. They also set up tents, issued urgently needed medical supplies to docs and nurses and assisted in emergency operations. At the same time, the team's combat controllers worked shoulder-to-shoulder with still dazed locals to clear a runway. As soon as it was open, the controllers used their modular tactical systems—lightweight, rugged radio/computer systems integrated into their uniform packs—to call in aircraft.

One thousand US Marines landed in the first wave to assist with rescue and recovery. Troops from Canada, Venezuela and neighboring islands arrived hard on their heels. Follow-on cargo aircraft delivered tons of medical supplies, water, food, generators and heavy equipment. US Seabees blew up mangled docks and constructed temporary port facilities. Dredges from Venezuela, Colombia and Panama pumped around the clock to clear the shipping lanes.

Within twenty-eight hours, a combined UN/Dominican Command and Control Center had been set up to coordinate the activities of the many civilian relief agencies that now began to arrive. As one of the senior noncoms on scene, Pete was detailed to the CCC to coordinate the USAF units providing disaster relief. Including, he discovered, the just-arrived elements of the 26th Special Tactics Squadron out of Cannon AFB, in New Mexico.

Taking his first real break since he and his men had touched down, Pete jumped in a utility vehicle and rattled over the newly cleared road to the airport. He found fellow Sidewinder Dave Carmichael and his team still unloading their gear from the belly of a C-17.

"Yo, Duke!"

Carmichael broke into a wide grin. Cutting through the pallets of off-loaded equipment, he hammered Pete's back.

"Winborne, you ugly son of a diseased coyote. Heard you flew in with the 23rd." His sun-bleached brows waggled. "Also heard some wild tale about you playin' footsie with that hot babe who sang at Josh and Aly's wedding. You'd think someone that classy would have better taste."

"You'd think."

"Anna told me to get all the details if I ran into you down here and she'll pass 'em to the rest of the wives."

"What, are they all on some kind of news loop or something?"

"Facebook," Duke said mournfully. "They've got their own page. The Sidewinder Follies or something like that. It's private. So private none of us guys have been able to hack into it yet."

"How is Anna? She still with DIA?"

"She is. Got a promotion when she nailed that systems administrator job at Cannon." Grimacing, Duke rubbed the side of his nose. "Next assignment for both of us will probably be the Pentagon."

"What about Jack and Josh and Travis and Dan? Seen or heard from any of them lately?"

"Saw Jack a few weeks ago at Fort Bragg. Travis and Dan are still back in Texas, and Josh is pulling down big bucks with that high-powered engineering firm in Hawaii. But get this. Anna texted a while ago that Aly and Caitlin have volunteered their services with one of the big civilian medical relief agencies here in Dominica."

"No surprise there. They're both highly skilled in their own fields. And if they fly in, you know Josh and Dan will come with them. Hell, we could have a mini-Sidewinder reunion right here."

"Be something, wouldn't it?" Never one to be sidetracked for long, Duke refocused his sights. "Back to this opera singer. You two for real seeing each other?"

"Maybe. We're supposed to reconnect in..." He took a quick look at his watch. "Twenty-nine days, eight hours and some minutes."

"Whoa!" Duke blew a slow whistle. "Sounds to me like there's not much 'maybe' in your end of things, pardner."

"A lot less than I thought when we left Oman," Pete admitted wryly. "And I'm the idiot who proposed we take some time to make sure that wasn't just a near fatal case of horniness."

"You didn't actually use those words, did you?"

"Pretty much."

Duke shook his head. "You are one smooth dude, Winborne. C'mon, let's go over to the TOC and grab some coffee. You can bring me and my guys up to speed on what resources we've got to work with here."

Pete knew most of the men from the 26th. Air Force Special Ops was a small and extremely select community. When he left to head back to the Command and Control Center, Duke walked him to the utility vehicle and thumped him on the shoulder. "That took some time off your countdown."

"Right," Pete drawled. "One whole hour."

A week later, Pete and his team were packing up for their return flight to Florida. The devastation was still horrific, but most of the homeless were now sheltered in tents, the sick and injured were being treated, mortuary teams were processing the dead and hundreds of cubic tons of relief supplies were arriving daily.

Pete and his men had put in sixteen- and twenty-hour days. Waded through snake-and-rat-infested water. Rescued stranded families from homes and villages cut off by mud and debris. Helped direct the steady stream of aircraft ferrying in supplies and equipment. So he was ready to shake off the dust of Dominica when Duke showed up just hours before his team's scheduled departure and demanded Pete accompany him to what was left of the Roseau soccer stadium.

"They've rigged a big screen with satellite hook-up. Anna says they're going to broadcast from studios in New York, LA and London."

"Who's going to broadcast?"

"A whole slew of rock stars and country singers. They're doing a concert to raise money for Dominica, like the one they did after the Haiti earthquake and Japan tsunami."

"Good for them."

"Willie Nelson's headlining."

"Can't do it, pal. We've got wheels up at nineteen thirty."

"I'll get you back in time."

Pete thought about it for another moment, then caved. After all the death and heartache of the past week, he and his team needed to kick back for a few minutes with a good ol' Texas boy.

"Let's go."

Duke's team was crammed into one utility. Pete's piled into a second. They had to navigate mountains of uprooted trees and demolished cars but eventually made it to the soccer stadium. Like everything else in Roseau, it had taken a major hit. Bulldozers had shoved the debris to the far end of the field to make room for a hastily erected giant screen and wooden stage. A crowd of thousands desperate to escape the devastation around them for a few hours sat hip-to-hip on pieces of cardboard or plastic bags. Thousands more squatted on the hillside above the stadium. The sun was already starting to sink behind the island's chain of volcanic mountains, throwing the stage in stark relief.

The program was aleady underway when Pete, Duke and their men parked on the sidelines and climbed out of their vehicles. Some rapper wearing a bright red Dreams for Dominica T-shirt was broadcasting from a TV studio in Rockefeller Plaza in New York. Next came the cast of a hit London musical, all in the same red shirt, followed by a twelve-year-old Dominican who walked out on stage and brought everyone to their feet when he belted out a gospel song with a distinctly Caribbean flavor.

Pete glanced at his watch, thinking that he'd have to miss Willie after all, when the singer's craggy face flashed on the screen.

"Hey, y'all."

In his gravelly rasp, Nelson promised the Dominicans that he and the millions watching all around the world would help them dare to dream again. The crowd was with him all the way when he launched into two of his biggest hits—"On the Road Again" and "Whiskey River."

"Now that was worth waiting for," Pete said with the pride of a fellow Texan. "We'd better make tracks now."

"Wait," Duke urged. "He's not done."

Pete turned back around to hear Willie say he was proud to be doing a duet with this next performer, a pretty young gal who was a big hit in her own field but would surely be making her mark in country. Then the ponytailed star strummed a few chords on his guitar and sang the opening lines to Kris Kristofferson's "A Mo-

ment of Forever." The melody was haunting, the senti-
ment in the lyrics stripped down to the basic.

Pete echoed the words in his head, thinking it really was the hand of destiny that had thrown him and
Riley together. Then a second voice joined the chorus,
and the object of his thoughts walked out on the stage
in Dominica.

"What the...?"

Dressed for the occasion in jeans, tennis shoes and
the red T-shirt, she sang to the man on the screen first,
her clear, soaring soprano somehow blending perfectly
with his weathered sound. She then turned to the audience for a repeat of the first and second stanzas. Then
she went solo. Willie accompanied her on the guitar,
his head nodding to the beat, his blue eyes admiring.

When Riley got to the line about how good it was to
know dreams can still come true, she made everyone
in the crowd—Pete included—feel as though she was
singing to them.

Well, damn! She *was* singing to him.

Took him a moment to realize Duke and his guys
had flipped on the utilities' headlights. He was caught
like a deer in their cross beams, clearly visible to the
performer on stage.

That was pretty much his last coherent thought. He
didn't hear the final chorus. Didn't listen while Willie
said something about a new country star in the making.
Barely registered the grin plastered across Duke's face.
Every atom of his being was focused on the woman who
blew Willie a kiss, took the stairs at the side of the stage
and wove her way through the crowd.

"Hello, Cowboy." Her smile cut straight to his heart. "Surprised?"

"Like you wouldn't believe."

"I know we still have three weeks left on our ninety-day contract. I couldn't wait them out."

She cocked her head, her long hair shining in the glow of the headlights. Her brown eyes brimmed with a laughing challenge.

"How about you? Still need the extra time to be sure?"

He didn't hesitate, couldn't think how he'd kept his hands off her this long. With a low growl, he caught her upper arms and pulled her against him.

"No way in hell!"

Pete feasted on her warm lips and the hot, sweet promise of things to come while his troops hooted their approval. When he raised his head, both he and Riley had to fight for breath.

"Okay, here's the deal," she breathed after a moment. "Aly says the church in Rush Springs is available the third of next month. I talked to your parents and that date works for them. Anna said she'll contact the other wives and make sure they can make it. Duke here will take care of coordinating with the guys." Her nose wrinkled. "I even left a message for my mother, so she would know where and when."

It took a lot to rock Pete back on his heels. She'd just knocked him clear to Tuesday. "You've been busy," he said when he recovered.

"Yes, I have." Her eyes held his. "Seems like I remember someone saying that if we're going to have a shot at something real, we've got to give it everything we've got."

"Seems like I remember that, too."

"Good! Then I guess there's only one small detail left to take care of."

To the raucous delight of his troops, she sank down on one knee.

"I love you, Pete. You're my hero, whether you want to be or not. Will you marry me?"

"Yes! Now for God's sake…"

When he tugged her to her feet and into his arms again, neither of them registered the fact that their images now filled the giant screen.

Duke, however, was gleefully aware that Riley's proposal and Pete's half embarrassed, half laughing acceptance had just been beamed around the world. He vowed to get a copy of the broadcast for each of the other Sidewinders in case they'd missed it. And between the five of them, they'd make damned sure this little scene went down in the annals of Special Ops history.

* * * * *

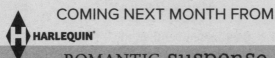

REQUEST YOUR FREE BOOKS!
2 FREE NOVELS PLUS 2 FREE GIFTS!

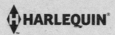

ROMANTIC suspense

Sparked by danger, fueled by passion

YES! Please send me 2 FREE Harlequin® Romantic Suspense novels and my 2 FREE gifts (gifts are worth about $10). After receiving them, if I don't wish to receive any more books, I can return the shipping statement marked "cancel." If I don't cancel, I will receive 4 brand-new novels every month and be billed just $4.74 per book in the U.S. or $5.49 per book in Canada. That's a savings of at least 12% off the cover price! It's quite a bargain! Shipping and handling is just 50¢ per book in the U.S. and 75¢ per book in Canada.* I understand that accepting the 2 free books and gifts places me under no obligation to buy anything. I can always return a shipment and cancel at any time. Even if I never buy another book, the two free books and gifts are mine to keep forever.

240/340 HDN GH3P

Name _____ (PLEASE PRINT) _____

Address _____ Apt. # _____

City _____ State/Prov. _____ Zip/Postal Code _____

Signature (if under 18, a parent or guardian must sign)

Mail to the **Reader Service:**
IN U.S.A.: P.O. Box 1867, Buffalo, NY 14240-1867
IN CANADA: P.O. Box 609, Fort Erie, Ontario L2A 5X3

Want to try two free books from another line?
Call 1-800-873-8635 or visit www.ReaderService.com.

* Terms and prices subject to change without notice. Prices do not include applicable taxes. Sales tax applicable in N.Y. Canadian residents will be charged applicable taxes. Offer not valid in Quebec. This offer is limited to one order per household. Not valid for current subscribers to Harlequin Romantic Suspense books. All orders subject to credit approval. Credit or debit balances in a customer's account(s) may be offset by any other outstanding balance owed by or to the customer. Please allow 4 to 6 weeks for delivery. Offer available while quantities last.

Your Privacy—The Reader Service is committed to protecting your privacy. Our Privacy Policy is available online at www.ReaderService.com or upon request from the Reader Service.

We make a portion of our mailing list available to reputable third parties that offer products we believe may interest you. If you prefer that we not exchange your name with third parties, or if you wish to clarify or modify your communication preferences, please visit us at www.ReaderService.com/consumerschoice or write to us at Reader Service Preference Service, P.O. Box 9062, Buffalo, NY 14240-9062. Include your complete name and address.

HRS15

"You, Brett Colton, are as slippery as a snake-oil salesman."

"I prefer to think of myself as stubborn and single-minded. Not so different from you."

The suspicion on Hannah's face melted away a little bit more and she closed her lips around the fork in a way that gave Brett some ideas too filthy for his own good.

He cleared his throat, snapping his focus back to the task at hand. "When my parents remodeled the big house, they designed separate wings for each of their six children, but I'm the only one of the six who lives there full-time. You would have your own wing, your own bathroom with a big old tub and plenty of privacy."

For the first time, she seemed to be seriously considering his offer. Time to go for broke. He handed her another slice of bacon, which she accepted without a word.

"Where are you living now?" he said. "Can you look me in the eye and tell me it's a good, long-term situation for you and the baby?"

She snapped a tiny bit of bacon off and popped it into her mouth. "It's not like I'm living in some abandoned building. I'm staying with my best friend, Lori, and her boyfriend, Drew. It's not ideal, but with the money from this job, I'll be able to afford my own place."

"And until that first paycheck, you'll live at the ranch." He pressed his lips together. That had come out a smidge more demanding than he'd wanted it to.

Their gazes met and held. "Are you mandating that? Will the job offer depend on me accepting the temporary housing?"

Oh, how he wanted to say yes to that. "No. But you should agree to it anyway. Your own bed, regular meals made by a top-rated personal chef, and your commute would be five minutes to the ranch office. The only traffic would be some overly excitable ranch dogs."

"I know why you're doing all this, but I really am grateful for all you're offering—the job and the accommodations. In all honesty, this went a lot better than I thought it would."

"The job interview?"

"No, telling you about the baby. I thought you'd either hate me or propose to me."

Brett didn't miss a beat. "I still might."

Don't miss COLTON'S COWBOY CODE
by Melissa Cutler, part of
THE COLTONS OF OKLAHOMA *series:*

COLTON COWBOY PROTECTOR by Beth Cornelison
COLTON'S COWBOY CODE by Melissa Cutler
THE TEMPTATION OF DR. COLTON by Karen Whiddon
PROTECTING THE COLTON BRIDE by Elle James
SECOND CHANCE COLTON by Marie Ferrarella
THE COLTON BODYGUARD by Carla Cassidy

Available wherever Harlequin® Romantic Suspense
books and ebooks are sold.
www.Harlequin.com

HRSEXP0615R2

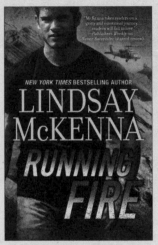

THE WORLD IS BETTER WITH

Romance

Harlequin has everything from contemporary, passionate and heartwarming to suspenseful and inspirational stories.

Whatever your mood, we have a romance just for you!